Seeking Neopolis

THE TRIDENT'S RECKONING

BOOK ONE

ELIZABETH A. DRYSDALE

Stag Beetle Books

To my sweet sons: David, Erik, and James
You help me remember what it means to be young and to dream.
Thank you for all the hugs, distractions, and words of
encouragement over the years.

I love you more than you'll ever know.

Chapter One

Battling against the biting winds that howl down the shadowed streets of Brooklyn, I defiantly pull up the collar of my jacket. Time to step beyond the safety of my doorstep to join up with Nick for school. Just as I muster the courage, Aunt Nina intercepts my escape, grabbing my hand to pull me back for another hug.

"Good luck today. I know you were worried about your test, but you're going to nail it," she says, her words add a palpable weight in my stomach.

"Thanks." I give her a grin void of confidence.

She pats my cheek, her hand lingering for a moment. "I packed a cookie for you, just in case."

Now my smile is genuine. "See you tonight."

"Good luck, kid." She closes the door behind me, leaving me to the mercy of the street.

Even after five years I'm still not completely used to living in the big city. The towering buildings just aren't what I think of when I picture home.

Closing my eyes against the cold, I remember warm

summer days along the Maine coast, so different from where I am now. The water was always too cold to swim in, not that it stopped us from jumping in anyway.

Just thinking of *us* hits me in the hollow space in my chest that's been empty since I left. It's just another reminder that I'm basically alone. Maine makes me think of Mom; the scent of her amber perfume wafts up through the lining of my jacket, her old jacket.

My heart clenches, and my jaw tightens until the pain in my gut eases. Mom's been missing for almost as long as I've lived in Brooklyn. Aunt Nina would tell me to say something besides *missing*. Something more like *passed*, but I still can't believe that. The police never found a body. There's no reason for me to give up.

The toe of my sneaker clips a jagged edge of sidewalk, almost sending me to my knees.

"You'd miss less of those dips if you kept your eyes open." Nick's half-grin belies his stern reproach.

As I give him a playful shove and he nudges me back with his shoulder, the breeze tousles his short brown curls.

He ducks his head into his collar as the wind picks up. "Thinking about her again?"

"Yes." I keep my voice sharp enough that he knows to abandon this line of questioning.

Nick and I have been friends for a long time now, but that doesn't mean I want his lecture on how I need to let it go and move forward with my life. I hear enough of that from everyone else.

He shrugs his shoulders and slows his pace to walk next to me. "You ready for Ms. B's history test?"

"I think you know the answer to that already." A laugh bubbles up my throat.

"I still don't understand why you have such a hard time

with that class," he says, his lanky torso bending as he tries to look me in the eye.

"I think it's just Ms. B." My voice is earnest as I try to plead my case.

Nick laughs, blue eyes sparkling. "Of course, it's the teacher. It's not your fault you can't remember dates to save your life."

I laugh with him. He's not wrong. For whatever reason I can't for the life of me remember the date anything happened, even if I can remember exactly where it happened and who participated in whatever it was. It's beyond frustrating in a class that only cares about dates.

We turn the corner and the school looms in front of us, the wrought iron grates over the window looking disapprovingly on the students as they filter through the double doors. Built in the early 1900s, the building's brick exterior still contains much of the charm of earlier years. With all the growth New York has gone through, I still enjoy seeing something older. Something that feels more like home.

Nick gives me a little shove to get me moving up the steps, pushing me inside the building and killing my nostalgia.

"Ready or not, class is starting," Nick teases as we unpack our heavy backpacks into the long line of rust-colored lockers. His still looks new while mine sags off my shoulders in a rumpled heap. "I'll meet you at lunch, okay?"

Busy students crowd around us as we push our way closer to the wall. The interior of the school had a facelift over fall break, and the fresh coat of paint shines under the fluorescent lights.

Sighing, I grab my books before slamming the locker closed. "Sure."

I know I should be grateful that I get to be here, and grateful that my aunt took me in after Mom disappeared, but pressure and abandonment press around me tighter than the crowd I surge through. The crowd that doesn't see me.

Slipping into the classroom, I hunch over in my seat. Shoulders tucked in, I make myself as small a target as possible and slide into complete obscurity, or at least, I *would* if Ms. B would let me.

"Avi." She smiles at me as she holds the stack of tests at the front of the classroom. "Are you ready for the test today?"

Having her echo Nick's earlier question, and in front of *everyone*, makes my face turn bright red. My throat feels thick and I can't find any words, so I give her a weak nod that I hope will make her leave me alone.

"Hmm." She starts handing out tests, her gaze still trained on me. "I guess we'll see."

She places the test on my desk and my mind can barely read the words, let alone process the first question. **What was the date of the Boston Tea Party?**

My chest feels tight and a thin trickle of sweat runs down my temple. I studied for this test and yet, with Ms. B still watching me, I can't think of anything.

In the desk next to me, Nick starts scribbling something down on a scrap of paper. The sounds of his pencil scrapping across the note makes it even harder to focus on the question.

My mind is still a swirling blank of nothingness, no matter how much I wish I could come up with something, there's nothing there. Ms. B glances away and I can finally think again. Nick coughs, drawing my attention back to him and the slip of paper he's discretely holding out for me to see. **December 16, 1773**, stands out in thick letters.

I know it's wrong to take the answer he's offering me, but I have to do it. I can't confirm that I'm a screw-up in front of her. I can't fail another test.

My hand shakes as I write down the date. Even knowing I

have the right answer from Nick isn't enough to make me confident that I can pass this.

There's nothing but the sound of pencils moving against paper to break up the noise of my heart beating against my chest. I don't dare look at Nick again. I know he'll try to help me and once was enough. I have to do this on my own.

It feels like an eternity passes before the bell rings and I can bring my made-up answers to the front. Ms. B. smiles at me as I hand over my test.

"I saw what you were doing, Avi. Unfortunately, you know that we don't abide by cheating. That will be detention for you. I'll see you after school."

* * *

The city streets feel empty after the chaos of school as I wind my way home. Without Nick to walk with me, everything feels empty. I was hoping he might have stayed after for one of his clubs to wait for me to come out of detention, but no such luck. I pull the cookie out of my backpack and finish it in two bites as I attempt to fill the hollowness.

Aunt Nina's apartment leans over me as I pass under the stale yellow light of the Chinese takeout we live above. My knee pops as I climb the stairs, an old track injury I haven't been able to shake. The smell of the restaurant clings to me and to everything in the apartment, but I can't really complain. Aunt Nina says we're lucky to be able to afford two bedrooms; not everyone can. She shudders every time she thinks about what could have happened when I came to live with her. Her worst-case scenario: the suburbs.

Mom never understood Aunt Nina's obsession with the city, preferring instead the quiet joy that came from our small oceanfront property. Not that we were wealthy either. It doesn't take much to live next to an ocean that far north, not like it does where I live now.

I climb the stairs two at a time in the tiny stairwell. My sneakers squeak against the clean but worn-down wood of the hallway as I stop to unlock the apartment door. The handle gives under my hand before I can even insert the key into the lock and I freeze. The door swings open with a long creak and the apartment sags in the stagnant air. Aunt Nina isn't home yet. From my position in the doorway, everything looks normal. I must have forgotten to lock the door before I left this morning.

Grabbing an apple off the counter, my teeth sink deep into the sweet flesh trying not to notice how still the apartment is. It's hard to find real peace in the city. The usual noises of cars and people are deadened and faint, even the bright colors coming through the window from the neon sign outside fade away throughout the room.

I move to the window, wondering if a detour has been put up on our street, but the road below is still bustling with cars. I move my jaw, trying to pop my ears. There's no blockage there, I just can't *hear*.

Turning back to the kitchen, the lack of color continues. It's like I'm walking through a vintage photograph with every-thing darker and out of focus.

The floor behind me squeaks and the apple drops out of my numb fingers, the piece I'd already bitten off sitting forgotten in my open mouth. The fruit rolls across the floor, coming to rest against the toe of a black sneaker.

Long, slender fingers pick up the apple, palming it before raising it to parted narrow lips. The breath leaves my lungs as I gape like a fish at the tall, pale boy with slanted eyes who calmly starts eating my apple. The sounds of his moist chewing fill my ears as they try to compensate for the rest of my muted senses.

"So." He tosses the unfinished apple into the trash behind me and rubs his hands off on his dark-wash jeans. "Are you ready to go?"

My hands reach out blindly behind me, gripping the green-tiled counter. Pulling myself up, I come to enough to remember to close my mouth. I shouldn't have come inside when I noticed the door was unlocked. I should have just waited downstairs for Aunt Nina to get home.

The boy continues looking at me. Tucking one hand into his leather jacket and running the other through his spiky black hair. My blood pumps sluggishly through my veins as shock fills my system.

"Did you hear me?" He waves his arms in front of me to get my attention, dark hair flopping over his eyes.

My brain refuses to catch up to what's happening, but even so, my fingers wrap around one of the long butcher knives Aunt Nina left on the counter. Mom always told me the city was dangerous, and I refuse to be another statistic. If I can get out of here, I'll be able to find help. Maybe Nick will be walking back and can call the cops. The boy doesn't see the knife as I move with it hidden safely behind my back. I'm not sure what I intend to do with it yet, but I have it just the same.

"Good grief." He turns his back to me as he mumbles under his breath. The words don't sound like English. I stop trying to figure out what he's saying as he pulls out a slim cell phone and holds it up to his ear.

I decide to make my escape as he continues speaking in his strange language. Slipping along the counter and hugging the outside of the fridge, I slide into the hallway and sprint for my room.

The window by the bed has a fire escape, a place where I've spent many warm evenings in the summer but may now hold my salvation from the intruder.

He mutters a curse in English this time as I slam the door

behind me, twisting the lock in place and flinging myself at the closed window. The knife clatters to the floor as I pull at the frame. The runners are older, refusing to work in tandem as one side moves up faster than the other faster than the other. Sweat pours down my back as I hear him approach the door. The window's opening is still too narrow to crawl through.

"What are you doing in there? Come out so we can talk. I had no idea you didn't know I was coming." His voice presses through the cracks in the frame. It's only a matter of time before he jiggles the handle and realizes it's too old to keep the door in place, locked or not.

Finally, the window slams against the top of the frame, catching my thumb and making my eyes water as I climb out onto the iron terrace. I try to close the window behind me to hide my escape, but it's stuck again.

I can't waste more time on it. Instead, I practically slide down, my sneakers slipping on the cold metal rungs as I go faster than I should.

"Avi!" His head pokes out of the window as my feet hit the ground. "Where are you going?"

He knows my name. Isn't that a kidnapping statistic? Something about being taken by people who know you, but I have no idea who he is.

I take off running, my breath coming in heavy gulps as my feet take me in the direction of Nick's house. He's probably not home, but I can't come up with a better idea.

My pursuer isn't dressed for a run. The thought passes from one side of my head to the other just as the squeaks of his leather jacket reach me. Three years of track taught me to run, sure, but it also taught me how to pick a struggle. When to sprint, and when to run for distance. Now called for a sprint —at least until I put some space between us.

There's a line of old apartments down the street and

around the corner, and I spin in that direction. Builders have been renovating them, and more often than not, when I pass the door it's wide open for the workers to get in and out. Sweat trickles down my temples and with my last remaining strength, I book it for the door. If luck is with me, I'll be able to get in and close the door before he sees where I've gone.

The metal grate on the door rattles as I slam it closed, making my whole body cringe. Keeping my feet as light as I can, I run up the empty stairs and slip into the apartment on the right side of the alcove at the top. My heart bangs out of my shaking chest. My gasping breaths are so loud I'm afraid he'll be able to hear me from the street below.

The low hum of a group of men talking on the floor above me does little to reassure me. It's probably the workers, and I don't want to have to explain why I'm hiding in their project. Although, trespassing can't be any worse than the kidnapping I feel certain is coming for me.

The front door of the apartment building creaks open just as I'm about to poke out and run upstairs. I freeze in place, my breath caught in my lungs as all rational thought of finding witnesses locks up and becomes impossible.

"Avi?" he calls in a hushed tone.

Through the stair railing I can see the top of his dark head. Saw dust floats around in the ray of light coming from the open window opposite me, blurring my vision. Slinking down until my butt hits the floor, I press my hand against my chest to try and still my pounding heart.

"Avi?" he tries again, still walking around the first floor.

If I could scream right now, those men upstairs would defi-nitely come down.

The metal stairs protest his weight as he climbs upstairs, my heart climbing with him. As he gets to the top, we make uneasy eye contact. I didn't go far enough into the apartment.

"Hey," he says, his muscular body still hunched over as he approaches me. "Can we talk for a minute?"

His words free my body and finally, I'm screaming. A blood-curdling scream that I don't recognize pours out of my throat. He startles, stepping back and standing up while watching me with wide eyes.

The construction workers flood down the stairs, their heavy boots hastily rattling the building.

"Good grief." The boy raises his hand in the men's direction with an easy smile.

They slow down, their legs moving as though through invisible molasses before coming to a complete stop. It's like staring at a picture of them coming to my rescue. Their faces are still screwed up in surprised determination, their limbs poised to grab us. The color leaches out of them and the sounds of the city fade away.

Looking at the boy again, a startled screech rips from my throat. While I've been looking at my would-be rescuers, he's taking the opportunity to close the distance between us.

"Can we talk now?" He extends a hand toward me to pull me from the floor.

"What's happening?" My voice is breathless and hoarse from screaming, but I'm just glad it works.

He gives me a side smile, his brown eyes sparkling. "That's what I've been trying to tell you."

He grips my trembling hand and pulls me to my feet. With a grin, he ushers me down the stairs and out the door before I can properly process what's happening.

As we cross the threshold, life springs back into our surroundings. Color, sound, and movement rush back into focus. He pulls me through a dense group of tourists waiting for the light to change on the corner. Loose tendrils of hair whip across my face while the world shifts around me. Everything is spinning and I can't breathe. When it all stops, I'm left in a cavernous room with a stained wood ceiling and a marble floor.

The boy drops my hand and walks away gasping, his chest heaving. Feeling dizzy, I stare blankly at his retreating back. My knees hit the cold floor and then I'm alone.

Again.

Chapter Two

I don't know how long the boy who knew my name leaves me in that room. The lack of windows makes it impossible to keep track of time, but it feels like hours from the amount of time I have to rethink the decisions I made when I ran and if I should have gone in a different direction. Laying on my back, I stare up at the vaulted ceiling. The cold floor numbs me, keeping my tears from making their way to the surface.

Not only have I been kidnapped, just like Mom always feared, but I think I'm going crazy too. There's no other explanation for what happened. I'm either going crazy, or having some sort of psychotic episode with hallucinations that led to me blacking out and ending up here. Since nothing like that has ever happened before, I'm going with crazy.

"Hello?" the boy's familiar voice calls, echoing in the empty space.

I'm too worn out from overthinking to care anymore. Lifting a hand, I give him a dirty gesture as my reply.

"Sorry about that, I just had to tell her you were here. Would you like me to take you to your room?"

I swear I'm listening, but the words don't make sense. I lean up on an elbow to look at him. "My room?"

"Well, yeah. She figured you'd want to stay here. It's easier to not have to go back and forth all the time." His sneakers squeak against the tile floor as he comes to stand next to me.

"I thought you were going to explain what the heck is happening," I remind him.

"You're still mad at me?" he asks.

I don't respond.

"You don't know who I am." His his voice full of surprise and disappointment.

I pause before I speak. "Why would I?"

He nods, spiky black hair falling over his dark eyes. "You need to stay, so she can explain everything."

"She?"

"Come on." He reaches out a hand to help me up.

I brush his hand away with a scowl. "I want you to take me home."

He smiles at me with down-turned eyes. "Just let me make you more comfortable while we figure everything out."

I'm a prisoner. That's what they call it when someone takes you and won't let you leave. So why don't I feel more scared? Why does my curiosity outweigh my terror? I see no weapons. He's made no threats. Maybe I'm an idiot but I don't push the boy away as he approaches me. He strong-arms me into standing, leveraging me against his broad shoulders. He closes the heavy oak door behind us as he leads me from the room.

Doors pass by in a blur of stone, dark polished wood, and splashes of gold that blend together until we stop in front of a door that stands at least ten feet tall with a large raven knocker in the center.

"This will be your room while you're with us." He pushes me inside with a large hand as he swings the door open.

He's nudged me inside a stone-walled circular chamber with a King size four-poster bed sitting in the middle with long maroon drapes hanging from it. The smell of dust hangs heavy in the air. My footsteps echo against the slate floor, the sound reverberating through my chest as my spirits continue to fall.

I turn but he doesn't follow me in. He leans against the doorframe while my heart beats in wild desperation.

"You said you were going to talk to me. Aren't you coming in?" I'm not sure I'm ready to be alone again.

"I thought you might want some time to put yourself back together." He shrugs, his shirt pulling taught over the tight muscles lining his chest.

I try to form a coherent sentence, but the fear that I've been pushing back makes my tongue stick to the roof of my mouth. "B-b-but—"

He recoils from my screechy voice, closing his slanted brown eyes. I take a deep breath and push my hands out from my torso, holding them open in supplication. "If I calm down, will you stay?"

I can't explain why I want him to. But he's the most familiar thing in this place. If he leaves will someone or something more terrifying take his place. He's promised me answers, or lies, but either way I need to hear them. He quirks his lips, smiling at me and I bite my bottom lip to keep from begging. Stepping into the room, he closes the heavy door behind him and leans against the door frame.

"What would you like to know?" he asks while folding his arms over his broad chest.

My hands shake and I push them into the front pockets of my jeans to keep my promise. *I will not fall apart,* I tell myself, which is a huge task after being kidnapped. "Why am I here?"

"Really? That's your first question?" He chuckles softly, a strand of dark hair falling over his eyes. "I would've thought your first question would have been who am I, or where you are, or something like that."

"I'm here for a reason. What is it?" My hands form tight fists that cut off circulation to my fingers as I hold my chin higher.

"Let me ask *you* something," he says as he steps closer to me through the shadowy beams of light coming from the cracks in the thick curtains covering the windows. "How much do you know?"

"How much do *I* know?" My voice comes out high-pitched and incredulous, but I can't hold it back. I can only imagine how unappealing I must be to him at this moment, standing there with my short stature and reddening face resembling more and more of a little girl. Not that I should care. "What are you even talking about?"

"Well, that answers that," he mutters under his breath. The leather in his jacket crinkles as he stretches his shoulders with a frown. "Okay, so apparently you don't know anything, which kind of makes you useless if I'm being honest."

"Gee, thanks."

He frowns as my face starts to crumple, my promise to him rapidly dissolving. "I'm not trying to be rude." He rubs his hand over his square-shaped face, massaging his temples for a moment. "I just thought this was going to go down differently."

"Believe me, no one is more surprised about what is happening than I am." I brace a hand against my hip even as I suck in a breath, trying to prevent a sob.

He gives me a grin and sits cross-legged on the floor a foot in front of me, motioning for me to do the same. "I assumed that with everything that happened with your mother that your aunt would've—"

"Wait a second." My usually strong legs give out as I fall

onto my knees in front of him. "What do you know about my mother?"

He waves me off. "What I know doesn't matter. I just thought your aunt would've said something to you about all of this. I mean, she's crazy if she thinks you would remain uninvolved just because your mom isn't around anymore."

My mind spins in a dark circle but he doesn't give me a chance to ask what he means before he starts again.

"Of course, we were going to reach out to you, that was part of the agreement. We need any information your mother could've left you. I thought that talking about this would be easier because I assumed you'd already know the game and the players." His mouth hangs open for a second too long, like he has something else to say before he slams it shut.

The hard tiles cut into my knees as I wait for him to continue. He grabs my hand, dwarfing it as he pulls us to standing in a fluid motion.

"Just let me show you."

The world shifts around us, fading to black once again.

* * *

My stomach heaves as my feet slam into the pavement. He lets go of my hand and I'm immediately colder as he walks away. The sight of tall buildings rising around us plants me firmly back in reality.

"You need to stop doing that!" I yell to his retreating back. My vision swirls and my mind grows increasingly more impaired from whatever illusion he keeps creating.

Turning around, he grips me under the arm with a low chuckle. "Believe me, my methods of travel are the least of your worries right now."

He uses his grip to direct me through the heavily populated streets. I try to figure out what he means, but the rapidly growing headache forming at the back of my head only throbs harder.

My body tingles as he leans over to whisper in my ear. "Just calm down. It's only going to get worse."

The taunt feels personal. Hand tightened into a fist, I try to punch him in the face, but my arm is pathetically weak. He avoids my swing with a graceful swoop and pushes us into a brown brick coffee shop, leaving me fuming.

The bell over the door jingles as we walk in, revealing a clean, if cluttered room filled with over-stuffed chairs and mismatched coffee cups left on ring-marked tables. The people on the street don't even notice the small disturbance and push past us like we're not even there. A plump woman behind the counter gives us a huge grin as we walk over. The rich smell of coffee washes over us in waves.

"Donovan! This that girl you were talking about?" she asks.

I blink in surprise. I should've asked his name a long time ago. It just didn't seem that important compared to the fact that I'd been kidnapped. A reminder that currently has me wanting to tear off his fingers now shifting to curl protectively over my wrist. Apparently taking me as a hostage is considered small talk where he's from.

"You've mentioned me?" I ask with a stiff jaw.

"This is her." He gives the barista a sly smile that barely shows his teeth while I glower under his grip. "I'd like the special."

"Coming right up! One dark roast with a shot of charisma," she yells even though we're the only ones in the shop.

"A shot of charisma?" I mouth to Donovan who just turns his crooked smile on me. Despite everything, I can't help the creeping curiosity that makes me go along with him. Fear should be gripping me tighter than he is, but either something in my gut is right, or something in my heart is horribly wrong.

The barista hands Donovan an unassuming disposable white cup, steam drifting over it in hazy ribbons. Staring at it, I will it to do something unusual. My breath stills in my chest and Donovan just laughs, reminding me to be irritated with him.

"Something wrong?" the woman asks, concern etched into every wrinkle.

"No, no. It's just her first time." He tilts his head at me. "This *is* your first time, right?"

"First time what? I don't even know what you're talking about." I scowl at him, lips pursed. "It's my first time here, if that's what you mean." I throw a glance around the room again, my eyes lingering on an expecially large chair covered in fabric that looks like scales. I would have remembered that.

"Really?" The barista turns her attention back to me. "I'll whip you up something special."

She gets back to work, her back turned so all I can see is the apron strap flush against her rounded hips. When she hands me a plastic cup, I can't help but feel underwhelmed. The outside of the cup isn't even warm.

"Just try it. I've got something special in there for you, you look like you could use it." She gives me a wink and motions for me to take a swig.

Donovan takes a deep sip of his and I follow suit. What's the worst that could happen at this point? Poisoning? If he wanted to kill me, he would have long before now. The sweet berry drink is warm in my mouth, shocking my taste buds. Still, warm or not, it's just a drink.

"Very funny," I tell them as I try not to be upset that his little joke actually got to me a little.

Donovan doesn't say anything, just continues to watch me over the rim of his cup as I take another gulp.

I move to tell him off, but my fingers start to tingle.

Glancing down at my hand, I bite my tongue to keep from screaming as beams of light shoot from my fingertips.

"What is this?" I ask the barista in a weak voice. I can't stop blinking as I stare at my hands.

She laughs. "I thought you could use a little light to jump-start your day."

Donovan thanks her before pushing me back outside.

In the chill New York air, what just happened in that shop doesn't seem possible. Already the light has faded and the people around me don't seem to notice anything wrong. Not that they'd say anything if they did. Still, I stick my hands in my pockets and watch Donovan with wide eyes while he sips his drink.

"Just a witch who's been able to commercialize her brews," he says between sips.

I stop short, the people on the street moving around me like I'm a traffic cone. "A witch?"

"You're not alone," he says in an ominous voice, wiggling his fingers in the air before barking out a laugh. "Sorry, I can't take myself seriously when I talk like that."

"Forgive me if I don't join you." Poking my hands out of my pockets, I watch my fingers fade further and go back to normal as his laugh echoes through my mind.

Donovan doesn't seem to notice my discomfort and instead grabs my pale hand as he drags me through the street. "I've got some other stuff to show you."

My mouth hangs open as we push through people, forcing our way against the crowd. All my confusion centers on Donovan's bizarre explanation for the coffee shop's eccentrici-ties. It just doesn't make any sense. In no rational world does any of what he's been saying make sense.

"I know you probably think I'm crazy right about now," he says like he's read my mind, his dark eyes wide with excite-ment. "But I promise you, this will all come together by the

time I take you back. I mean, I remember this one time you—
"

I freeze, my heels digging into the uneven pavement. "You're going to take me back home?"

"Not home." He slows down, even though I've felt enough of his well-muscled arms through his jacket to know he's strong enough to pull me forward. He looks down at me with a tight jaw. "I was under orders to bring you there in the first place, and I really shouldn't have taken you out to begin with."

"Then why did you do it?" My voice is sullen as I watch my freedom flit through my grasp.

Donovan shrugs. "This just seemed like the easiest way to show you exactly what you've been missing. Consider this your refresher."

My chest falls even as my blood pumps more fiercely, but Donovan's already started walking. We shove through the people lining the streets. They don't even notice us passing, which is weird because I walk directly into one slender woman in a black suit, and she doesn't so much as blink in my direction.

Testing out a growing theory, I punch a man in the shoulder as we pass as hard as I can. Donovan pulls me forward with a jerk as I pause to see his reaction, but what I can see is absolutely nothing. He does nothing. It's like it never happened. Like I don't exist.

"Can they not see us?" I ask him, my voice squeaking as panic gets the better of me.

"Oh yeah," he says, not even turning around to look at me. "It's a simple trick, one I should've used more of with you."

He chuckles under his breath, but I don't join in. I'm sure it would've been much easier to kidnap me if I hadn't been able to see him coming. He probably expects me to be grateful he didn't use his little mind tricks on me before. My face burns, anger filling the voids that have been growing during my short imprisonment.

We pass a grubby dumpster, and he loosens his grip on my wrist to throw his cup away. I take advantage of his distraction with a chop to his wrist with my free hand that has him releasing me. I spring through the people waiting for the light to change, my heart beating hard against my chest.

"Help!" I'm all too aware of Donovan's heavy footsteps gaining on me. "Help! Fire!"

Mom always taught me to shout fire if I needed something. She said it was a guaranteed way to get attention. *Well, she was wrong.* No one so much as glances at me.

I push through two heavy men in black suits and Donovan catches me by the hand, yanking me against his hard chest.

"Let me go," I plead, tears welling in my eyes.

Donovan shakes his head and reaches out his free hand to run it through my flyaway white-blond locks. Heat blooms in my chest at his touch. "I can't do that."

He must see my terror. A hint of sympathy flashes across his face.

"Just let me finish your little tour, okay? I promise you won't get hurt." He bends down to look me in the eyes. His slanted eyes open wider, revealing a weakness I haven't seen before.

Without waiting for me to respond, he pulls us forward again, lacing his fingers through mine. It feels weird, but at the same time, there's something about it that feels... right. We walk a few paces and I decide to voice my building anger with him, regardless of how he feels, when Donovan stops short and I walk right into his back. Peeling my face off his leather jacket, I peek up at the sign hanging at a slant above the door.

Affordable Blood Work, Same Day Results.

"We're getting blood work done?" Confusion softens the edge of my turbulent feelings.

"No, no, no. That would be stupid. I have someone here I want you to meet."

The smell of bleach singes the hair in my nose as Donovan opens the door. White paint flakes off the trim and around the doorways, sitting in pathetic piles on the grey-tinged tiles.

"Is Vince in today?" Donovan asks the receptionist where she's slumped against the front desk.

She snaps her gum and stares at us with a vacant expression, her red lips hanging open. "He's in room three."

"Thanks."

Donovan walks down the fluorescent lighted hallway, my sneakers sticking to the floor as I follow him. He stops in front of a door with a red flecked *3* painted on it. Slamming the door open, he reveals a pale man in a white lab coat hunched over several vials of blood.

"Donovan?" he asks, his English clear with the slightest trace of an old world accent.

"I'm surprised you remembered me. It's been a few months at least."

Donovan leans against the counter and waves me closer. I stand next to him, my hands hanging loosely by my side as my stomach grows heavy. I keep my gaze on Vince, his slicked back brown hair reminding me of old 50's tv.

"Vince, can you tell Avi about your job?" Donovan asks, spinning one of the vials on the counter around with a long finger.

"Sure. I examine the blood samples and get back to our patients about what is wrong with them, if anything. Half the time they are just hypochondriacs looking for a quick answer." Vince shifts his focus back to the blood before I can get a good read on him.

Donovan slaps the vial, clinking it against the counter as

he stops it from spinning. "Tell her what you really do." His voice is low, his eyes creased with impatience.

"Please Donovan, you know I do not like to talk about it in front of normal people. The more people that know, the more likely they are to tell someone and then I'm out of a job and on the run." A whine enters Vince's voice as he pleads for Donovan to change his mind.

"It's okay, she's one of us even if she doesn't know it yet," Donovan says with narrowed eyes.

A strangled huff pushes through my throat but gets cut off as Vince speaks.

"It is easier if I show you." He pulls the stopper of the full vial in front of him and chugs it down before slapping the empty vial on the counter.

"What the ---" I gag, turning to find a garbage can and to stop looking at him. There's nothing to help me in the empty room, and my posture grows rigid as Vince puts the stopper back on the vial. A dribble of blood runs across his pointed chin.

He ignores me, reading his notes aloud as he types them on an old laptop. "AB positive, slightly anemic, potential for leukemia in the next five years."

"You really can't beat the speed here," Donovan says as he picks at his fingernails.

"There is no freaking way you could know that just by drinking blood." My face is frozen, my thoughts fuzzy, causing my words to come out stiffer than I intended.

Donovan leans over me as Vince takes more notes. "It's very possible. You see... Vince is a vampire."

Vince shushes him. "Keep it down and do not use that word."

I feel the blood drain from my face as Vince finally looks at me. His eyes are dark, almost black, with a pale red ring around the outside of the iris.

"It's not polite to stare," Donovan says with a laugh at my horrified expression, his laugh tighter than before. "You should be more grateful for Vince. He does a great service around here. Now this woman will be able to get help right away for her leukemia or find a way to avoid it altogether because of his warning."

He's right. I don't understand what's going on here, but I do know I'd rather know about the probability of an illness as quickly as possible, no matter the methods. I just can't get a clear thought together. It's like I'm seeing my life from the end of a narrow tube.

"What is her story?" Vince asks. "She looks pretty pale." He glares at Donovan with shifty eyes, the metallic smell of blood filling the room as he picks up another sample.

Donovan turns his back to me as I slink against the dingy walls. "I'm not entirely sure to be honest. She's a part of our world, but says she knows nothing about it. I've been trying to jog her memories, but I'm beginning to think she might be telling the truth. How else do you explain her genuine surprise despite all the things I know she—" He stops himself with a cough.

Vince gives me a long look then shrugs and turns back to his work, his black hair shining blue in the yellow light.

"Thanks for your help." Donovan guides me back out the door. "Ready to go and talk now? Or would you like to see some more?"

"I don't understand what's happening." *How could there possibly be more?* Witches, vampires, people thinking I'm invisible, and strange spinning trips through space. I don't think I can handle anything more.

Donovan smiles at me, his lips pulled to the right. He slips a gentle arm around me, fingers curling against my waist and the world around me disappears again.

Chapter Three

As much as I hate my imprisonment, there's relative safety in the heavy stone and wood walls of my bedroom. At least there aren't any fairytale creatures waiting for me here.

Just thinking about it makes my stomach heave. I feel physically sick as my mind spins, the soles of my feet slamming against the unforgiving stone floor. Body shaking, my chest heaves as I gag and slide down onto all fours.

"Shaken up from the trip?" Donovan asks.

"Shaken up? Like all we did was drive down a bumpy road?" I stand on unsteady legs, my mouth pulling into a scowl. "You parade me around the city to show me crazy things with no explanation, and you just expect everything to be normal and fine?"

Donovan shrugs and puts his hands into his front jean pockets. He stares at me with narrowed eyes as he leans against the bedpost.

Emboldened with adrenaline, I poke him in the chest. "What's going on here? Don't bother showing me anything else, just tell me in simple words what's happening."

He grabs my hand as I move to poke him again. The dark

room swallows me up, only Donovan's bright smile stands out against the dark paneling and closed curtains. I stare into his topaz eyes, my anger ebbing away. He mesmerizes me and I can feel my emotions draining out of my body like a painting underwater. I don't know how he's doing it, but I know that he's taking my emotions away, and he's doing it without my consent.

"Let's just calm down for a second," he says while smoothing down my arms with his large hands. "I took you out today to show you that my explanation isn't crazy. If I hadn't done that you would never believe me. Do you understand? And I just—"

He clamps his jaw shut and I nod at him, my lips tightening. My feelings are still muted, and I don't trust myself to speak. *Will he take that away from me too?* Despite the wall he's put in place somehow, I can feel anger building behind it.

Donovan nods, his dark hair falling over his forehead for a second before he pushes it back. "Good. Now, we brought you here because we need your help with something."

"But I don't *know* anything." My voice has been taken over by pathetic pleading, but I can't help it.

He sits me down on the narrow wooden bench in front of the bed. The two of us barely fit with his much larger frame taking up over half the seat.

"I understand that. I mean, I wish it was different, more like it used to be." He looks away and clenches his hand into a fist. "But I can see that things are far more different than I thought they'd be. If I'd known your mother had done this, if I'd known you wouldn't remember...jeez." He runs a hand through his hair.

I grind my teeth together. "What do you know about my mother?"

"She used to work for us. Back before my time obviously," he says as I open my mouth to tell him how impossible that would be. "She knew things that were important to my organization. We thought you might have known what they were, or even where she could have hidden her plans."

"My mother is dead." The words fall out of my mouth in dry syllables.

Donovan's mouth thins, his eyes narrowing with sympathy I don't believe. "I heard. I'm so sorry."

Sorry. Everyone is always sorry when they find out, but what does that even mean? Are they sorry I have to live the rest of my life without a mother? They have no idea what that's like. Or are they sorry she was taken from this earth? Are they sorry I'll never feel the warmth of her hugs or lay out on the beach with her under the stars while she tells me stories? Hot tears prick the corner of my eyes and I hold my head even higher.

"She was a great woman, and did a lot for us," Donovan continues in somber tones. "I know bringing you here seems like an interesting 'thank you for your service,' but things have gotten a little tense, and we couldn't wait for you to approach us on your own."

"You could've just talked to me like a normal person. How long do you expect me to be here anyway?" I gesture to the bed. On top of the black comforter with a blood-red floral pattern embroidered across the top sits a small pile of clothes. Pajamas probably.

"Avi, you have to understand. There are bigger things going on right now than where you'll sleep tonight. Especially considering how little you remember. We're going to have to spend some time sifting through your memories to see if we can find anything useful."

"How little *I* remember?" My heart pounds harder despite his emotional block.

Donovan shifts uneasily. "This isn't the first time we've met, you know."

My stomach drops. "So, you're trying to tell me that not only is there a secret world I don't know about, but that I'm supposed to be a part of it?"

"I guess so."

The words hang in the air between us. My mind is blank. I have no idea how to overcome this.

"Do you need me to leave you alone?" His gaze travels over my rapidly falling face.

"I think that would be best." Despite not wanting to be alone in this mess, I don't think I can handle being around anyone either. I have to get a handle on what's happening before I can placate anyone.

He pats my leg as he stands. "We'll work through this together. Try not to worry too much about it."

He gives me one last dazzling smile and then closes the heavy door to my room behind him. The quiet that settles in the air after he leaves hangs heavy around me even as the click of the lock sliding into place resonates through my chest.

With an exasperated breath, I get up and pace through the room. The rubber of my shoes squeaking against the tiles echoes through the room. I keep moving until my legs cramp, then throw myself onto the bed. My body sinks into the mattress and my breathing grows strangled. I miss my own bed. I miss Aunt Nina and the life I had before. Nothing will ever feel the same again.

One of the hardest ideas to stomach is that I've met Donovan before. The idea of a mystical underworld full of magic is dubious, but there is more supporting evidence with each passing moment. The idea of a whole past and group of people being wiped from my memory? *Impossible.*

The sun sets and the room is thrown into pitch darkness. I hold my hand out in front of me, but I can't even see the edges of my fingers. I guess I'm not going to be served dinner.

A tear leaks out the side of my eye and I roll over and bury my face into the pillow. *Mom worked for the same company as him? She was a part of this secret life?* Betrayal burns through me as I think of my past life being erased making it hard to breathe. My shoulders shake and I curl in on myself until my knees touch my chest. Still, I don't know what to do now without her.

I don't know if there's anything I can do without her.

* * *

Time passes slowly, moonlight filtering through the closed curtains. Leaving me to my devices all day isn't going to help whatever "cause" Donovan thinks he's a part of. Instead, my gaze travels to the open window where a soft breeze flutters into the room.

With the only room I've really seen in this building being my own, I don't know too much about where I'm at. Stepping lightly to the window, I decide to get a better look at my surroundings. A dark green lawn spreads out before me in the moonlight; the winking of waves glimmer in the distance. Maybe if I'm lucky, I'm still somewhere off the coast. Maybe home isn't that far away.

The stone wall of my room continues along the outside of the building, reminding me of an old castle. Although, no old castle I've ever been in was this well maintained.

It's this level of maintenance that provokes me to pull the curtains from the rod and press against the window's glass. I can't see anyone outside, and I hope whatever guards I might have been given are only posted outside my door.

My breath catches in my throat as I grab the curtains and swing out the window. My feet hang in the air over a two-story drop. I screw my eyes closed and keep my thoughts focused on Aunt Nina, on getting home.

Only the distant sound of waves breaks up the silence of

the night as I rappel down the side of the building. It only takes a second to travel too far down to use the curtains anymore and I'm forced to use the uneven surface of the stones to grip as I make my way down the 8 feet to the ground. My breathing grows heavier the longer I hang over the ground. Track never prepared my arms for something like this and all my muscles from running have only made me heavier.

When my feet finally sink into the dewy grass, I collapse into it, arms burning. I'm so grateful to be on solid ground that I even think about kissing it. With adrenaline making the blood pump loud in my ears, I take off through the grounds.

Running towards the ocean seems like the best option. I can't see anywhere else to go and there might be the possibility that a boat has been left on the shore, and if not, I can at least track the coast and find some other house. A lighthouse. A cottage by the sea.

The distance is deceptive as I stare across the rolling expanse of grass, lungs burning. I try to even out my breathing, reminding myself that this temporary pain is a much better option compared to remaining Donovan's prisoner, even if he has been kind to me. I won't be anyone's prisoner. A wild grin spreads across my face as I pound down the last mile at a sprinter's pace.

I breathe in the saltiness of the ocean and strain to see the sand that builds just over the last swell of grass.

"Out for a night run?" Donovan's familiar voice jolts me out of my daydream as he keeps pace with me. I tear through the last few yards of grass, my sneakers sinking into the sand.

I glance at Donovan and stop watching my feet. My toes catch on a hole in the sand and fling me face-first into the sand, grit digging into my skin.

"You all right?" he asks.

There's concern in his voice as he lifts me out of the sand. I wish I could just bury myself in it.

I groan. "Go away."

Donovan sets me down and flops next to me as I spit out wet sand. Wiping off my face, I stare out at the flat stretch of beach. There's no boat waiting for me here. Just water and more sand spreading out in either direction.

My chest sags and a strangled sob bubbles up my throat. Donovan gives me a sidelong glance before slinging an arm around my shoulders.

"Shhh, it'll be okay," he whispers into my hair as my body shakes against his chest.

He waits with me until my sobs subside and I'm left with hollow emptiness as the hope of escape flees once more.

"How about I take you back?" he asks gently.

I give him a weak nod. I don't know what else to do at this point.

In another flash of his magical swirling darkness, we're back to sitting on the side of my bed, pajamas still sitting untouched atop it. Donovan stands up and swings my legs onto the bed, sliding me up so my head hits the pillow as he gives me a soft push.

He gives me a sympathetic smile as he tucks the blankets around my shoulders. I'm grateful he doesn't try to talk to me about what just happened. I don't think I could keep it together long enough for that.

"It'll get better." His voice is quiet in the still night. "I promise."

My body grows sleepy as the adrenaline drains from my system, putting me in a half-awake state. He gets up to leave and I think he gives me a feather-soft kiss on my temple as he goes, but my mind is too far gone to be sure.

* * *

"Hello?" Donovan's voice echoes through the room, disrupting the faint bird songs coming through the open window.

I haven't moved from where I fell asleep last night. Moving at this point will awaken the cramps currently lying dormant from sleeping with my back twisted up. It's easier to just stay where I am, nestled into the four-poster bed with the curtains surrounding it tightly closed.

"Are you awake?" he asks.

His footsteps tap closer to me until he stands next to the bed beside my face. He draws back the heavy curtains, gazes down at me. I have nothing to give him, my mind just spiraling farther and farther down. I'm drowning in the hopelessness of my imprisonment and the past that was never mine.

"I brought you something to eat. You want to get up and join me?"

I can't open my eyes, let alone respond to his question. There's a rattle as he sets something down. The mattress sinks next to me. My body rolls into the depression, moving me against my will.

"Hey." Donovan pushes the limp hair out of my face and turns my head so I'm looking at him.

A few stray tears trickle down my cheeks as I glance at him. He stares at my wilting face, sympathy clouding his dark eyes.

"I didn't realize you'd take it this hard," he whispers to me as he rubs the rough pad of his thumb against my cheek.

His pity draws me out of the depths where I've been hiding. Energy surges into my limbs and I wrestle myself out of his soft grip. I refuse to be pitied by him.

"What did you think was going to happen? You would just tell me my whole life was a lie and I would smile at you and ask how I could help and what was for dinner?" I sit up, feeling my long hair hang suspended from where it was bunched up against the pillow.

He raises his hands in mock surrender. The leather jacket has disappeared this morning, exposing his muscled arms in a navy blue V-neck shirt. "I didn't mean to turn your life upside down. Seriously!"

I raise an eyebrow in disbelief.

"I knew it would be a shock, I just didn't think it would be *this* much of a shock." He shrugs.

"Well, surprise!" Spit flies from my mouth.

Donovan gets off the bed and sticks his hands in the front pockets of his jeans. We stare at each other in a depressed and heavy silence until I can't take it anymore. Flinging myself back onto the bed, I want to scream. I don't. Staring up into the canopy, I hope that if I ignore him, he'll go away again.

Instead, he drops a tray next to me, the dishes rattling again. "I don't know about you, but sometimes a good meal helps me feel better."

Waving a piece of buttered toast in front of my face, he tries to tempt me to go through the motions of daily life, but I don't feel ready to move forward. With a sigh, he takes a bite of toast, showering the dark bedspread with crumbs. He finishes the piece and brushes his hands against each other, leaving more crumbs behind as he starts toward the door.

"Are you leaving?" I hate how weak my voice sounds.

"You made it clear you didn't want me here. What else am I supposed to do?" He leans against the door frame and watches me with a relaxed face.

I don't know why I bothered to say anything to him. Didn't I want him to leave? While he hasn't been able to get me to eat, he has been able to awaken a small sense of self-preservation that tells me not to let myself be alone to spiral back into the depths I spent the last night in.

"I'm ready to hear more," I whisper.

"I really don't know what else there is to tell you," he says, not budging from his position.

I roll to the side so that he's in my sightline. "What else do you know about my mom?"

He runs a hand through his dark hair. "I don't know what you're looking for me to say. I mean, I didn't even know her personally."

"She worked with you guys though?"

"Yeah, yeah. Minna did a lot of work with us." He slides over to lean against the bed's foot board.

Minna.

Just hearing her name makes me have to breathe deep before responding. I have to make sure I can keep my voice calm as I swallow the growing lump in my throat. He knows Mom's name, that means something. "If my mom trusted you, then I guess I do too. What do you need me to do?"

Donovan grins at me, his bright teeth standing out starkly in the dark room. "I was hoping you would say that."

Sitting up, I finger comb my hair back into relative straightness and look over the tray. It's a basic plate covered with a piece of toast, a glass of orange juice, and some scrambled eggs. Not too bad for a prisoner.

I bite into the toast, savoring the bits of butter melting on my tongue. My stomach growls as I swallow. I didn't realize how hungry I'd been until this moment.

Donovan smiles, his pale collarbone peeking out through the v of his shirt. "What can you tell me about your mother's routine before she died? That might tell us where to look for her notes."

"I don't remember very well what she did for work." I screw up my face as I try to remember, my mind feeling hazy and my stomach growing sick. "When I came home from school she'd already be done for the day. We'd drink a cup of tea on the beach and talk about our dreams."

I try to ignore the pain creeping up my spine as I think about her. She'd been my best friend, my closest confidant. I haven't recovered from her leaving, and I don't think I ever will. I'm lost without her.

Yesterday, having to tell Donovan that she was dead... made it too real. I wanted to shock and guilt him and instead subjected myself to a whole new round of agony.

He's quiet for a few minutes, his brows furrowed in concentration as he mulls over my words. I dig into my eggs as my stomach cries out for more.

"So, you never saw your mom working at all?" he finally asks, his voice mirroring the disbelief on his face as he scratches his jaw.

I shake my head. "She always told me home was a place for rest and fun, not for business."

Donovan exhales noisily and I glance over at him, my fork hanging suspended with its load of eggs. "What did you think I was going to be able to tell you? 'Hey sorry I know nothing about this side of my mother's life, but here's the safe where she kept all her notes?'"

He frowns, muttering something under his breath about making progress, but my annoyance sparks a memory. It drifts up through my mind like smoke: Mom locking her old wood desk with an elaborate brass skeleton key, her bright blonde hair falling in her face.

I open my mouth to tell him what I've remembered, but he stops me by throwing himself off the foot board. He punches the sturdy stone walls with a curse.

I bite my lip as he paces in front of me. What he did should have brought him to his knees in pain at the very least, maybe even broken his hand, but he moves like it was nothing. My stomach feels sick. There's something different about him, just like the rest of the 'people' he's introduced me to. I have to distract myself from this revelation, so I ask him a question that's been pressing against my mind. "How is it possible that my memories could be taken away?"

He whips around and stares at me, mouth hanging open. "What do you mean? With magic of course."

"With magic," I repeat back to him, absorbing the words and still coming up short.

"Yeah, nixies like magic. Not as much as witches, but, you know."

"I don't know! What are you you talking about?"

"You don't know—" he stops. "You don't know anything about it." I can't tell if the tone in his voice is irritation that I'm helpless to him or sympathy for my complete ignorance.

"What is a nixie?"

"Your mom was a nixie. I think of them like fancy mermaids, if it helps. It's how they can live on land. There's no reason to think that she couldn't get her hands on a spell or two in order to alter your memories." He offers me a shrug of his broad shoulders.

I stare at him, jaw suspended while he looks at me with a frown.

"Will this ever end?" I ask, my voice small as I knit my hands through my hair. "Will you ever stop dropping these kinds of bombs on me?"

Donovan has the decency to look ashamed, his neck flushing red as he turns his face from me. "I really am sorry about what you're going through, but if you don't know about any of this, then how can you help?"

"I just want to go home." I pull a blanket around my narrow shoulders. "Can I go home now?"

"I can't take you home right now. Is there something else I can do?" He's practically begging as he leans over me.

I shake my head. There's nothing he can do to make up for what's been done. For the kidnapping, for showing me an underworld of magic I still don't understand, for the pain of Mom's betrayal.

"Am I a nixie too?" His words have continued to work

their way through my mind, and I have to know where all this ends. Where is the truth in all this?

Donovan sighs. "I really couldn't tell you. Only you would know that. I mean, we could probably give you a few tests, but we don't really have time for it and it's not really necessary."

"That's what I want." I keep my voice firm and decisive. "I'll try harder to work with you if you can take me and do some testing right now."

Donovan's black brows pull together, wrinkling his forehead. "I don't actually have the clearance for that, and we don't have time for it."

I cross my legs under me, finding a firm base in the face of my constantly churning life. "Well, then I guess this process is going to take a lot longer then."

He paces back and forth in front of the bed while I gulp down the orange juice, pulp sliding down my throat. It feels good to finally find a place of power in this situation. He runs his hands through his raven hair and pins me under his dark gaze.

"Fine. Come with me." He frowns. "And move quickly."

Springing from the bed, I race to the door. He guides me through long hallways with curtain-shrouded windows. I still don't have a clue where I am, and it doesn't look like I'll find out any time soon.

"Keep quiet," he hisses, pointing to my feet.

My shoes have been slapping loudly against the floor, but the rubber soles demand nothing less. I try walking on tiptoe until he nods at me in approval.

He stops short in front of a large metal door at the end of several stone hallways. The door looms over us at twenty feet tall, with a spiraling design running down the length of it. We stand there a moment, my wheezing breaths cursedly loud in the immense space.

With a groan, Donovan steps forward and pulls on the

circular handle of the left door. The muscles in his arm stand out with strain before the door glides open. With just enough room for us to get through, he waves me through the open space before jumping in himself as the door swings closed on silent hinges.

A huge tank, bigger than the ones I've seen holding orcas bubbles in front of us. The water inside is a beautiful teal, like pictures I've seen of the Caribbean.

"Wow." I stop walking to stare at the water as Donovan marches past me and around the glass enclosure.

"What's this for?" I have to run to keep up with his longer stride.

The back of his neck grows tight. "Nothing that concerns you."

I want to scream in frustration but hold it in. It's pointless to try and argue for rights when I'm still just a prisoner here.

He approaches a long panel of blinking buttons, reading off the screen in the middle of them. Turning, he grabs my wrist and walks me closer to the tank.

Questions freeze in my throat as shapes materialize in the cloudy water.

Flickers of brightly colored scales shimmer in the bright opaque water. I take a step back with shaky legs, but Donovan holds me in place. A webbed pale green hand presses against the glass before a face streaked with gold hair comes into view. A smile grows across my face as I stare at what has to be a mermaid before she gives me an ugly grimace that shows her pointed teeth. She turns to swim away, turquoise tale flapping back into the hidden depths of the tank. My hand reaches for the glass, disbelief making me want to touch it.

Donovan leads me further around the perimeter. "They're mean little things."

"What are they?" My voice is breathless after seeing the face of a creature I've only ever seen in animated movies. I can't stop looking at the tank, wondering what else might be hiding in its depths.

He doesn't answer my question. Reaching the back of the tank, there's a metal ladder leading up to the water's edge. I hesitate and Donovan pulls on my arm as he walks up the first few steps. My sneakers clang against the thin metal and I grip the railing with my free hand to force him to slow down.

"Do you want to know or not? You asked me to test you." He gives me a smirk as he releases my arm.

I shake my head, beads of sweat growing along my forehead. "I don't want to get any closer to anything you might describe as 'mean'."

"You wanted a test, here's your test." Donovan grabs me by the waist.

"I--- I know. I just didn't expect a test to look like *this*." I spare a glance at the deceptively still water. "What do I have to do?"

He helps me up the rest of the stairs, my breath coming in short gasps as we get closer to the platform at the top of the tank where there is no railing.

At the top, Donovan presses a sequence of buttons on a panel just beside the tank. The sound of glass sliding in a track answer's his request. We stand beside the open water, my gaze tracking it for any hint of movement.

"The test is simple," his voice is quiet as he leans closer to my ear. "You just have to get in the water."

I glance up at him, my face panicked and eyes wide. "I'm not getting in there!"

He moves us closer to the edge or the platform. "I promise, I won't let anything happen to you."

My sneaker slips against the slick metal of the platform. I want answers, I do, but not this way. Getting into that tank would be the same as jumping into the water with a shark. I wouldn't do that, and I can't do this.

"No." I shake my head vigorously. "I won't do it."

"You can do this." He looks into my eyes, taking me by the hand. "You'll be fine and we'll have answers."

I close my eyes, torn between moving closer to the edge and running away. Donovan moves his hand to my back, massaging it in small circles before giving me a slight push. My eyes flash open seconds before my body hits the cold water.

Bubbles leak out of my nose as I thrash around the water, my white-blonde hair looking blue as it floats around my face. The weight of my pants and shoes tug me down like an anchor despite my efforts to pull myself back to the surface. Kicking wildly, I get close to pulling my body through the water. I have to get out of here before the mermaid lurking in the tank can find me.

Breaking through the surface, all I can see is Donovan's arm as he leans over the edge of the window of the tank. His brow furrows in concentration as I gulp down a breath of delicious air and ease the sharp pain searing through my lungs.

"Get me out of here!" I got in the water, that should be enough.

"Avi, behind you!"

A scaly hand wraps around my ankle. I glance down just before being yanked under the water again.

My hair streams above me and my mouth fills with water as I'm swiftly taken to the middle of the tank. The water burns my eyes as I force them open to stare down at the creature swimming with me. Pulling me.

Drowning me.

Her long sea foam green hair streams behind her as she kicks, her legs a blur. *Legs?* I stop thrashing long enough to squint and see thick fins along she sides of her calves blur as they propel us deeper to the bottom of the tank.

My lungs burn. Air. I have to get air.

I try kicking towards the surface and she gives me the same

ugly grimace as before. Her sharp teeth scare me into submission. Her mouth is jagged like a shark's. Like those videos of shark attack victims Mom and I watched one summer after a broken leg made it impossible to get in the water. *Too bad I'm not that lucky now.*

Looking up through the water, I can't make out Donovan's outline anymore, just my own wild hair coursing above me. Panic encourages me to breathe out. Only years of living by the ocean and listening a million times about what to do if you're caught in the undertow keeps me from following through and breathing in water. *I should have paid more attention in those stupid classes.* nN number of lessons in the world keeps the pain in my chest at bay as the last of my air bubbles past my lips.

My body burns where she's grabbed me. My lungs beg for air. Black spots speckle through my vision.

I don't want to die here.

Something brushes the side of my arm and I twist around, my movements jerky and frantic. I catch a glimpse of an amber fin in the corner of my eye before it disappears into the water.

The water around me slows and the creature releases my ankle, leaving me to float alone in the murky depths. I kick my legs, moving to swim back to the surface again, but she floats in front of me, her lipless mouth curved in a demonic smile.

Shock has me opening my mouth, but there's no more air to leak out. She reaches out a hand and runs it through my hair. The short fins on the side of her hand snag in the water-formed tangles. I push her away with a weak hand. My lungs scream. Worry claws at my mind. I'm going to die at the bottom of this tank while Donovan watches. He must be a devil. A demon.

The mermaid's lips move as she stares at me, sharp teeth poking out. I stare at her, waiting for her to attack but her mouth just makes the same movements again.

Black spots tamper with my vision and I reach weakly up toward the sky. I keep my finger pointing up, begging her to bring me back.

She doesn't seem to notice, still looking at me the same way as before. Things start to go fuzzy, and I realize belatedly that she must have been trying to talk to me.

I look back at the air waiting at the top of the tank and let darkness consume me.

Chapter Four

Something slaps against my face and my head whips back and forth as I come to.

"Come on," Donovan grunts as I cough up what feels like gallons of water.

I roll on my side and water continues spilling out of my throat. Blinking blearily at my surroundings, I find myself on the metal deck beside the glass tank.

The creature who almost killed me perches in the tank window. My heart beats irregularly as I scuttle away from her, my legs too weak to stand.

"Calm down." Donovan tries to reassure me as my shoulders shake. "She's not going to hurt you. I don't think she was ever trying to hurt you. She's the one who brought you back to the top of the tank after you passed out."

"—don't trust—won't do—again," I gasp out, my throat burning from all the water.

Donovan laughs but doesn't meet my gaze. "I figured if anything were to pull the nixie out of you, it would be this. You know, hanging out in a tank with so many of your cousins."

I can't even manage a weak smile as I stare at him. He's just done an experiment on me. A stupid, not well-thought-out experiment. Not at all what I thought would happen when I asked to be tested. An image of a sterile room and lab coats flashes through my mind before I can shake it away. Donovan definitely never planned on doing anything that scientific.

"I guess you've found your answer then." I stand up with a snarl, staying as far away from both of them as I can on the narrow metal deck.

"Oh, come on." He's still smiling. "Don't be like that. It's not like you're hurt or anything."

"You didn't know if I would get hurt or not! I could've died in that tank, and you would've been standing around like an idiot watching it happen." My blood is boiling, ringing through my ears.

The yelling burns my strained throat and creates an ache in my chest. Donovan runs a hand through his hair as his cheeks grow pink.

"You never would've died." He holds his hands out as though he's calming an animal. "We have safety precautions set up on this tank."

"You don't think that would've been something I might want to know before you tossed me in there?" My breathing grows harder against my sore throat as I glare at him.

He gives me a side grin. "I thought it would be more fun this way."

Shaking my head, I use the railing of the deck to stand against. My knees shake, but my disgust empowers me as I walk down the steps and cling to the railing. Donovan calls after me, but I don't slow down. A splash announces my new 'friend's' disappearance. Reaching the bottom, I lean against the side of the tank and stomp back toward the giant metal doors.

Creatures make faces at me as I pass by their home. The

one who almost dragged me to my death follows me, her eyebrows pointed down as she mouths something through the glass. I purposefully keep my eyes focused on the door and don't try to figure out what she might be saying to me.

Only after I place my shaking hands on the handle of the door do I realize I won't be able to open it, I don't know how to get to my room, and Donovan hasn't followed me. My pride burns but I know pulling on the handle will be useless. Even if I hadn't been on the brink of death only minutes ago, seeing the strain Donovan went through just to crack it open for us is something beyond my strength level.

"Waiting for me?" His mouth is pulled to the side in a way that makes me want to slap him.

I gesture to the door with wide arms and step back, leaving him space to open it. He looks at me, grin growing wider.

"Don't you think you should say 'please?'"

A scream threatens to erupt from my wounded throat. The last thing I would ever want to do is say 'please' to him.

We just stare at each other. Donovan raises an eyebrow at me. I cross my arms over my chest, refusing to rise to his bait.

He pushes off the door and saunters back around the side of the tank, his long legs moving steadily away from me. Panic sets in. *He's really not going to let me out of here unless I say please to him.*

"Wait," I finally call.

Donovan stops walking and leans against the tank, the blue water reflecting off of his black hair. "Yes?"

"I would really like to go back to my room now." I deliberately avoid the statement he's looking for.

He raises both brows. "Don't you think you should say something to me then?"

I grind my teeth, violent thoughts flashing across my mind. But all of this is fruitless. I have no power here.

"Please."

"I would love to help you out with that." His voice booms across the large room.

Walking past me, he pulls on the handle. His muscles almost pop out of his skin with the force required to get the door moving. He gets it farther open than last time, linking his arm through mine before leading me back out to the hallway.

He walks with his shoulders thrown back, none of the timid worry he had earlier bleeding through. Maybe he knows he can't hide me from anyone else as my shoes continue to slap wetly against the tiled floors, leaving soggy footprints trailing behind us. Maybe he feels more confident now that he's had a question answered.

The trip back is more direct, leaving us standing in front of my bedroom door in no time. Donovan opens the door and nods his head to me in mock respect as he releases my arm and gestures for me to move inside.

It's that little gesture that breaks me. I punch his shoulder, my hand in a tight fist as I give him all the strength left in me. My hand throbs from the impact and I look up at him with a scowl. My efforts don't even elicit a wince. He uses his arm to push me the rest of the way into the room as a deep chuckle rumbles in his throat.

He can't be human. I'd ask what he is, but the question would come as a compliment his inhuman strength. I can't give him the satisfaction.

Determined to solve it on my own, I march over to the bench at the foot of the bed. With a huff I lean against the foot board and cross my arms over my chest. "What now?"

Donovan closes the door, ambling over to me. "What do you mean?"

"I mean now you know I'm not any kind of nixie. So, what do we do?" I speak slowly so he can't misunderstand. It's hard not to grind my teeth together.

"It's not so much that we found out you weren't a nixie.

It's more that we found out you can't change," he says. "The others in the tank recognized you as one of them."

"Yeah, that's why they pulled me down and tried to drown me, because they wanted me to be one of them." My voice is sour.

Donovan slides onto the bench. "You realize they weren't trying to kill you right?"

"No, I don't realize that. From where I'm sitting, it definitely seems like they were trying to kill me."

He runs a slender hand through his dark hair. "If you were a full nixie, dropping you in that tank wouldn't have done anything to you. I mean, you would've been able to breathe. It was just a game to them."

"This isn't a game, it's my life!" I fling myself from the bench to stand in front of him. "I'm tired of you treating everything that happens to me like a joke."

Donovan's mouth pulls down. "I'm not saying it's a joke. I'm just saying you shouldn't be so quick to assume anyone who does anything to you that you don't like is out to get you."

"Forgive me if I assume things in this building are less than pleasant where I'm concerned. You know, considering I'm being held here against my will."

He rubs his closed eyes with his thumb and forefinger. Silence sits like a heavy blanket over us, but I don't take back my words.

"Can we move past this?" His voice is quiet.

I nod, my brows still pulled tight. I need more information, but it doesn't mean I'm ready to forgive him.

"Okay, great." He claps his hands together and stands up. "Are you ready for me to lay things out for you then?"

"I thought you never would."

He's been so evasive up to this point, only giving information when it suits him. I never thought he would ever be willing to hand anything over to me.

"We're looking for something important," he says. "Something we believe your mother may have given to our...enemies."

"Your enemies?" I chuckle, the hit of a smile softening my face. "What is this? A comic book grade school rivalry?"

Donovan shakes his head. "This is bigger than anything like that. Surely you must realize that with all these creatures and all this power there would be a darker side to it. Even in your own human history people have rarely been able to hold out against the lure of power."

"Are you saying you have a good and an evil side?" I scratch my head while he nods. "Because this still sounds like a children's book."

"Just because we can't all get along peacefully doesn't mean we're childish." His mouth pulls into a frown.

I nod sarcastically. "Oh, I'm sure."

"If you can't take this seriously then maybe we shouldn't talk about it at all," he says. I do my best to look doleful so he'll continue. "To sum up, we're looking for a relic and your mother was the last person to have it in her possession. She was working on it for us and now we really need it back."

"I'm sure you do," I say as his dark eyes watch me. "Why can't you just find another relic and call it good? What's the point of looking for something that I honestly won't be able to help you find?"

The muscles in his face pull taut. "There's only one like this. We have nothing that could replace it."

I sit back, doing my best to absorb all this nonsense.

"What does it look like?" I run my mind over the many different knickknacks I remember from our beach house.

He slumps to the floor and crosses his legs. "We were really hoping you would know. I'm not supposed to give you any clues."

I bark out a laugh. "You want me to tell you where it is, but you won't tell me what I'm supposed to be looking for?"

He raises his arms to the side in an awkward shrug while I continue to laugh.

"Seriously, if you're looking for my help, you're going to have to give me a lot more to go off. I didn't know about any of this before yesterday."

Donovan stands again. "That's just the thing. You used to know all about this. We've talked about it before. We planned on you spending some time here working with us. Why else would I be the one that came to get you?"

"Cause you're a kidnapping demon?"

"No. Because we're friends...We were friends."

Shoulders drooping, his jaw slackens, and I feel my heart soften. But it doesn't change anything. I know it doesn't. He still brought me here as a prisoner. "I don't remember any of that."

"I know," he says, voice soft. "Patrice told me this could happen to you. I just never believed it."

He opens and closes his fists, standing lost in the big room. I'm tempted to move; my body aching to comfort him, but I hold back. My hands grab the bench and dig into the wood.

"I have no idea what I'm supposed to do." My voice is apologetic for more than just my lack of knowledge.

Donovan nods. "We'll have to figure this out together."

"I'd like that."

* * *

Days pass with no noticeable improvement. Donovan spends hours each day talking with me about my life in Maine, but I never remember anything important.

At this point, I'm dying of boredom and the tired repetition of days. The bed is my most constant companion and where I spend too much of my time. It's there nestled among the pillows that I wonder if Aunt Nina is looking for me. Nick must be going crazy wondering what's happened to me. At least, I hope he is. I don't dare voice my dark fears that everyone is relieved now that I've seemingly run away.

After a week and a half of Donovan's quiet prodding, I have to wonder. Someone should have come across this building asking about me by now. I mean there must be some kind of trail that could lead the police to me, right?

Donovan's gaze lingers on my drooping form where I'm becoming one with the bed as he comes into the room. "Rough night?"

I groan and roll over, burying my face in a pillow. There's not a single good reason to get up. It's not like I'll be going anywhere.

The bed sinks under his weight. "Too worn out to work?"

"What's there even left to work on? Every day it's the same questions and every day I don't have any answers for you," I say, voice muffled in the pillow.

Donovan sighs. "I know. I know this has been hard. Why don't we get out today? Would that help?"

I nod, keeping my face in the pillow as Donovan laughs. He pats me on the back, the sound echoing through my hollow chest as my back burns from his touch.

He gets up but I don't follow him. I know I agreed with his plan, but I can't bring myself to get up today. Not even for the promise of a new location. I'm just too far down this spiral. All I want is for Mom to come and fix everything. I didn't ask for any of this to happen, and being kept here with almost nothing to do but think about it is a cruel punishment for not having any memories.

Donovan doesn't wait more than a minute before grabbing me by the waist and hefting me out of bed. My sock-covered feet hit the floor with a thump, sending a jolt all the way to my neck as my breath hitches.

I take a second to adjust my clothes when he puts me down, the unfamiliar silky fabrics that I've been provided twisting weirdly against my body. It's been a nice-ish thought to give me clothing, but just one glance into the closet would tell anyone who knows me that my captors do not. The rows of bright colors and shimmering fabrics are so far away from the typical faded cotton neutrals that I usually wear that even after a week I'm not used to how these clothes feel against my body.

"Want to change?" Donovan turns his back to give me privacy as my cheeks flame.

Having a boy in the same room makes my body clench up and my mind war with indecision. But if we're going somewhere then I'd rather not be paraded around in pajamas. I grab one of the many flowered blouses and do my best to put it on while shimmying out of my pajama top so that I'm completely covered throughout the process. With a vicious smile, I grab the pair of jeans hidden in the bottom of the closet and slip those on too.

When I first got here there were a few quiet girls who would come in to clean and try to confiscate my stuff. When my shirt didn't come back from the laundry, I didn't dare let them take my jeans too. I tried to get them to help me run away, but they moved around me like I didn't even exist. My heart clenches at the memory of hope being quickly eradicated from my system.

Donovan turns around as I'm just finishing zipping up my fly, grabbing me by the hand and dragging me out the door. I try again to find familiarity in his grip, but nothing surfaces. He must have lied about being my friend.

I almost have to run to keep up with him as we speed

down the long hallway. He doesn't say a word about the level of noise I make today, which is great because my sneakers were one of the first things to go. The strappy sandals they left me clap in wild abandon against the tiles as I run after him.

The hallways twists and turns and then we pass through a set of French doors off an immense dining room with twenty seats lined up around an empty marble slab table. The sun blinds me for a moment as we walk onto a flagstone deck. The sound of the waves beating against the beach takes over my senses as I use my hand to shade my face until my eyes adjust.

"Come on!" Donovan lets go of my hand and runs across the deck to the stairs set into the stone wall.

The lack of tread on my sandals has me slipping after him as I suck in a quick breath. As I get to the stairs, Donovan's already reached the bottom and is pulling off his shoes and socks. Cutting to the chase, I pull off my ridiculous shoes before running down the stairs.

Donovan runs down the beach, flinging sand up in his wake. "Come on slow poke!"

Skin tingling, my track training kicks in, and I fly across the sand. My breathing finds its rhythm, arms swinging as my face cracks into a smile.

Donovan peeks over at me with wide eyes as I catch up with him. This only spurs me on until we're running shoulder-to-shoulder into the surf, all the depression of earlier momentarily forgotten.

With a wild look in his eyes, he grabs me by the waist. Pressing me tight to his chest, our breath mingling before he throws me into the water. A primal scream rips from my throat as panic hits me in the gut. Memories of the tank press in on my mind making my chest squeeze tight. Then my butt hits the sand and I spring up, gasping for air.

Donovan laughs as I pull limp strands of hair out of my

face. The smile from our run warms my face again and I send a splash at him, laughing as it hits him in his open mouth.

He shoves water back at me and then we're having a full-on splash fight and rolling in the warm water. I can't remember the last time I was able to enjoy myself without feeling like the weight of the world was resting on my shoulders.

With a sly smile, I grab a handful of sand and rub it into Donovan's still partially dry hair. It dribbles down his forehead as he sputters at me, but I can't stop laughing. Falling on my knees, I laugh so hard I can barely breathe. My face turns red with the effort and my chest hurts.

Donovan kicks water into my still-open mouth and I choke on salt water. The taste of brine nearly overwhelms my taste buds. Swallowing some of it, I gaze at Donovan with wide eyes, my mouth frozen in a face-splitting smile. He laughs, the tension running out of his body as he closes his eyes.

His laugh might not be familiar to me, but I don't feel threatened by him anymore. What I feel is fear of myself. Fear that I don't know my own mother. My own identity.

Does he know me? He knew I needed a day out of my room. I sigh, leaning back into the water.

I may not be a 'nixie' like Mom, the thought no longer stopping me in my tracks, but I feel myself recharging in the water. Even without being kidnapped, if I'd spent over a week in my room at home, I would've ended up with cabin fever too.

Donovan struts onto the beach, wringing water out of his shirt as it clings to his body. "Feeling better?"

I want to choke back my smile, but I can't help it, I do feel better. My lips pull so wide that I'm sure he can see all my teeth. "Thanks for getting me out today."

"I'm sorry it has to be like this." A small frown grows on his face as he trudges through the sand.

Following behind, I speed up to face him. "So, let's not have it be like this then."

He shakes his head, wet black hair falling into his eyes as he looks away from me, my heart flip-flopping in my chest. "There's nothing I can do. I told you that."

"I don't understand!" My voice cracks as my hands curl into fists. "I've been here forever, and I've only ever seen *you*. You talk like someone else is making you do this, but where's the proof?"

Donovan sighs and runs a hand through his hair. He plops into the sand to pull his shoes back on, and I have to look away from his skin-tight shirt before a blush can finish creeping up my cheeks. "You really shouldn't rush this. There's no way you're ready to meet Patrice yet. She doesn't want to see you until you've been able to remember something useful."

"Well, Patrice won't get anything until I meet her." I decide, sitting straight-backed in the sand beside him.

"Are you crazy? You have no idea what you're dealing with. You think sitting in your room for days is horrible? She can make you truly miserable." His eyes narrow, blocking their emotion from me.

I shake my head. "I don't trust you."

He looks away from the ocean to stare into my eyes, my reflection in them stern and unforgiving. My damp hair lays lank against my shoulders, but I refuse to shiver. I can't let myself soften. Being soft has gotten me nowhere.

"Take me to Patrice."

Donovan stares out at the water again, swallowing hard. "Please don't make me do this."

I cross my hands over my chest, staring down at him with narrowed brows as I stand. I'm getting answers today, regardless of what Donovan says. This ends now.

"Fine." Donovan marches back up the stairs, his shoulders hunched.

"This is for the best," I whisper. He doesn't even glance my way. I bite my lip, needing him on my side. "We can still be friends, right?"

He stops short. "Friends? Friends trust each other, Avi. You've already made it perfectly clear that you don't trust me."

"I would've thought you'd be happy I considered you a friend at all after you *kidnapped* me." My face feels hot and tight.

"Whatever," he says under his breath as he climbs the stairs.

* * *

Donovan guides me back through the French doors, and I stop to run a finger over the smooth surface of the dining room table. I've never been around such wealth before. What else could be lurking behind the other doors we pass? It's almost like Cinderella's castle, except that I'm the one locked away in the attic.

"I thought you wanted to see Patrice." Donovan comes up behind me, his forehead wrinkled.

Wrenching my hand away, I follow his taut back down the hallway. His shoulders tense and despite everything, I have a building desire to run my hand across his tight muscles.

He takes me around to the other side of the building, the world outside the open windows full of lush green grass and flowered gardens, a hedge of rosebushes filling the room with their scent.

"It's so beautiful here."

Donovan shakes his head. He stops in front of an engraved door and gives it a quick tap.

"Yes?" a stern alto comes from the other side of the door.

Donovan gives me a look that says *last chance to change your mind*. I mouth a quick 'no' back and he squares his shoulders and faces the door again.

"I've got Avi here. She wants to speak to you directly."

"Let her in."

Chills spread down my spine as he opens the door and pushes me through. He slams it closed behind me and I'm instantly alone with this mystery woman. Maybe I should have listened to Donovan after all.

"Do you have something to tell me?" she asks.

A severe woman with pale white-blonde hair and clear blue eyes looks down at me from behind her practical desk. The top is completely devoid of personality. There are no framed pictures or paperweights to help me figure her out. Her nails click against the black keyboard, not stopping for our little impromptu meeting. Scratching the back of my leg with my foot, I try to work out what to say. After all, there's nothing I've remembered that I can tell her.

"Are you going to waste my time all day?" She gives me a cold look.

"No, of course not. You're Patrice?" I ask and she raises a brow at me.

"Yes. Is that all?"

"I need to know why I'm here. What is it I'm supposed to be looking for?" My words are halting and less strong than they were with Donovan back on the beach.

She stands behind her desk, revealing a lithe body with legs wrapped in black leather pants that just keep going. "Let me understand this. Donovan brought you to me with no information. You remain completely useless, and have the nerve to disturb my work with mundane and pointless questions?"

Her frown actually makes me flinch as her thin lips pull impossibly down.

"I just can't work under these conditions," I say while she

sneers. "I don't know anything about my mother's work. Asking me about it over and over again won't help me remember things I've never known."

"Donovan," she calls over my shoulder as she brushes silky hair away from her face. The action reveals a delicately pointed ear. "Get her out of here and give her the serum. We're done waiting."

"Yes, ma'am." Donovan stands before the newly opened door, his face drained of color.

I back out of the room on swift feet, not taking my eyes off Patrice until the door is securely shut.

"What is she?" I whisper to Donovan while backing down the hallway.

"Just one of the Dark Fae," Donovan says with a dismissive wave. "They think they're better than everyone else."

The power I felt in her presence seems to confirm that opinion, but I keep that to myself. Donovan curses under his breath and I let the questions go, not wanting to find an argument.

He leads me farther away from Patrice's office, his shoulders softening with every step. We get twenty feet away and he stops, grabbing my hand.

"You have to understand, what's about to happen isn't my fault," he says in a hurried whisper as he bends down to stare into my eyes. His breath is soft on my face. "I don't have a choice. I... I'm so sorry. I never thought it would come to this."

"Come to what?" I ask as the blood drains from my face.

"The serum." His eyes are tortured as he reaches towards me then stops and pulls his hand back. "It's going to force you to tell her about your mom and the process of pulling that information from your mind makes your brain unusable. Think of it like an acid that destroys as it searches."

"Uh-uh." I take my hand out of his tightening grip.

"You have to believe me, this is it. In about ten minutes you'll be drooling into a pillow with no chance of recovery." The words tumble out faster and faster as he reaches over to grip me by the shoulders.

"You're hurting me," I complain, but he doesn't hear me.

"I always thought you'd eventually remember. Just a few days would be all it would take and then you would remember everything. Remember your life, remember us."

Us? My mouth goes dry. "What are you—"

Donovan uses his grip on my shoulders to pull me forward, planting his lips firmly on mine.

Shock races through me, and for a moment I'm too stunned to respond. His lips are firm against mine, pressing into me with intent like he thinks he can force my memories back with a kiss.

No matter how attractive I might find him, this is not something I'm ready for. My life is confusing enough right now.

His fingers thread through my hair, pulling me even closer. Donovan's breathing grows heavy against my cheek. I bring my arms up against his chest and then gently push him away from me, breaking our faces apart.

His dark eyes stare at me, unfocused as he comes back down after his moment of passion. Chest rising and falling at a quick pace, he stares at me as he waits for me to say something.

"Thank you for the kiss." My words are slow as I process his actions. *Thanks for stealing my first kiss.* At least the first kiss that I can remember if he's right and I have memories I can't access.

Tears burn behind my eyes. This has all been way too much. And now this too... Why did he think this would be a good idea?

His face drops, the smile that had been perking up at the sides of his lips pulling down to his chin. "That's all?"

I shrug my shoulders to hide the pain. "What am I supposed to say?"

"I just thought... I just thought if I could remind you that you might... you might..." Donovan buries his hands in the hair on the back of his head so I can only see his arms pressed against his face.

"I don't remember anything like that." My chest falls as I come to terms with the fact that I may never remember my real first kiss. "I just met you."

"Maybe this is for the best then," Donovan says, jaw clenched as he looks away from me.

He doesn't glance back at me before heading down the hallway again. The slapping on my sandals against the tile floor grates my ears as I speed up to him.

"Were we...?" I taper off, not sure what to ask him. I'm almost afraid of what he might say.

Donovan doesn't look at me, his black eyes trained on the tile in front of us. I wait a few moments, but he still doesn't say anything.

"I didn't mean to offend you." I keep my voice earnest despite the disastrous kiss that still tingles on my lips.

He laughs, the sound reverberating deep in his chest. "Offend me? We have years of history together and you're worried about offending me."

"Has this been going on since I've been in New York?" I ask as my mind tries to piece together some sort of timeline.

"No, not since you've been there the last three months."

My heart threatens to stop as my mouth goes dry. "Three months? But my mom has been missing for years now."

He gives me a sidelong glance and reaches but he's not fast enough. My legs give out beneath me, my knees scraping the edges of the tiles as I collapse.

My entire life is a lie.

No wonder everyone's been so confused as to why I know

nothing about Mom. I literally don't remember anything about her life because somehow that's been taken from me.

"Avi?" Donovan's voice grows gentle as he kneels next to me. "It's really not that bad."

My breathing is strangled, sporadic as tears drip down my cheeks. I don't know what to say to him, but even if I did, the lump in my throat wouldn't let me.

"That's why Patrice wants you to have this potion, to fill in some of those holes you're living with." He places a soft hand on my back and swirls it around in small circles.

I draw in a shaky breath. "The potion that will melt my brain as it goes through finding these memories?"

His hand tenses on my back before he grabs me by the upper arm and pulls me to standing. My knees buckle as he lifts me up. His hand grips underneath my arm, forcing me to stay upright even as my chin trembles.

He marches forward, my shoulder drooping in the silence that grows between us.

The door to our destination hangs open on limp hinges. Donovan sits me down in a cool metal chair next to a long white counter-height table. The seat sends chills along my legs, making me more and more numb. Looking at Donovan with dead eyes, I watch as he pulls lavender-colored vials out of one of the upper cabinets.

The glasses clink together, their contents sloshing around inside. Donovan asks me something, but my mind has withdrawn too far into itself to answer. After a few more attempts at communication, he stops trying. We're both resigned to my fate. I already know I can't get away from him, and we both know that he's going to do exactly what Patrice told him to.

He holds a paper cup with two tablespoons of purple liquid sliding around the bottom. Staring into its depths, my breath slows as I wait for him to force me to drink it. Donovan sighs like he has something he wants to say, his tight grip crinkling the cup. But it doesn't matter. My brain is already too far gone to care anymore.

Glass shatters, sprinkling across the counter-top and over the floor, slamming me back into myself. Donovan jerks in surprise, his hand still holding the cup hanging suspended in the air between us.

"What the—?" he sputters as four large men in black uniforms with sparkling gold insignias over the right breast swing in through the window they just broke.

The one closest to Donovan reaches out, clocking him on the side of his temple. Donovan crumbles and the man walks around him like he's nothing more than a piece of furniture.

They swarm around me, still not saying anything. One of them takes the cup out of Donovan's hand. He crumples it in his massive fist, throwing it on the floor. I stand to run, but he grabs me, lifting me into his arms. Shock permeates my system, leaving my body trembling.

The men glide back out the window and sprint across the manicured lawns surrounding my prison. The man carrying me breathes easily as I jostle in his arms, like he always runs while carrying seventeen-year-old girls.

We reach the edge of the yard, where wilderness threatens to reclaim its territory. The man holding me whispers something. My world turns black.

Donovan is gone.

Chapter Five

I'm surrounded by a plushy warm heaven as I wake up. The light is soft and yellow with a few beams staining the wall with its rich color. The bed I'm in is piled high with cozy blankets and the comfort makes me never want to leave. The ceiling I can see is smooth, no stone to be seen. I know I'm not home, but this already feels better than where I came from.

"Hey, welcome back."

I sit up with a jolt. "Nick?"

He's seated in a chair next to me, a wide grin splitting his face. I throw myself at him, wrapping my arms around his neck. He stiffens for a moment before hugging me back. My chest feels with warmth and my body relaxes into his arms.

"What are you doing here? Did they take you too?" My voice is high and breathless as I finally release him and sit back in the bed.

"Like I was going to let my best friend go missing and not hunt her down myself," he says with an easy laugh. His wide smile is so contagious that I feel an answering smile pull at my cheeks.

"How did you find me?" My body is practically vibrating.

Am I really free? I want to trust that the nightmare I've been living in is over. No more sloshing around in giant tanks of mermaids. No more phlebotomists drinking blood. I want it to be over.

Nick lifts a shoulder. "I have my sources."

"I'm sure you do." I laugh and lay my head against the headboard. "I'm so happy to see you."

His smile falls a little, nothing a stranger would notice, but I can see the stress my disappearance has caused him. "I'm happy to see you too."

I can't stop grinning at him. I'm sitting in a real bedroom. It feels too good to be true. A warning sound at the back of my mind that reminds me I still don't know where I am, but at least I'm with my best friend. Everything was in shambles when I blacked out, but now I just know they'll be better. Tension melts from my shoulders. The tightness in my chest that's been there since I first met Donovan relaxes.

Donovan.

My heart falls. What happened to him? Is he okay? Did Patrice punish him for my disappearance?

Part of me is disgusted with myself that I would even care. He kidnapped me and now I'm worried he'll be in trouble because I got away. I shake my head, irritated that I could be this stupid. I will not be a victim of Stockholm Syndrome.

He said we were friends. But he kissed me like we were—

The door swings open, revealing one of the men from my rescue as he pops his head into the room. "Is she okay?"

"Yeah, we're doing great." Nick turns his face away from me to respond.

"Get any information yet?"

Nick shakes his head. "Not yet just give me some more time."

My breath comes faster, and my palms grow sweaty, as the

man shuts the door. Nick turns his easy smile on me, but I don't feel like returning it anymore.

"What?" The smile stretching across his face looking more like a mask now.

I shrink back against the headboard, my blood turning to ice in my veins. Donovan had said I'd been gone for months, not years like Nick wanted me to believe. *How well do I even know him?* I may have switched a tank full of mermaids for one full of sharks.

Nick reaches out to grab my hand, but I wrench it back from him. His forehead wrinkles as he stares at me.

"What's wrong?" he asks as his hand curls into a fist in his lap.

The one window set high in the wall sends yellow rays of light across his face as he leans forward. My hands fidget in my lap as my gaze darts around the room for a potential escape. Everything is cement walls and the only furniture in the room are my metal bed with its pile of blankets and his chair. The only obvious door is the same one the man came through. There's no way out.

"Avi, what's going on?" Nick's blue eyes follow the bead of sweat growing on my temple.

He's a part of this, whatever this is. He's been part of it all along. A small tear slips out of the corner of my eye. I knit my hands together and still myself as I wait for Nick to explain. We're friends, right? He'll tell me what's going on.

Nick moves closer to me, but I wave him back. I don't want his comfort right now.

"Let me help you. I know you've been through a lot." He keeps his voice slow and calm.

"You're just as bad as him."

Nick visibly flinches at my quiet accusation.

His gaze drops to his lap where he opens and closes his fists in slow repetition. "It's really not like that."

"Oh, no? What've you been lying to me about, Nick? What've you been hiding from me? What is it that you need from me?" Questions drip out of my mouth like venom. I know Nick doesn't deserve *all* my anger, but there's no holding back now.

The close-cut curls lying against his head shake as he scratches the back of his neck. "This isn't how it was supposed to happen."

I bark out a crazy laugh, and I'm sure my eyes have gone equally as wild. "And you think this is how I wanted things to happen?! You better start telling the truth."

Nick's brows slam down over his bright eyes. "I never lied to you!"

"Then why are you looking for information from me?" I ask, my voice sickly sweet as I tilt my head at him.

"I don't know any more than what you've already told me," Nick says, still trying to profess his innocence.

"Then what makes you think I have information you need?" I cross my arms over my slight chest.

"I literally know as much as that guy just told me."

I don't believe him. The guys that took me from Donovan don't seem like the kind what would let anyone in to see me just because they asked nicely. Nick knows something. I don't back down as he stares at me, open hands in his lap still pleading with me.

A knock pounds on the door before one of the uniformed men swings it open. It smacks against the wall, breaking our standoff as we both flinch.

The man's broad chest fills his black military shirt, showing off his firm muscles. He hands me a breakfast shake with an easy smile, his brown eyes sparkling. "Thought you might be hungry.

"Thanks." I give him my most brilliant smile as I crack off the top of the bottle and take a big swig. Chalky chocolate spreads across my tongue as I force myself to swallow it down.

I don't give Nick a second glance as he glowers at me behind the newcomer's back. He's had his chance to talk to me and didn't take it. I'm ready for a fresh start with whoever this nice man is.

"How are you feeling?" He shifts so his large torso completely blocks Nick from my view. "We worried how you would recover after we found you in the lab."

"You came just in the nick of time," I tell him, my voice breathless with thanks. "Donovan wasn't able to do anything to me yet."

There's a thump as Nick kicks the wall with the back of his foot at the sound of Donovan's name.

"That's really good to hear."

I reach out a hand and lay it on his arm, feeling bad for him even though I shouldn't. "I really am so grateful that you came when you did. They were planning on giving me something that sounded like it would turn me into a vegetable. You saved me from a fate worse than death."

Nick's face grows purple as the man gives me a shy smile. This guy can't be much older than I am, but the uniform he wears with the same insignia as the men who saved me from Patrice ages him with a wave of authority.

"What's your name?" I ask. I can't decide if I want to know just to know or if not knowing Donovan's for so long has me thinking of simple things like names a lot quicker. And partially because I know it will bother Nick. The longer I focus on this guy, the tighter Nick's shoulders become.

"Jack." He holds out his hand for me to shake. "Nice to meet you, Avi."

"Is there a reason for your visit besides the drink, or are you ready to leave?" Nick's voice is sullen as he crosses his arms.

Jack looks over at him but doesn't apologize for prolonging his visit. "We're still talking."

"It sounds like you're done." Nick stands to challenge him, his jaw tight.

"Oh, calm down!" I turn to Jack again. "I'm sorry he's being so rude. I don't know what's gotten into him."

Jack shrugs his large shoulders with a grin. "Nick's had a stick up his butt for a few weeks now."

It only takes seconds for the timeline to snap into place. Ever since I was kidnapped. Which means that Nick's known about this sub-level kingdom for longer than he was letting on. My blood pumps rapidly in my chest as I stare at his unrepentant face.

"At least have the decency to look ashamed," I snarl. He needs to feel something about the way he's treated me.

We've been friends for years, at least I thought we'd been friends. I thought it had been years.

My mind spins with all the changes and I almost miss the rude gesture Nick gives Jack as he leaves my room.

"So, you *do* know about everything." I feel hollow as the words leave my chest.

"It's not what you think," Nick protests as he takes a step toward me. "I was assigned to you after you were moved to New York."

Assigned. My heart falls and I have to grip the side of the bed to keep myself upright. Nick's face pales as he realizes his mistake.

"I mean, that's how it started, but you're not just an assignment to me anymore. We're friends." He holds his hands out to me in supplication.

"Just leave me alone." I can't take any more of his half-hearted lies and explanations. I bite the inside of my cheek until the coppery taste of blood fills my mouth. He squirms under my gaze, but I don't look away.

He nods and strides for the door without looking back at me. Alone again, I bury myself under the blankets. My shoulders shake with heavy sobs.

I may not be with Donovan anymore, but nothing has changed.

* * *

"Good morning!" a bright voice breaks over the small piece of calm I've found in my solitude.

I grip the blankets around my head as I roll over.

"I brought you something to eat and some better company than all those boys you've been forced to hang out with. Ugh, I can just imagine how horrible that's been for you."

I peek through the blankets at a red-haired girl carrying a tray by my bed. She's right, I *am* relieved not to be spending another day with a bunch of backstabbing boys. *Boys who lie and pretend to care about me.* Even in my mind the words come out bitter.

Sitting up, I let her place the tray in my lap. She settles herself at the end of the bed, leaning against the cold metal frame. A bright smile creases her thin lips.

"I'm so glad you made it here. It's been so dull just waiting for you all the time. And meetings, so many meetings! I thought I would die of boredom! But you're here, so now the real fun can begin." She talks at a rapid pace that's almost too much for me to keep up with.

She has an easy way about her, and my body relaxes in her presence more than it has since I got here. I have no memories of her, so I don't have to worry about her confessing anything to me. There's something so reassuring about knowing that she's not about to drop some heavy bomb on me about my forgotten past.

The tray she brought is overflowing with pancakes, still

warm from the stove. Thick rivers of maple syrup form a moat around them. My mouth starts to water as I stare at her offering.

"Oh sorry, you might want these." She pulls a fork and knife out of her white apron pocket. "I grabbed them just before they closed the kitchen for lunch."

My stomach rumbles and I dig into my plate, barely acknowledging the bright sun of almost noon coming in through the window.

"My name's Sarah. I haven't been here very long, and there's not many of us. Girls I mean. These men think we're not as essential. Imagine my surprise when they went through so much trouble to find you! I'm so glad they did though, I'm not complaining. I'm sure we'll be great friends. I'm excited to have more company. It can get soooooo dreary around here," she says without taking a breath.

Surprisingly, I actually *do* hope we'll end up being friends. My heart flutters hopefully at the idea of a real friend. I need someone who'll fill the awkward space in my life with noise and not expect anything more from me. I'm exhausted from trying to keep up with everyone's agendas. At least if she betrays me, it won't mean anything, not like Nick...

"So, what do you want to do today?" she asks when my plate is almost empty. Sarah's been talking almost constantly, so it's really the pause as she waits for my answer that alerts me to her question.

"What?" I ask through a mouthful of pancakes.

"What do you want to do today?" she repeats with a smile, brushing a few curly strands of hair behind her ear. This must not be the first time someone's zoned out while listening to her.

I wave my fork at the empty room. "Isn't this it?"

Sarah laughs, her voice high and easy. "Of course not. You're not a prisoner here. In fact, I think they're hoping you'll end up working here. Some days we could use all the help we can get. Plus, they like to recruit us young, so we'll grow used to the workload and material. It's a little messed up, but who can blame them?"

"What's the material?" Maybe this is the moment when I'll finally get a clear answer.

"Just the usual," she says as she picks lint from under her fingernail. "Magical objects, hidden creatures, stopping evil. Pretty basic."

My laugh echoes against the blank walls. There's nothing basic about stopping evil, and I can't begin to imagine what kinds of magical stuff they must deal with on a daily basis. This will be all brand new to me.

"Want to check it out?" she asks, her green eyes flashing as she hops off the bed.

"Definitely." I give her a vigorous nod. If there's a chance to leave the room, I need to take it.

No one has bothered to provide new clothes for me, so I'm stuck in the same flimsy wardrobe from Donovan's. Sarah doesn't comment on it even though she's dressed in some kind of dark medical scrubs. It's a loose olive crew neck with matching pants and it's ridiculous how jealous I am of them.

I breathe a sigh as we leave the room, breaking free from what I thought would be my next prison. The hallway we enter has big skylights set in the ceiling, which combined with the white tile floor and the white walls flood the space with light. It's so different from where I stayed before that for the first few steps, I can't stop myself from blinking. The modern, clinical feel is miles away from the dark castle vibe where I stayed with Donovan.

"Where are we?" I ask Sarah.

"Still in New York." The pant legs of her scrubs swish as she walks next to me.

"Still in New York?" My face grows red. "You mean I've been in New York this whole time?"

Sarah lays a supportive hand on my arm as she keeps me moving down the hallway. "You've been sequestered on an island off the coast. It's been a magical sanctuary for some time, but we didn't realize Amaro had moved in. It's supposed to be a place where creatures can live and recover without fear, not some crazy dark corporate headquarters. In hindsight, we really should've thought about looking there sooner. I mean, there's not a huge radius that Donovan can disappear to."

"So, I've been in a secret hideout for the past few weeks that everyone else knew about but no one thought to actually look in?" I feel a headache blooming in my temples. Personally, that sounds like the first probably place to look, so what stopped them?

"Think of it like a national park, you don't usually run there looking for kidnap victims." Sarah gives me a shrug.

I know she believes what she's saying, but it still doesn't make sense to me. It seems like every summer I've heard at least one news report of someone missing in a national park. The police would never just avoid looking there because it was so obvious. Still, I need to be more grateful that I'm getting some information.

"How many of these parks do you have that you wouldn't have thought to check the one-off New York?"

"Don't be testy." Sarah stares at me with her big green eyes. "Everyone did the best they could to find you. It all worked out."

"I'm not testy." I rub my sweaty hands on the leg of my jeans. "And I'm not trying to make a fuss. I've just been tripping around for the last few weeks, and I feel like there's been no one to help me."

"Yeah." Sarah gives me a sidelong glance. "It's really too bad about the potion your mom gave you. I'm sure things would've been far less complicated if you'd just known every-thing in the first place."

"The potion my mom gave me?" My head jerks back as hot waves of betrayal travel over my body.

"Well yeah, how else do you think you lost so many memo-ries? Spells can take away a few, usually something specific, but you'd need a serious potion to do the thorough wipe she's done on you."

Stopping mid-stride, I force her to face me. "What makes you think it was my mom who gave it to me?"

"Who else had something to hide?" She raises her brows.

Linking arms with me, she forces me to keep pace with her. "I bet there's something we can do to help you out with that. There's usually a way to reverse these things, even the more complicated ones like yours."

"No thank you." I give her a dry laugh as my thoughts turn to Donovan. "I'll just stick with the way things are. I've had enough problems trying to get my memories back."

"Oh yeah, I heard about that. It's been the hottest gossip since you were brought in." Sarah squeezes my arm as she leads us down the right side of a split in the hallway. "Nasty stuff. We would *never* do something so barbaric."

I'd like to believe her, but human history has taught me *all* people are capable of outrageous types of cruelty depending on who it's being done to. We just call it something different to justify it. Justice, mercy, any number of words that say we're doing something cruel because we feel it's necessary.

Just like Donovan with me.

My heart aches as my mind glances over the image of him with pain in his eyes as he led me to my doom. I can still feel the pressure of his lips on mine as he desperately tried to help me remember my life from before. My life that included him.

His reluctance to hurt me resonates on my mouth. It shouldn't I should forget him. Just like I did before.

"Are you coming?" Sarah tries to move me forward as my steps slow and my thoughts linger over the last few weeks.

"Yes, of course."

My body follows her, but my mind doesn't. Nick had to have known about my history with Donovan. I mean, he's known me for five years now. Donovan said we'd been together up until the last few months. Why did he never say anything?

Sarah pushes open the swinging doors at the end of the hall and ushers me into the next room. Immediately I'm assaulted by noise: people talking, laughing, metal clanging and scraping. It takes me a second to process it, enough to look up from the floor. Sarah's brought me to a cafeteria. A cafeteria full of people. They laugh and joke, shoving spoonfuls of heavy lasagna into their wide-open mouths.

"I thought you might be hungry, maybe for more than just food." Sarah gives me a knowing smile that shows off a dimple in her right cheek.

"Thank you." My voice is quiet in the chaos of the room and there's a part of me that wishes I could melt into the floor.

Sarah beams at me, flashing bright white teeth. Handing me a tray, she pushes me into a line. The array of choices quickly brings me back to life, jolting me from my thoughts. My stomach keeps me fixated on the assortment of desserts: cheesecakes, pies, chocolate cake, and cookies the size of my head all sit behind the shiny glass case.

"Go for it." Sarah nudges my elbow. "You only have this great metabolism once, put it to work."

I give her a real laugh before loading up my tray. I don't even bother looking at the lasagna as I head back into the dining area. Sarah leads me to a table on the left side of the bright room, close to the middle. There're a few empty seats here, so I don't have to sit right next to my neighbor. Yet another thing I'm grateful to Sarah for.

Eating as quickly and as noisily as the people around me, I barely take the time to savor any of the wonderful flavors filling my plate. It's something so small, just the ability to choose what I want to eat, but I haven't had the opportunity in weeks. I run my hand along the side of the tray, marveling at the small freedoms granted me here.

Sarah doesn't bother trying to talk to me while we're eating. I watch her in the side of my vision as I eat, marking how she doesn't attack her plate as ravenously as I do. Even so, I'm grateful for the moments of silence she's giving me, something I wasn't sure if she was capable of.

My gaze roves over the sea of scrub-covered backs sitting at the tables around me. I wonder if Nick is hiding out in here. I should be angry with him, but I find the feeling ebbing away. We've been friends for years. I must believe that somewhere in his heart he is truly my friend. I can't even begin to contemplate what it would mean to me if everything were a lie.

"Looking for someone?" Sarah asks, noticing my distracted staring.

I shake my head. "Guess not."

"It's okay if you're looking for someone," Sarah says with a smile as she looks over the crowd. "There's a lot of cute boys here. We're pretty lucky, the options here are much better than the average high schools. It's probably all the training we have to do."

Nodding, I try to smile back at her. I'm not interested in looking for cute boys. I just want some answers.

I move to turn my attention back to my tray so Sarah doesn't think I'm looking for romance at a time like this and catch a glimpse of the back of Nick's head as he dumps his tray at one of the trashcans under the glowing green exit sign.

"I'll be right back." I don't even glance at Sarah as I leave the table and beeline to where Nick just was.

The doors are still swinging as I follow him out. "Nick!"

He glances over his shoulder at me and stops. He leans against the white walls of the hallway, watching me with a raised brow. "You want to talk now?"

"Well, yeah." I wring my hands together. "I just want to know what's going on."

"I know, I know." Nick nods at me with sympathy in his bright blue eyes. "I wish there was something I could tell you, but your mom gave you this potion. There's really nothing we can do to reverse it. I just sincerely hope you can still trust me. We'll get through this, I promise." He reaches for my hand, but I'm just out of reach.

"But that's the thing." I raise my fists to my temples. "I don't want to *just get through this*. I want to be able to understand. I want to know what's going on and why it's happening. What was my mother trying to hide from me? What about my mother is so important that everyone wants to know what she knew?"

Nick's face crinkles into a frown. "That's the problem. None of us can tell you the answer to that."

I slam my fist into the wall, sending shocks of pain up my arm. "None of this makes any sense! How can no one know what she was working on?!

"It's not like she was this crazy mysterious woman. We had a simple life! We walked on the beach and made pancakes on Saturday mornings. She didn't work for some secret organization bent on overthrowing the government. She didn't hide magical things in the closet. We lived a simple, beautiful life, and I just want it back. I need *her* back."

Nick wraps his arms around me as sobs wrack my body. I never asked for any of this. My fingers pull at the knots in my hair, ripping out a few chunks before logic overrules my emotions and forces me to stop.

"Just make it go back," I cry. "Even just to last month

when things weren't the best, but they at least made sense. I can't take this anymore."

"I know," he murmurs as he runs a calloused hand along my back.

He slides us down to the floor, letting me lean against his shoulder as my tears dry up. My body shakes.

"We're going to help you get through this." Nick's voice is soft in my ear. "You're not alone anymore."

"I didn't think I was." I pull out of his embrace with narrowed eyes.

Nick frowns as he looks at me for understanding. Of course, it wouldn't make sense to him. He doesn't know about Donovan. Doesn't know about the time we spent together. He may not have always been the nicest, but he was the closest thing I had to a friend for the last few weeks. He took care of me. And there was something in that kiss. Something almost familiar.

Donovan did the best he could under the circumstances, I'm sure. The thought of what Patrice is doing to him now has me scooting away from Nick's outstretched arms.

"Are you talking about those *creatures*?" Nick asks as the silence stretches between us. His face distorts at the last word, his neck growing red.

I bristle at his tone. "If you mean Donovan, then you don't know what you're talking about. He was nothing but kind to me."

"Yeah, sure, *so* kind while he kidnapped you and tried to turn you into a vegetable. How could I forget that? He sounds like a real pal." Nick stands and points a finger at me. "Don't mistake his lies for friendship."

I scramble off the floor to look him in the eye. "You don't get to tell me who my friends are. You've lied to me too! Who hasn't lied to me in this stupid place?"

Marching down the hallway, I slam my open palms into

the wall as I go. My blood burns, consuming me like a raging fire. The slap of my sandals against the smooth tiles mocks my anger. I rip them off my feet and throw them against the wall. My body weakens and I collapse in a pile as my legs give out from under me. I have no more tears left to cry, my shoulders shaking silently.

I slump down further, shoulders sinking into my lap until my head can rest on my knees. The turmoil of the last month has been far too much. If Nick thinks everything can just go back to the way it was between us, he needs to wake up. He *lied* to me. He wants me to hate Donovan, but Nick is the only one who lied. Donovan isn't perfect, but he's stood by his promises to me.

Honestly, I would like nothing more than to go back to my life in Maine when I didn't even know he existed. If I could wake up tomorrow and be back in my own bed with the smell of burnt toast wafting up the stairs while Mom sings in the kitchen, I could happily pretend that all of this had been nothing but a bad dream.

"Psst."

I glance up, swollen eyes widening. The door to the left of me cracks open, slender fingers beckoning me into the darkness. I curl up tighter, wrapping my arms around my knees and pulling them in close.

"Psst."

The sound echoes in the empty hallway. I look up just in time to see eyes reflecting against the darkness of the room.

When I still don't move, the door opens a little further. Its hinges squeak as it swings into the hallway. Leather creaks as the figure in the room leans forward enough for the light to catch on his black hair, creating a shining dark blue streak.

Donovan.

My heart leaps. He waves me over again, his eyes down-turned and pleading. Worry and pain etch his features and I'm desperate to help him.

I crawl over to him, his slender fingers wrapping around my bicep and pulling me into the dark room. He slams the door shut as soon as I'm inside.

"We don't have much time," he whispers. Our bodies are pressed close in the narrow space of a utility closet, leaving my heaving chest pressed up against his. "Have they been taking care of you?"

My chuckle is soft in the darkness. "I could ask the same of you."

I feel him shrug against me, but there's a stiffness that wasn't there just a few days ago.

"I'm fine, really. Now, how are you doing? What have they done to you?"

"Should they be doing something to me?" I ask. Nick's angry eyes flash through my mind.

"No, no," he breathes into my hair. "At least I hoped not. You never know how they'll react to these kinds of situations. I've known them to be a bit vindictive."

"Seeing as how I didn't get to choose to go with you, no one's really held it against me." I keep my voice low, trying not to think of Nick's accusations.

Donovan stiffens beside me. "I'm really sorry for how everything went down. I know you might not believe me, but I really didn't think things would go the way they did. I thought you'd remember me and when you didn't, I was so sure you'd eventually regain your memories. It never crossed my mind you might never get them back.

"I never wanted to do what Patrice was making me do, you have to believe that. You have no idea how happy I am that Nick's guys came when they did. I'm unbelievably grateful for their interference. Without them, you'd be gone."

I knew the drink would fry my mind, but I don't like

thinking about how serious it could have been. Just how close to being eliminated I came.

Donovan's arms wrap around my back, his fingers looping together to keep me close. He rests his head against my hair, his breathing slow and content. We don't have the kind of relationship he wants, but the softer side of me can't take away this moment of peace.

"I'm so sorry, baby." His words are muffled against my head, making them almost incoherent even as my heart jolts from his term of endearment.

My scalp tingles as fat, wet teardrops soak into my hair. My heart threatens to tug out of my chest. I hug him, my fingertips barely touching behind his back. His body slumps even farther into me, gasping sobs accompanying his tears.

The sound of laughter and loud footsteps from the hallway slips into our hiding place, sounds of the outside world forcing Donovan to pull himself back together. He stands straight and releases me from his arms. I let go too, my body not quite ready for the embrace to be over despite any misgivings I have or should have. My hands hang heavy at my sides as we stand together in the darkness.

"I don't know when I'll get to see you again." His head is bent to try and see my face in the black room. "But I'll be looking out for you. I won't let them hurt you."

I open my mouth to ask what he's talking about, but the door opens instead. Light floods my eyes and even blinded I try to shelter Donovan from the intruder. Blinking against the light, my hand searches for him to push behind me, but he's gone. There's nothing but empty space around me.

"What're you doing in here?" Nick's voice fills the closet, forcing me to turn towards the door.

I blink more furiously, the tears I thought long dried up now doing their best to make an appearance. "What does it matter to you?"

Nick gapes at me like a fish. "Were you crying in the closet?"

"What does it matter? I don't answer to you." I rub my face with the back of my wrist.

He keeps watching me, so I shove past him, my hand pushing hard against his narrow shoulders to make him get out of the way. He leans against the wall and watches me with solemn eyes.

"What's gotten into you?" His voice is soft, but the muscles in his jaw tighten.

I shake my head and continue down the hallway, leaving him burning in my wake.

Chapter Six

"What's gotten into you?' I mutter to myself as I stumble through the seemingly endless rows and rows of matching white, clean hallways. What's gotten into Nick? Why won't he help me? But there was no way I was going to ask Nick for help. I still can't bear the thought of seeing his face knowing he lied to me.

I push open a door I think is mine, but the room that greets me is nothing but an empty office. It's hard not to scream in frustration. I have to bite my lip to keep my emotions inside.

Muffled voices drift from under the gap in the solid wood door from the hallway. I stumble to my knees, moving over to the crack between the door and the doorway.

Sarah and Nick stand in the hallway facing each other.

"I'm here for you, you know," Sarah says, resting her hand on Nick's arm. "I'll be your friend if you let me."

I press myself closer to the gap, making sure that it's only open the barest amount.

Nick rests his hand on Sarah's and her mouth quirks like

she's trying not to smile. She holds his hand in silence, not trying to make him explain what happened.

Tension trickles down my arms. I thought Sarah was my friend, but now she wants to comfort *Nick*. They have each other and I have no one. It makes my stomach turn. I though Nick and I would always be friends. But now... I just don't know.

"I saved you something." Sarah leans forward with a sly smile.

From behind her back, she pulls out a large chocolate chip cookie, one of the cafeteria napkins folded around it already showing spots of grease. Releasing her hand, Nick grabs the cookie, smiling at her like he's never really seen her before.

"I thought you might like that." Sarah laughs as he chomps down on the cookie, crumbs not quite staying contained in the napkin. "I know something sweet always makes me feel better."

She lets him finish the cookie before saying anything else. It's only when he's wiping the melted chocolate off his fingers that she broaches the next tender subject.

"Avi's been giving you a hard time, huh?" She stares at the toe of her sneaker where it taps against the tiled floor.

I frown. Nick doesn't seem to understand how confusing it is to learn that everyone's been lying to me. I guess there's also an aspect of his pain that's caused by Donovan, but I hope he doesn't say anything to Sarah about that.

Nick sighs. "I'm not sure what she wants from me. I'm just trying to help her."

"Girls can be a little crazy sometimes." She still doesn't look at him. "I thought you were going to lose your mind the last few weeks when we were looking for her. I've never seen you so stressed before."

"It was really hard to not know what was happening to her," Nick whispers.

"Are you guys together or something?" Sarah draws out her words as she plays with her slim hands.

He shakes his head. "No."

She visibly relaxes, her small shoulders dropping low as the tension leaves them. He reaches out and grabs her hand, giving it a squeeze.

"There's nothing going on between us. We're just friends, I promise." He bends closer in an attempt to get her to look at him.

"That's good." Her gaze remains firmly glued to the floor and I can only see the frame of ginger lashes around her eyes. "Not that it's any of my business or anything. It just doesn't seem like a good idea to get involved with anyone when you're still figuring things out."

Nick sighs. "I just don't understand why it's so confusing for her. I feel like all she can think about is how she might be betraying her mother instead of how she's really *helping* her."

My eyes narrow and I clench my fists. He's gone too far if he feels like I should be choosing his little organization after all the lies he's told me over my own mother.

"It's not a betrayal to her mother though," Sarah says. "It's just doing what's best for our people."

"Exactly, and it's not that her mom was a bad person, she just had a very dangerous object in her charge. That's why we can't have Amaro getting their hands on it. The ramifications of the Trident in their power would be detrimental for everyone, not just our people," he says in a single breath.

"She had the trident?" Sarah asks.

"Yeah. Her mom had it in her care. I guess it had something to do with her being a nixie and all. Water creatures usually have better luck at keeping water artifices under control. It just makes sense." He shrugs and she steps closer.

"So, her mom is the last person who saw the Trident, and

now we know Amaro is looking for it. You can see why we might be concerned."

Sarah reaches to take his hand, but he moves his, running his hand through his hair. "Speaking of that. I need to get back to work. I'm supposed to be helping figure out where Avi's mom went. She covered her tracks well, so I have no idea when I'll have good news."

Sarah nods and smiles even though I can see her hand curl into a fist. Nick's footsteps echo down the hallway and she waits until he turns a corner before she sinks to the floor.

I'm going to be stuck in this room forever, or at least until Sarah decides she's pulled herself together.

"Avi?"

I can't breathe. Does she really know I'm in here?

"Avi, you can come out. I know you're there."

I open the door, my face bright red. "I didn't mean to eavesdrop. I was looking for my room."

Sarah gives me a tired smile. "You don't know this place well enough to have picked this room to listen in on us. I believe you."

"How long did you know I was there?" I can't get the blush to leave my face. I'm mortified that I wasn't as sneaky as I thought I was.

"I thought I heard someone in the hallway ahead of us but then there was no one there. It wasn't hard to assume it was you that was hiding. No one else would think twice about us talking." Sarah leans her head back against the wall and closes her eyes.

The embarrassed part of me wants to explain how I wasn't hiding, and it was all an accident, but I know that's not what's important here. "You don't mind that I was listening?"

"Why would I? It's all stuff you deserve to know. Not knowing what's going on won't help you and it definitely won't help us." She opens her eyes to look at me, her lips quirking into a small smile.

"So...why would Amaro want a trident? It can't be that cool." If she doesn't mind me knowing what they're looking for, then I have nothing to lose by asking.

"It's not that it looks cool or anything. It's what it can do, that makes it so special," Sarah explains as I sit down next to her. "King Reizei used the Trident when he first formed Ret over two hundred years ago. He stole it from the sea and harnessed its power to overthrow all the small Lords that had sprung up throughout the country. We were so disorganized then that it was easy for humans to persecute us which led to the retaliation of several of our more...interesting species.

"King Reizei stepped in, got us to stop fighting with each other and helped us realize that by taking a backseat and concealing our nature, we could live with humans, work with them, and everyone was happier. It only makes sense that we take the next step and completely hide ourselves.

"As for how Ret is going to use the Trident to do that is above my security clearance. Apparently, I don't need to know what it does to know we need to find it."

I throw my head back onto my pillow, ignoring her fairy-tale story in favor of the facts that matter. "Sounds like what everyone else says to me."

"Well, it makes sense, you know? I mean, you're not a part of us. You're only here because of circumstances outside your control. They don't want to give you any information you might use as a weapon against them later," she says. "I, on the other hand, have basically sold my soul to them, not that they care."

"What made you join?" If someone like Sarah joined, then there might be a reason for me to work with them too.

"I'm not sure that *join* is the right word. My mom was a Fae who decided she didn't want to look at a half-breed anymore," Sarah spits out. "There are not many places for people like me to go. We can't exactly hide in plain sight. But the King found a place for me."

"Why can't—" I stop as Sarah brushes back a lock of her hair to reveal a delicately pointed ear.

"It's unobtrusive enough to go out occasionally, but I can't make my life out there. It's too dangerous." She lets her hair fall back over her ear.

"Is your dad here, or..." I trail off, feeling uncomfortable about the intrusion into her life but feeling too curious not to try to ask at all.

She shakes her head, brows furrowed. "I don't know who my dad is. I don't really know who my mom is either if I'm being honest. I wandered around a lot when I was younger, before one of the guys here found me and brought me in."

I give her shoulders a tight squeeze. "I'm glad you're okay."

"Yeah." Her body is tense, but she doesn't shrug me off. "It could have been way worse. I *know* it's a lot worse for so many other kids."

"I wish I could help you." I can't help but feel guilty for being annoyed at being here when Ret's government has been responsible for saving so many people like Sarah. It even saved me in a way.

"We all know you want to help. It's so frustrating to not know how to help each other." She sighs. "I've never dealt with a memory issue like yours before."

My mind wanders back to the trident. "So, you really have no idea what this trident might be able to do?"

Her emerald eyes glitter as she looks back at me. "Like I said, it's classified information, but there's a lot the internet can tell you. If it's the same trident Poseidon had, then there's not much it can't do, at least where water is concerned. Although, it has been known to create earthquakes."

"Earthquakes?"

"Well, you know, it can make tsunamis, hurricanes, and control any creature in the sea. That's a lot of power," Sarah explains while I chew my lip.

"Control over the water doesn't seem like that much power."

Sarah leans forward, eyes gleaming. "It's a lot for the people moving against us. With the Trident they could use the water to wipe out any human who opposes them, control the sea creatures to make them come to the surface and fight us."

"Why not just let them choose to fight on their own?" My mind swirls around the history of armies who used slaves as their fodder. Not a whole lot of them are still standing.

"The Sea Fae are notorious for keeping to themselves. There have been wars in the past where they've abandoned their commander halfway through. So, you see, they don't make very reliable allies. But with the Trident..."

"They won't have the opportunity to be anything but," I finish. Sarah gives me a knowing nod and taps the side of her nose with a slender finger.

I file the information away for later. The idea of my often-forgetful mother having an artifact that powerful in her control, has me more than a little nervous. Not because she couldn't handle it. I just have a very clear memory of her melting a plastic cup in the microwave once because she 'just couldn't understand how to use technology.' There were many times growing up when I was raising her just as much as she was raising me.

"So, you can understand why getting your memory back is so important," Sarah presses.

"Do you think there's someone I could talk to who has experience with something like this?" I can't help but go back and forth on wanting my memories back. I want to know my past, my real past, but I'm afraid of what it might cost me.

Sarah pushes herself off the bed. "Let's talk to Ramsey. She might know more about this, although I'm sure she's already been consulted. I can't imagine Nick hasn't tried her yet."

She grabs my hand and sends us running through the hallways. I curse my stupid sandals for the thousandth time as they slide on the slick tile. Sarah doesn't slow down for me, her short legs making the distance with half the effort of mine, something I have to attribute to her Fae mother. But she *does* hold me steady through the halls.

* * *

Hesitating outside the heavy metal doors that I'm sure lead to the outside, I let out a slow breath. Even though I'm not treated as much like a prisoner here, I'm not stupid enough to think they'd just let me leave.

Sarah grunts as she opens the doors and pulls me outside, cutting across a small grassy walkway. Cars honk on the nearby street, and my senses feel like they're coming back to life. A squat row of brown brick townhouses lay stacked behind the tall steel industrial building we came out of. Sarah stalks towards them with heavy purpose.

Little bronze plaques sit into the wall next to the front doors to announce the occupants, which is not unusual in the city. Still, it looks a little odd on the obviously residential homes.

Sarah jumps the couple steps leading to the home labeled 'Ramsey' and raps on the door three times before leaning against the door frame. Standing on the front step, I like my lips and try to straighten out my pale pink satin blouse that has obviously seen better days.

The door opens just a crack and a light female voice protrudes from the opening. "Sarah, I told you not to bother me anymore."

"Nice to see you too." Sarah plants a wide smile across her face. "I've got a *real* problem for you to work on today."

The tips of vibrant green hair poke through the door as the woman inside shakes her head. "I don't have time for your problems today. Go back to the compound and leave me alone."

She tries to shut the door but Sarah sticks her white sneaker into the crack before it can close. "Did you see who I came with? You're being awfully impolite in front of our guest."

Her head peeks out around the door, floppy hair and thin nose proceeding long before the rest of her face.

"This is my friend, Avi." Sarah's freckled smile is becoming a permanent fixture on her face. "Avi, this is Ramsey."

"Nice to meet you."

I hold out a surprisingly steady hand to shake. Mom always taught me to be polite, even though I have no idea who this woman is or what the proper protocol for meeting her would be.

Ramsey steps out the door, black dress shoes gleaming as she takes my hand in her long thin ones. "Finally, someone with manners."

She shakes my hand but doesn't say anything else. We stare at each other for longer than is polite, my eyes drawn into the swirling circles in her blue irises.

"Avi here has a problem, and we were wondering if you could help us with it." Sarah breaks the spell between us, and I take a deep breath.

Wrenching my hand away, I shove it into the pocket of my jeans. Her eyes continue to swirl, moving like a hurricane as she stares at me. My shoulders grow tight under her scrutiny.

"What can I help you with Avi?" Ramsey asks.

"My memories have been taken away." I stare at the

shoulder of her crushed purple velvet smoking jacket. "And my mom is missing."

If I'm going to get help, I might as well get the help I've been really wanting. Plus, finding Mom would clear up all my other issues and free me from this never-ending nightmare.

"Sounds like quite the problem." Ramsey leans against the door frame, watching me with her unsettling eyes.

"Yeah." I nod. "Now I have to deal with all these people wanting me to tell them about things I have no memory of. Which might not *sound* like such a pain, but they keep kidnapping me to do it."

Ramsey cracks a smile, her snow-white teeth shining in the midday light. "So, what do you want me to do about it?"

"We thought you might know a way to reverse the spell, you know seeing as how you're a witch." Sarah folds her arms over her narrow chest.

Ramsey shakes her head. "I don't know enough about the spell to be able to change it."

"So why don't you invite us in and we'll get to know each other better," Sarah says, running her hand down the door frame.

I blink at her change of tactics, but let it slide when Ramsey opens the door and waves us into her home.

Ramsey's sitting room walls are covered in dark oak panel. A long leather studded couch sits in front of a crackling fire.

Sarah slips past me and makes herself at home on the couch. Stepping into Ramsey's house is like taking a trip back to the 1800s. My mind keeps reeling over every little detail and it keeps me from getting comfortable. Ramsey crosses in front of me to lean against the mantle, her fluorescent green hair looking out of place in our new surroundings.

"So, let's get to know you." Ramsey pins me with her complete attention, and I struggle not to shift on my feet. "What is it about you that makes you so curse worthy, because let's be honest with ourselves, this isn't a spell that's done this, it's a curse. To lose your memories is to lose your identity. It sounds a lot like a curse, doesn't it?"

My mouth hangs open at this realization. She leans forward to tap it closed, her fingertips cool against my skin.

"What makes you special?" she whispers, her face close to mine.

Sarah coughs. "Not to interrupt this love fest, but are we actually going to work on the problem or are you just going to flirt all day?"

Ramsey stands tall, looking down her nose at Sarah. "This is part of my process."

She snorts. "Sure it is."

"There's nothing particularly special about me." I try to ignore their banter. "I grew up in Maine with my mother. To my knowledge, she went missing five years ago and I've been living with my Aunt ever since."

"You say to your knowledge, but how long has your mother really been missing?"

"Three months." My voice is small in the richness of the space.

She rubs her chin with her long fingers. "Something happened in the last five years that your mother doesn't want you to know about."

"How can you be so sure of that?" I hate the grin that's steadily growing across her face. How can she solve something in five seconds that I haven't been able to figure out for weeks?

"Why make you think she's been missing so long if it's only been a few months? There's a reason the rest of those memories left with her. So the question you need to ask now is why. Why were the last five years so important? What happened to make your memories a threat to have?"

"She knew something about a trident. That's what everyone's been asking me to remember," I blurt out. Ramsey's eyes grow wide.

"The Trident? Your mother was The Guardian of the Trident?" I can't tell if she's asking me or talking to herself. "Your mother was Minna?"

"Did you know her?" My eyes narrow as I try to focus on Ramsey and not on the shifting flames beside her.

"A long time ago," she says, stormy eyes clouding over in memory. "I was there when she was given guardianship over the Trident, that must have been at least thirty years ago."

"My mom was given the trident when she was only fifteen?"

"Oh no, no." Ramsey runs a hand through her hair. "Your mother's a nixie. She's probably over two hundred years old, not that I ever asked her. Even in our world it's rude to ask a woman about her age."

"Two hundred years old?!" I squeak. "Don't you think I'd know if my mother was ancient?"

"My dear girl, just because she's old in human years doesn't mean she looks it. How old do you think I am?" She gestures at her lean form.

My lips twist to the side. "Twenty–five?"

Sarah laughs, slapping her leg as she struggles to breath. "Twenty-five, that's great." Ramsey rolls her eyes as Sarah wheezes.

"Yes, yes, laugh at the old woman," Ramsey says with a groan. "Let's just say I'm a little older than that."

"Yeah, you were only off by this much," Sarah says, holding her hands as far apart as her body will let her.

"Do I have siblings?" I ask. My mother lived so much life before I came into the picture. There's so much I don't know. With that much time anything is possible.

Ramsey shakes her head with narrowed brows. "No, I feel pretty confident you're her only child. Nixies can't usually have *any* kids, so I doubt you have a sibling hiding in the attic somewhere."

"If they can't have kids, then what would make Minna abandon her miracle child?" Sarah asks as she wipes the tears from her eyes and leans onto her thighs.

My heart breaks for her. Of course, that's what Sarah would focus on. Her mother had made no qualms about not wanting a half-breed daughter. It would kill me if I ever thought my mother had left because of who my father was.

"I guess that's the question you'll want to answer. What would make Minna leave you behind and wipe out a quarter of your life with her?" Ramsey asks, not looking at me anymore, her questions turning introspective.

Sarah's scrubs tighten across her shoulders, tension lining her mouth. A part of me wants to reach across the couch and grip her hand in mine, my heart wants to tell her she's not alone anymore. We won't abandon her like her mother did. I keep my hands clasped in my lap though, not feeling close enough to her to offer myself as comfort. Especially since we've only known each other for a day.

"I don't know how to answer those questions. The memories that would probably answer them have been wiped out," I remind Ramsey, keeping Sarah in my peripheral view as her face turns red.

"Are you sure you can't just wave a magic wand and bring her memories back?" Sarah asks, pushing herself off the couch.

Ramsey blows out in exasperation. "I've told you before, just because I'm a witch doesn't mean I have a wand. After so many years of perfecting my craft, I don't need it anymore. The fact that you are always asking me to use it is insulting."

Sarah grins, goading her on purpose. Ramsey pouts back with tight pink lips.

"So, what can we do?"

Ramsey shakes her head. "I'm not sure how I can help

you. Nixie magic isn't the same as wizard magic. We're quite literally like oil and water. I don't think anything I do will stick enough to be useful."

"Whelp, you heard her. Let's get out of here." Sarah throws her arms up and starts marching for the door.

"Hey! I didn't say I couldn't help at *all*. Don't get your panties in a wad," Ramsey says, brows turned down.

"Then what can you do?" I'm still planted in the couch. Something Ramsey can do is better than the nothing I've been able to accomplish.

"I think we should explore your ancestry a little before we do anything. It might answer some of those questions for us."

"You mean like my grandma?" I knead my forehead, feeling the beginnings of a headache blooming. "This might come as a shock to you, but I never knew her. I do have an aunt though," my voice trails off as I realize how worried Aunt Nina must be. I've been gone for weeks and now that I'm not under complete house arrest, I never even thought to call her. "Do you think I could see her? Let her know I'm okay?"

I look back at Sarah as I ask permission, but she turns her head away, red curls hiding her face.

"Can I go see her?" I repeat.

Ramsey walks closer, putting a comforting hand on my shoulder. Her face goes tight with remorse.

"What's wrong? What happened to her?" My voice becomes more frantic as all the worst-case scenarios flit through my mind, starting with her being attacked in the alley by our apartment. I can't remember how many times I've asked her not to use it. The lack of lighting through it just screams 'come and get me!'

"There's nothing wrong with her," Sarah says at last, not meeting my gaze. "She just doesn't remember you."

"How is that even possible?" I ask without giving myself time to completely process her statement. "She's my aunt, she wouldn't just forget about me after a few weeks. I'm sure she's been worried sick about me."

Ramsey gives my shoulder a squeeze as Sarah looks away from me again. "She's not really your aunt. We have no idea who she is. As soon as Amaro took you, it was like you'd never existed. Your aunt doesn't remember you, no one at your high school remembers you. There's no record of you ever living in New York."

"What are you saying?" I can't breathe.

"Your presence in New York was just another one of your mother's spells," Sarah says.

"I guess that's another question I need to answer then. Why New York? Why Nina?" I ask softly. If I focus too long on what I've lost, I think I'll explode.

The room quiets, only the pops from the fireplace interrupting my thoughts. I try to remember the last time I saw Mom, but the images are blurry, and my thoughts grow hazy. The longer I try, the more pressure builds in my head. Dark spots flutter across my vision and I have to stop.

"Would you like to try to find out who your actual relations are?" Ramsey asks me. "It might give you a better foundation if you know exactly where you came from."

I nod blankly. My mom is gone. I'll never see my aunt again. She isn't even my aunt and wouldn't even remember me if I passed her on the street. No one would. I have no one left. I can't breathe, I can't feel my hands.

I need to find out who I am, but what else will it cost me? I'd rather be alone, but that's not an option. I'd like to be with people who know me, but that's not an option either..

Ramsey releases my shoulder and grabs my hand. "I'll personally make sure that you find the answers you're looking for."

Tears lurk behind empty eyes, but I refuse to let them out. At this point, I'm completely sure things will only get worse before they get better, and I can't help the burning behind my eyes as tears try to force their way out. *Don't cry, don't you dare cry*, I force my thoughts to cut through the pain and take the tears away.

Squaring my shoulders, my mouth tightens even as it pulls farther into a frown. "Okay, let's do this. Test my blood or do what you need to do. I'm tired of dancing around the problems in my life."

Sarah gives me a curt nod. I'm not alone in my suffering here. I need to be better at remembering that.

Ramsey leads me from the room and down a short panel-lined hallway into an office space. She sits behind a large mahogany desk, gesturing me to sit in a low back chair in front of it. Fingers steepled under her chin, she gives me a long look.

"I'm going to try to dig through your memories first," she explains. "It's possible Minna left clues there that you haven't been able to access on your own."

"Okay." I lean back in the chair, tilting my head.

Her swirling eyes close, head resting on her too-long fingers. I shift in my seat, not knowing where to look or what to do.

A tingle spreads across my temples, then I'm whisked back through memories. The growing pressure in my head making me white knuckle the wood armrests of my chair. The room around me fades away, replaced with images of Mom and my home.

Flung into the past, I stand in the white-washed kitchen of my childhood home, watching Mom stirring something in the old red mixing bowl while my five-year-old self looks up at her with unabashed admiration. My past self doesn't even come up to the countertop, just hangs on Mom's skirt, watching her work with wide grey eyes.

"Want to help me Avi?" she asks, eyes watching me with pale blue focus while a bright smile plays across her lips.

I nod at her and she hands me the spoon she's been using.

"I need you to taste this and tell me if it's ready," she says, resting a slender hand on the top of my bedraggled hair.

I don't hesitate to stick the dripping spoon into my mouth, licking off the remnants of brownie batter. My phantom mouth tingles with the remembered taste of chocolate, this faint memory becoming more real the longer I stand here.

Mom smiles at me, my five-year-old self smiling back with a missing front tooth before the image is ripped away and replaced with another moment from my past.

My feet sink into the sand of the beach by our house, and my younger self and my mother stand closer to the water.

We're splashing in the ocean. I'm ecstatic in my brand new sparkly pink bathing suit, running up the beach and back into the frigid water with youthful delight.

Mom stops and stands away from me, her blue dress floating around her waist as she stands in the water, facing the open ocean. Her arms hang limp, hands lost in the water as she continues to stand there.

My childish self continues to play without noticing the difference in my mom's attention, but I see the change and a tingle runs up my spine. Her empty eyes as they stare out past the waves. What was she looking at?

My younger self turns around and runs up toward the long grass that grows just past the beach, Mom far out of my view.

I wonder what could've been going on as I stand on the beach as a silent spectator. Sand grinds into my feet where it squishes between my skin and my sandals before the vision changes again.

It's the day Mom disappeared. This memory is one that still lingers in my mind even after all these years. Months? I'm standing in the kitchen again, staring at the pale blue fruit bowl sitting on the white counter, its contents nearly empty with the sour-sweet smell of rotting fruit emanating from what's left.

The room is still, my ears ringing in the silence. I'm twelve years old in this memory and I've just come downstairs to find my mother missing. The back of my throat closes off, my voice gone as I walk through the empty rooms of our beach house.

The living room is just as barren, with only a rumpled blanket at the end of the shabby couch to say anyone has ever been through here. I walk over to it and hold the thin weave blanket to my face, breathing in the smell of her amber perfume as it fades away.

Sinking to my knees, I cradle the blanket against my chest. The screen door slams open, its springs squeaking as it continues to rock back and forth in the salt-heavy breeze.

Standing, I sprint to the door and hang on the frame as the sounds of ocean waves blast through my skull.

"Hello?" I ask with a small voice.

Only the ocean answers. Tears run down the cheeks of my phantom body. This was one of the worst days of my life and reliving it hasn't shown me anything new. It's only raked me raw with more pain.

Walking back to the kitchen, my blurry gaze lands on a small piece of paper poking out of one of the kitchen drawers. My brow furrows. I don't remember seeing that before.

I haven't tried to change the past in any of my other memories, but now I pull my feet towards the drawer, my younger self continuing along the same path I walked so long ago. My fingers itch as I reach for the corner of the page.

Then I'm gone, the pressure in my temples flows out until my fingers unclench. I open my eyes in Ramsey's office again. She leans forward, staring at me with a frown.

"What was that? Take me back!" My fingers curl toward a piece of my past that's now a full day's drive away at least.

"I can't do that," Ramsey says with a shake of her head, green hair flopping back and forth. "You can't actually change anything from the past. Like I said, I just wanted to comb through memories to see if you'd missed anything. Looks like I was right."

"Then what do we do with that information? Somewhere in Maine, a note's been sitting, waiting for five years. Am I supposed to assume it's still there? What difference would that make? It's not like I can just walk home and get it!" I fume, face turning red as my fingers still itch for the drawer handle.

"Maybe it's time for a road trip," Ramsey says with a bright smile. "I can only send you so far using my magic, so you'll have to go the rest of the way on your own."

"I highly doubt this place will let me out of their sight for that long," I remind her, mouth twisted in a grim smile. "They're kind of protective of me. And why can't you just zap us there? Since when is there a distance clause on magic?"

"Of course there are limits, just like you couldn't run all the way home, I can't just blink you there. No one has the strength to go farther than about twenty miles," Ramsey says while waving my excuse away. "As for leaving, they'll let you go anywhere if they think it will benefit them in some way. You've remembered something about the Trident and you have to go back, I can't see them saying no to that. Plus, I'm sure Nick wouldn't mind assisting you."

She rises from behind her desk and leads me back to the living room where Sarah stares into the fire with a blank expression on her freckled-lined face. As soon as she sees us, her usual wide smile forms, making me wonder if I only imagined the complete lack of emotion just seconds ago.

"You're about to go on a wonderful trip of discovery!" Ramsey announces melodramatically from behind me, her long arms swinging wide.

"Oh yeah?" Sarah asks, face brightening. "You find something interesting in her DNA?"

"No actually, do you think we should go over that before you push us right out the door?" I ask Ramsey as she propels us towards the exit with a hand on my arm.

"Nah, I don't see how that could help us any more than the information we've already gathered today."

"So, what did you find?" Sarah asks, looking at Ramsey.

"I remembered a note," I cut in, annoyed as they stare at each other and right through me.

Sarah keeps her eyes on Ramsey and shrugs. "So, you want us to head out after this note?"

"I think it's our best option," she says, opening the door. "I'll get Nick to meet you where my magic leaves off. Go get ready, and good luck."

Sarah walks out with a light step and I follow her as she cuts back to the building that will be my newest prison, the sign in front bearing the same gold insignia as the men's uniforms that came to rescue me. A gold crown perched on top of the three points of a mountain range.

She doesn't say anything as she marches us through the identical halls. Stopping in front of a door I don't recognize; Sarah takes a deep breath and raps her knuckles on it.

"Come in."

She motions for me to stay with an open palm before entering the room. I lean against the wall, the back of my head cooling against the shiny white paint.

I can't make out anything distinct behind the door, rumbling voices the only evidence Sarah's in there at all. Waiting for a few minutes, I close my eyes and let the memories Ramsey dug out flood through me. I don't know how I could've ever forgotten the look on Mom's face that day. I wonder how many other times she looked like that and I never noticed. What struggles was my mother going through that she kept from me? How long did she suffer alone?

The door swings open, snapping me back to the present as it hits the wall.

"Time to go." Sarah walks me back to my room. "You might want to rinse off, go to the bathroom, I don't know. Just get ready for a long trip."

She closes the door behind her, and I stare at the grooves in the white paint, unhinged by her coldness. I may not know her very well, but I thought at least we were becoming friends.

* * *

I try to shake off the feeling of being hustled and open the narrow door wedged between the foot of my bed and the main door. A small bathroom sits in the closet-sized space, reminding me of the airplane bathroom I used once when my mom took us to Florida. At least this one has a tiny standing shower.

Rinsing off in the warm water, I'm grateful for the small moment I have to recharge. Water splashes against my face, sticking to my eyelashes. I'm lulled into peace in the moist warmth before realizing I don't know when Sarah is planning on coming back for me.

I rush through the rest of my shower and wrap myself in a scratchy military-grade towel. Sighing, I reach for the clothes I'd discarded on the floor.

"I've put out some new clothes for you on the bed," Sarah's voice comes through the crack in the door where steam is escaping. "I realized you wouldn't have anything else to wear."

Reaching my hand through the crack, I grab the pile she's left before firmly shutting the door. The steam threatens to suffocate me as it fills my lungs. I dress quickly into the olive-green cargo pants and tan shirt she's given me.

"I got some new shoes for you too," Sarah says, voice muffled now through the closed door. "Figured you wouldn't want to wear those ridiculous sandals anymore. They're not really that great for an expedition."

"You make it sound like we're going off into the wilderness or something. We're only going to Maine." I frown, smarting even though I didn't like the shoes either. "Did you happen to bring a hairbrush?"

I open the door to find her flinging one through the air toward me. Grasping it with clumsy fingers, I drag its teeth through my messy brown hair. Her smile is back in place, but I don't trust it like I did earlier.

"I'm going to pack a bag for us just in case. You want anything specific?" she asks, hand wrapped around the silver doorknob.

"Nope. I'll just be waiting I guess." I give her a one-sided shrug.

Sarah nods and heads out the door. Sinking into the mattress with a sigh, my face is partially covered by my arm.

"I thought she'd never leave," Donovan says, jolting me from my rest.

I almost knock heads with him as I rise too quickly. He kneels over the bed next to me while tingles spread across my chest.

"What are you doing here?" I ask in a quiet hiss as his musky cologne fills the room.

"Are you leaving?" he asks, dark eyes boring into mine as he ignores my very direct question.

I push him back, hands shoving against his firm shoulders. "That's none of your business."

"It's really not safe for you out there," Donovan tells me with a frown. "Who's going with you?"

I cross my arms. "How'd you know I was leaving?"

"I'm worried about you," he confesses in a near whisper.

I stare at him as he sits back on folded legs, his eyes focused on the metal frame of the bed. My heart threatens to soften, but I will it back into place in the weak protection of my wounded chest.

"You don't have the right to be worried about me. You almost destroyed me," I remind him, body rigid, hand twitching towards an almost warranted slap. "If you'd had your way, I'd be back in Amaro with my mind wiped right now."

He looks up at me, brown eyes pleading. "It's not like that. I won't let her do that to you. Do you really think you could have been taken so easily from Amaro if I hadn't let them in? Hadn't whispered into stubborn ears where you might be?"

My brow narrows as my jaw opens and closes weakly, leaving me looking like a goldfish.

"Don't you understand? I'm risking everything for you ba —" he cuts himself off, leaving me wondering if he was going to say 'baby' again. His , hand hangs suspended in the air between us as if he wants to grab my hand but isn't sure if he can.

I shouldn't want him to reach for me, but I can't deny the ache that says I do.

"Where are you going?" he asks me again. "I won't be able to find you if you don't tell me. You're going to leave my radius."

If we leave his radius then he won't be able to check in on me anymore. My mouth slams closed. I know for a fact that Nick and Sarah won't want me to tell him anything. If Donovan's telling me the truth though, telling him we're going where can only help me. Doubts creep into my mind with dark clawing fingers.

"I just want to make sure you're safe," he says, hand fisting like a hammer as he lowers it to his side.

"I don't think they want me to tell you where I'm going," I say, thinking again of the memory I recovered but didn't share while in his care. When I get home, I'm going to have to go through that desk and see what else Mom may have been hiding from me.

Donovan stands and kicks the side of the bed, rocking me back on the mattress. "What makes you so loyal to them? What makes you so sure they have your best interest at heart?"

"I don't think it's so much why I trust them as why I can't trust you." My face heats up and I take a step away from the bed. "Do I need to remind you of what happened the last time I was in your care?"

Donovan shuts down, his eyes closed. "That wasn't something I wanted for you. I told you, I sent word to Ret where you were to prevent what Patrice had in mind."

He says Ret like I'm supposed to know what he's talking about. I dig through my mind for where I've heard it before. Mouth screwed up; I realize it's Nick's last name. Nick Ret.

"You talked to Nick?" I turn away and cover my mouth with a shaking hand.

"Not Nick personally. I just contacted Ret's officials to let them know where you were," he says, slinging his hands into his jacket pockets.

"What do you mean?" My mind spins with the answer, but I can't deal with it. I need Donovan to actually say it.

"Ret is where you are now. You know, this building, these people," he says, throwing his arms wide. "All the creatures and magical beings that live in this country are a part of Ret."

I punch the pillow next to me, trying to let out some of the blood quickly boiling to the surface. Just when I thought he'd finally told me something truthful about himself, I've been suckered again. Nick's a stranger to me. I don't know that I'll ever understand what's been going through his mind, but I can't imagine it's been for my benefit.

"We're going to Maine," I whisper, not meeting his prying eyes.

Out of the corner of my eye, I see him give me a curt nod before disappearing. Grabbing at the cool metal bed frame, my head whips around to see where he went and comes up with nothing. A shiver runs down my spine as I exhale.

Sarah throws the door open, tossing a backpack on the bed. "Ready to go?"

"Can we stop by my apartment before we head out?" My gaze shifts back and forth as I cover for my encounter with Donovan. "I'd like to grab my phone."

Creases line Sarah's brow as she stares at me, eyes narrowed in debate. "I really shouldn't let you go back. It's kind of a blacklist area right now. We don't know what will spark a memory or a change in Nina that we won't be able to control."

"She's at work right now," I tell her, pretty confident even without a watch to tell me the time. Nina spent most of her time working. "I'd just like some of my own things. I promise I'm not going to run away."

Sarah laughs. "That's kind of what we're doing anyway. Running from this dump to have a real adventure for once."

I give her a shy grin. Things are crazy enough without some sort of friend having my back. She may have secrets of her own, but I just have to hope that they don't have much to do with me. Obviously, there's something, but hopefully, it's not the 'I'm about to wipe your mind' kind.

"So, we can stop real quick?"

"Eh, why not?" she asks, opening the door for me with a flourish of her open hand.

I walk past her, gaze catching on Sarah's changed clothes. She's outfitted me like I'm about to go on a safari but she's wearing a casual pair of fitted jeans, a pink shirt, and sneakers. I know it's not super fancy, but I have to fight the urge to cover up my canvas-swathed body.

Squashing those feelings as we walk down the hall, I try to put on a happy smile and pretend we're the kind of friends I wanted us to be. Before we went to Ramsey's and she started to get weird. I'm not sure what's going on, but I know it's got something to do with me. Things would be so much easier if I just felt comfortable asking.

We walk out the heavy double doors and the city blooms around me. Typical New York smells of filth and the ocean floods me with calm after so much time closed off. Sarah hails a taxi and we slide in together.

I rest my forehead against the glass, something I've been told a million times by Nina never to do. My wide eyes take in the city, wondering if it's the last time I'll have a real view of it.

When we get to the apartment Sarah lets me go first. I run my hand over the worn banister as we head up the stairs, thinking about the last time I was here. I wonder if Donovan is watching me right now.

The door to the apartment is open when I reach the landing. My breathing slows. Nina would never have left the door open on her way out. I might have, but never Nina.

I cross the landing, feet moving like I'm trudging through cement until I get a full view through the open doorway. My chest relaxes as I take in the room. Everything inside is just as I left it, not a paper out of place and the curtains drawn tight. I'm not sure what I was expecting, but things have been weird enough to put me on edge at the slightest provocation. The apartment smells stale, like Nina's been gone for a while.

Heading right for my bedroom, I pull out a backpack and load it with jeans, underwear, a few decent shirts, and my spare sneakers. Leaning against the bed, I let my eyes tear up as they wander over the different aspects of my life that I'll never get back.

Homework is piled on the desk; spare hair ties are strewn across the nightstand. I have a poster up on the wall of some man dressed in full armor that caught my eye one day. Nina never could understand why I bought it. It doesn't match any of the rest of the décor. My shaking fingers trace the paper before I yank them away with a frustrated sigh.

A clang echoes on the fire escape out my bedroom window and I freeze, every muscle tightened in anticipation. After a few moments of silence, I walk over to the open window and stare down at the street. I don't see anyone right away, which isn't totally abnormal in the early afternoon. Then my gaze snags on movement headed around the corner and I catch a glimpse of dark hair and a leather jacket. My mouth pulls up thinking of Donovan crouched on the fire escape watching me pack for a trip he isn't even supposed to know about.

"Ready?" Sarah comes up behind me, her gaze traveling around the small room. "Ramsey wants to get us moving as far as possible before we have to stop for the night."

I give her a nod, the smile still painted across my face as I grab my phone and charger from off the nightstand. The face lights up for a second as I'm packing it, revealing no missed calls or messages. My nose wrinkles. Who's been checking my phone? I may not be the most popular person, but after so long I should have at least a few missed calls, maybe some emails waiting for me. At the very least I would have spam.

I'm about to ask Sarah if we have to go back for Ramsey to transport us when she shows up in a puff of purple smoke in the middle of my living room.

"Such a drama queen," Sarah mutters, adjusting the strap of her backpack against her shoulder.

Ramsey gives her a wide smile, teeth dazzling as they pick

up any hint of light in the closed-off apartment. "You girls ready to go?"

"Sure you don't want to come with us?" I tease, even as my shoulders shrink at the idea of being alone with Sarah for however many days this adventure will take.

"You'll be fine," Ramsey tells me, placing a reassuring hand on my shoulder. "You won't be gone that long and then you'll have more answers than you do right now."

I nod and her eyes crease in sympathy shifting between Sarah and me. I'm glad I'm not the only one who's noticed the change. With everything going on, it would be easy to dismiss the difference as something I've made up. After all, isn't everything I know about my life something made up anyway?

"Alright," she says, shaking out her shoulders. "Hold hands and we'll get this party moving."

Sarah grips my hand in her cool palm, giving me a slight smile. "This might make you sick the first time."

I smile back, lips tight. I'm not going to tell her how Donovan traveled with me this way before. I don't see it going over well.

"When you're ready to come back just stand in the same place where I'm about to send you. It has a sensor, so I'll know you're there," Ramsey says, cracking her knuckles. "Hold on tight!"

I grip Sarah's hand as my body jerks into temporary darkness. Sarah grits her teeth next to me, our bodies rattling against each other in the black abyss. I grit my teeth and daylight comes back as we slam to the ground.

Chapter Seven

Raising my head from the pillow of cool grass, I stare at the thick forest lining the road next to me. Definitely not in New York City anymore. Sarah stands next to me, brushing off her pants in quick movements.

"I'm hoping you remember where you're going." She turns to me with the blank face from before.

Lubec is almost as far north as you can get and still be on the water, so I imagine we'll just have to drive north and keep an eye out for the ocean.

"Are we walking there?" I raise a brow and point where the highway lies just to the right of us but there's no vehicle idling, waiting to be found.

Sarah laughs but it doesn't reach her eyes. "This'd be a pretty lousy road trip if we were going on foot. There should be a gas station just around those trees where a car will be waiting for us."

The tall grass swishes against our legs as I follow her to the road. I'm grateful for the cargo shorts I grabbed as sweat coats my back under my backpack. It's not even that hot yet but my body doesn't care. I've always had overactive sweat glands, just like Mom, one of the many joys of being in my family.

My smile fades. I guess I don't know what that means. Who is my family? What are our collective traits? Can I trust what Mom told me about them? I shake my head to try and clear out my thoughts.

We've gone half a mile when the trees on our left begin thinning out. A parking lot spreads in front of us with several people parked and going in and out of the half gas station, half Dunkins. My mouth waters, thinking about the hot donuts sitting just inside. I know better than to ask Sarah to go in with me. I grabbed my wallet from home, but I don't know what my meager funds will need to cover on this trip. A donut is probably a luxury.

"There we go," Sarah whispers to herself, waving down a black sedan sitting on the edge of the parking lot.

The car drives over, tires picking up loose gravel, and my chest clenches. I didn't realize anyone else would be joining us on this trip.

"What are two lovely ladies like yourself doing out in the middle of nowhere? You happen to need a ride?" Nick gives us a wide grin as he rolls down the window.

"Stuff it, Nick." Sarah throws the back door open and slings her bag inside without looking at him. She turns to me with a tight mouth. "You can have copilot."

I nod my thanks, not sure whether I'm thankful at all. Sitting next to Nick might test my manners more than I can stand. I don't know if I can trust myself for the next day of driving.

Nick smiles at me, his blue eyes open, happy. Obviously, I've been forgiven for my previous behavior. I smile back at him, even as I grind my teeth.

"While I was waiting for you guys, I took the liberty of

loading up on some road trip snacks," he says, pointing to the plastic bags by my feet.

With my backpack perched on my lap, I wish I'd known he'd already taken over my leg space before getting in the car. I debate asking Sarah to pass my bag back to the trunk but decide against it. I need her to get over whatever's going on first. Her little changes in behavior have the icy hands of anxiety reaching up my throat to suffocate me.

"Thanks Nick," I say out of politeness as I try to rearrange the bags.

"No problem!" He beams at me. I'm not sure if he's trying to ignore the tension between us or if he's just that oblivious.

He pulls us out of the gas station and onto the highway. Trees and more trees pass by, and I can't tell where we are without signs to guide me.

"How far away did Ramsey get us?" I ask as we pass another numbered exit.

"We're just south of Hartford," Nick says as he swerves out the way of a quick semi.

I sink into the leather interior. We have a long way to go before I'll be home, at least eight hours most likely. We didn't start out at the beginning of the day either, so I wonder if Nick will have us stop and stay the night somewhere.

I give him a sidelong glance, but he's happily humming along to the radio. My fingers clench into fists. I don't understand how he can be so content with everything. He has to know how mad I am at him.

"So how did you get dragged into this little excursion?" I ask while attempting to relax my hands after my fingernails leave puncture marks in the fleshy parts of my palm.

"Volunteered," he says, turning to smile at me for a second. "I thought you might like a familiar face instead of another stranger."

Grinding my teeth, I smile back at him and turn to the window. I don't know if there's anything he can do that will repair our relationship in my eyes, but then again, it's not like he sees any problem to fix. Sarah chuckles in the seat behind me. I'm pretty sure the only one who can't feel the tension is Nick.

Miles pass in silence as I keep my attention on the view outside the car. We don't stop until the sun is already starting to go down, bathroom breaks eliminated by the lack of water in Nick's snack pile. The conversation is kept to a minimum as well, encouraged by my turning up the radio anytime Nick tries to talk to me. I'm not sure what Sarah's doing, but I'm just glad to not have to deal with her either right now.

Nick pulls off the highway at an exit that proclaims gas and lodging around the corner. "You girls ready to call it a night?"

"Anything to get out of this car," Sarah says, practically yelling to be heard from the backseat over the AC.

"Awesome, let's stay here and I'll see about grabbing a pizza."

He hops out of the car and heads into the rundown building. Sarah stretches in the backseat, groaning as her back cracks.

She throws an arm over my shoulder from around the headrest. "It's going to be okay. Nick can't help it that he's an idiot. I'm pretty sure that just comes from being a boy."

I snort a laugh and throw open the door. My sneakers grind into the loose gravel parking lot as Sarah gets out behind me.

"Sorry I didn't tell you he was coming," she says with a half-shrug, not meeting my gaze.

"Yeah, a little heads up would've been nice." I walk up the sagging porch steps, and Sarah clomps along behind me.

Nick's just finishing up talking to a grizzled old woman

behind the counter. He flashes her a winning smile before turning to us and handing over the room key.

"I hope one room is okay," he says. "You guys make yourselves at home and I'll go get some food."

I give Sarah a sidelong glance. Does this mean we'll be sharing a bed tonight? There's no way Nick could think I'd share with him, but things have been just weird enough that I don't know if I can trust him to act normally.

Sarah leads the way down the mildew-smothered hallway, stopping in front of room 8 where she uses the worn keycard to let us in.

A blast of cold fishy air slaps me across the face as we walk into the darkness of the room. Sarah stops to pull on the light cord hanging from the ceiling.

"Home sweet home."

I laugh, but my face doesn't follow suit. I'm too afraid to even sit on one of the stained comforters, so I stand awkwardly in the middle of the room. This is my third bedroom in a week, and I didn't think it could get any worse than what I'd already experienced. Sarah shakes her head and runs her hands through her limp red hair, pointed ears poking out briefly before she covers them up.

"Whelp, I guess this is it." She turns around in a circle like we may have missed something. "Want the first shower while Lover Boy is gone?"

I give her a relieved nod, heading into the yellow-walled bathroom. A black bug scuttles behind the toilet as I turn the light on, but it doesn't surprise me at this point. The only thing I want out of this hole in the ground is a warm shower, cleanliness would be too much to ask.

Turning the hard water-stained handles in the shower, I strip off my borrowed clothes while steam fills the room, covering the impurities I'm trying to ignore. Climbing in, I let the burning water course down my face and chest and close my eyes against the stream. I use the generic soap I know will just dry out my skin, wishing I had packed some of my nicer stuff from home.

Once the suds have been rinsed off, I sink to the bottom of the tub. Ignoring the grime I can feel slipping against my butt, I dip my head into the water and focus on my breathing. Tomorrow we'll reach Lubec. There's no way we wouldn't. I'm pretty sure our little hotel is sitting between Hampton and Newport; at least that's what the last signs I read implied. Which puts us well into my home state.

This trip should have brought me the level of calm I've been missing, but I only feel increased tension as I get closer and closer to bringing my new present to collide with my past. I just want to get some answers. I just want to know where my mom is and why she left me. Is that too much to ask? I'll work with anyone I have to, even Ret, if it gets me any closer to the answers I'm looking for.

The water starts to turn cold, leaving me shivering in the bottom of the tub. I'm surprised Sarah hasn't come to check on me, but I'm grateful for the moment alone.

Wrapping a towel that's already soggy from the lack of a fan in the bathroom around my chest, I climb out of the tub and stare at my drooping reflection through the mist-wrapped mirror. My blonde hair hangs down my body in limp strands, my grey eyes staring out at the small girl whose body is slowly caving in on itself. The cheekbones in my face stand out sharply, the weeks of stress showing in the hollows of my body

I sigh, not ready to deal with Nick and Sarah but my time has run out. Even if they don't come in after me, hogging the only bathroom for three people is just rude.

The clothes in my backpack are as damp as the towel, pale yellow lines of old condensation running down the walls, further evidence of the lack of ventilation in this place. My clothes stick to me as I pull them on, and I feel more like I'm trudging through the jungle than getting dressed. Hiding out for a few more precious minutes, I pull my brush through my tangles. I might as well have not used the provided conditioner at all for the good it did.

When I finally emerge from my sanctuary, Nick's come back with two large pizzas which he's spread out over one of the beds.

"Thank goodness," Sarah says with a sigh as she sees me come out. She grabs her bag and brushes by me. "I thought you'd never come out."

She closes the door behind her, leaving me alone with Nick. He's switched on the tiny old tv and is eagerly watching a news program.

I sink into the bed opposite him, cringing as more and more of me touches the mattress. Grabbing a piece of pepperoni pizza out of the open box, I hold it out to keep the grease off my pajamas. I packed ones that were fairly nice, with no holes or stains, and I'd like to keep them that way.

"You excited to go home?" Nick asks around a bite of pizza. "I know you love it up here."

I nod. He's right, I've been missing Maine ever since I left, and not just because of losing Mom. Maine just feels like home; it feels right for me in a way that New York never has.

"I can't wait to get a look at the beach you've talked so much about."

"I don't know what it'll be like now. I've been gone so long, and there's been no one to tend it and make sure the grass and weeds stayed down," I say, my focus far away from the depressing hotel room.

"It's not been that long, I'm sure it will be fine," he says, taking another bite out of his slice.

My hand goes limp. He's right. I might have five years of fake memories, but I've only been gone a few months.

"How long have we known each other?" I ask, trying to figure out what parts of our relationship are actually real.

"Since you came to New York," he says, not looking away from the television screen.

"So only a few months?"

He nods, and I feel a little sick. The relationship I thought I had with him is almost completely fake.

"So, what made us such good friends so fast?" I pry, needing to know more about myself. Nothing makes sense anymore and I need some sort of foundation to fall back on.

"We had all the same classes, and I knew what you were going through."

I straighten up to get a better look at him. "What do you mean? I don't remember us having any shared history."

"Well, we don't really. I just knew what you were going through when you came here. I was assigned to you after all. It made me the only one who knew what you needed to hear. Knew what kind of support you were looking for," he says without a hint of remorse for treating me like an assignment.

"I guess we're not really friends then."

His face whips to mine. "What are you talking about?"

"If you only told me what you thought I needed to hear, then we were never really friends."

He gapes at me. "Of course we're friends. Just because I was assigned to you doesn't mean I don't care about you."

"There's no proof of our relationship being anything but a project. Does it feel good to know you sucked me in? I really thought we were friends for a while there." I slam the pizza box shut in my fury.

Nick drops his half-eaten piece on the lid and grasps my fingers in his greasy hands. His eyes bore into mine, and I narrow my brows in a glare. "I really do care about you, Avi. How can I convince you this is real?"

I rip my hands out of his. "Stop pretending this is

anything other than what it is. From now on I want you to keep it purely professional. I don't want anything else from you, and I don't want you to try for anything else either."

He lets his hands drop in his lap and looks away. He's not quick enough to keep the angry tilt of his eyes away from me before he does though. The wall of emotions I've been building in the last month keeps me from wanting to comfort him like I might have done in the past. I'm glad there's distance between us. I'm tired of pretending to be something that I'm not to any more people than I have to.

Sarah steps out of the bathroom with her red hair wrapped in one of the dingy towels. "Everyone doing okay in here?"

Nick ignores her question, but I smile. I don't need to trust her to appreciate that she's on my side. For the moment.

"We're all good here." I wave her over. "You sharing with me tonight?"

"There's no way I'm going to share with that slob," she says with a laugh pointing to the fresh grease stains spreading over the comforter from the cheap pizza boxes. "You better not snore."

"I prefer the term 'heavy breathing,'" I joke, earning a genuine laugh from Sarah.

She's in a comfy shirt and running shorts, and I envy the casual comfort she's packed with. Next to her I definitely look overdressed in my matching jammies. Again.

Nick pushes himself off the bed and heads into the bathroom without a word, his head turned away from Sarah's curious gaze. As soon as the door clicks closed, Sarah whirls on me. "What's going on between you two?"

She's tried to keep her voice calm, but her eyes are too intent for her question to just be idle curiosity. I shrug. "We just had a little heart-to-heart while you were in the shower."

"Oh really?" She starts braiding her liquid-fire locks. "What about?"

"I just told him he's not allowed to pretend nothing happened between us. He's lied to me too many times, and I'm sick of his happy smile while he tells me there's nothing to be worried about."

The grin on her face grows until I'm worried it will crack. "That's great! You can't let him get away with being such a butthole all the time. Boys think they can say whatever they want without any consequences!"

"Yeah," I agree slowly, not nearly as passionate as her about lying boys. After all, I've been burned by both genders, not just boys. Boys just happen to be my biggest problem right now.

Sarah leans back into the bed, tucking into a piece of pizza. "I'm glad you had that conversation before we got to your house. I can only imagine how obnoxious he would've been. 'Show me your bedroom', 'show me where you had brunch', 'show me every intimate detail of your old life'," she says, mocking Nick in a ridiculous little kid voice.

"What makes you think he'd be like that?" I frown.

"Because he's in love with you, of course," Sarah says, drawing out the word 'love' until it feels ugly.

I lick my greasy fingers. "What makes you think that?"

"You didn't have to put up with him while you were gone. All the whining about what could be happening to you and what he would do when he found Amaro. Honestly, finding you was a relief for the whole mission."

"I'm sure it was just because we were friends," I point out, irritated that any relationship I had with a boy had to have romantic implications no matter which side they're on.

"No boy gets *that* obsessed over a friend," she says around a mouthful of cheese. "You were all he ever talked about, day or night. Anytime you tried to have a normal conversation about anything else he immediately brought it back to you. I swear he lost weight from all the pacing and nagging he was doing."

I pull the comforter over my legs, feeling more exposed than before as she continues to complain about Nick.

"I'm sure the higher-ups dreaded the day they'd assigned him to you, which is something I never understood anyway. Why send in a boy when a girl would be the obvious choice?" she asks me with an incredulous shrug. "He went on every mission but the one when they finally recovered you. He didn't believe the source or something, so he was off on his own still trying to find you. You should've seen the look on his face when Jack brought you in."

She laughs, kicking her feet as tears run down her face. I give a weak chuckle but can't find it in me to agree with her. The pizza sits like a rock in my gut. Whatever else we were, Nick really did believe we were friends. He really does care about me. Even if it is in some messed up way that I don't agree with.

Nick comes out of the bathroom, towel slung low around his waist, and Sarah immediately shuts up, face reddening the longer he's in the room with us.

"Everyone still doing okay?" he asks, running a hand through his disheveled brown hair.

"Yeah, we're fine. Thanks for the pizza," I tell him in a quiet voice.

Sarah doesn't say a word until Nick walks back into the bathroom, water still dripping down his lean back.

"What was all that about?" I ask Sarah with a small smile.

She peels her eyes off the closed door and glances at me, her face still warm. "I don't know what you're talking about."

"I think you do," I wheedle, grateful that the attention is off my complicated relationships and on to Sarah's. "What's going on between you two?"

"Nothing, obviously," she says with a screwed-up face.

"Didn't you hear what I was saying before? He only has eyes for you."

"That can't be true," I continue to pry. "You wouldn't be that red if there had never been anything between you before."

She buries herself under the sheets. "There was one conversation, but that was almost a year ago. As soon as he was assigned to you, that was it. I might as well be dead."

"That can't possibly be true," I say, trying to encourage her to take Nick off my crowded hands.

Nick comes back out of the bathroom, and Sarah shuts her mouth and leans away from me. He's got on a pair of sweats and is still in the process of pulling on his shirt. I can see what Sarah finds attractive in him as abs ripple down his chest.

Sarah stays covered under the blanket, even as Nick turns out the light and we settle in for bed. He doesn't say anything more to me, and I don't try to start up a conversation. There's just too much going on in my mind right now to be able to soothe anything between us.

I roll over, my face turned toward Nick's bed. In the light coming off the tv I can see him turned toward me, his eyes trained on my face.

We look at each other for a second before I turn away, Nick sighing behind me.

My hand sneaks out from under the blankets, grabbing my discarded phone from the scratched nightstand. The face lights up, showing nothing but the time and my lack of messages. I pull up Mom's number, her face grinning at me in the small circular icon. I press the call button, but a notification quickly pops up to remind me that I need a carrier to make any calls. Cradling the phone, I swallow past my thick tongue.

"Mom," I whisper to myself, letting the word hang heavy in the darkness. "I'll find you."

Chapter Eight

Nick wakes us while it's still dark out, wanting to get an early start. Sarah moves groggily next to me, covering her face with her arms as Nick flips on all the lights he can possibly find.

I take a moment in the bathroom to pull on clean clothes, the nostalgia of the last time I wore them washing over me like a torrential downpour of pain. Just another representation of my life before everyone came and ruined it.

I try to absorb the smell of the familiar detergent and let the clothing give me strength, but it's harder than I thought it would be. Washing my face, I stare at my drooping features in the mirror and give myself a few light slaps to get me moving again.

Nick grabs donuts on our way out, only making a few offhanded comments about road trips needing donuts. Sarah makes a face at me, her head tipped toward me with raised brows, but I ignore her. Instead, I pull out my phone and wait for it to wake up.

Checking my messages, I'm surprised to find it blank still. My thumb scrolls through empty space and my brows narrow as I stare at nothing. If I needed any more convincing that someone's gone through it then this is it.

When I open my mailbox, the inbox looks eerily similar. Even my sent box is empty. I try to get on the internet, but my phone plan's been canceled, and I don't have Wi-Fi nearby.

Staring out the window, I clench my fists, right hand wrapped around the phone. Staring through the trees my frustration only grows.

"Anywhere you want to stop on our way up?" Nick asks, his voice gentle. His face is screwed up like he's ready to be denied.

"I don't know." I try not to come off as angry as I feel. "Have you guys ever been up here before?"

"Nope, I've never even really been out of New York." Sarah pokes her head through Nick and I's seats. "Let's see the sights before they make us come back."

"There's not really much up here, I mean there's lighthouses but not much else."

Nick looks toward Sarah. "I'd like to see some lighthouses. We should go to the beach too! Let's get some clam strips or lobster or something."

Sarah nods emphatically. "Yeah! Let's be full-on tourists."

I smile back at them, mouth weak. I just want to get in and get out and be done with it. Instead, it looks like we'll have to spend another night out on the road. Another hotel room where I'll be smothered by Nick's good intentions.

He takes the scenic route north, keeping the coast in sight and filling the passenger window with the ocean. The salty smell begins to permeate the car, my body relaxing with the sensory memories of being home.

We stop at the first lighthouse we see, Nick and Sarah jump out, running through the sand and whooping at the seagulls. Luckily for Nick there's a little shack selling fried foods, clam strips among them. He slurps them down after drowning them in tartar sauce, Sarah never taking her sparkling eyes off his animated face.

My stomach rolls, still not recovered from the rock it turned into yesterday. I sit in the sand and stare off at the waves while they continue their casual flirting.

The ocean speaks to me, the waves drawing me in until I'm walking towards the water. Eyes glazing with each forward step, I remove my shoes before my toes dig into the soft wet sand. Nick and Sarah laugh together, the sound muted as I stand knee deep in the briny water.

My sight focuses solely on the line where the horizon meets the ocean. An iridescent fin slaps at the water and still I'm drawn in like a fish on a hook, the water up past my waist. The icy bite of the waves pricks at my consciousness, but it's not enough to pull me from the ocean's spell. I wade deeper. Deeper.

"Avi?" Nick calls out, sounding miles away to my distracted body. "What're you doing?"

Logically, I know what I'm doing is crazy. I don't know why I'm out in the water, especially when I'm going to need to peel my waterlogged body out of the ocean and into the car for the next few hours. But my mind is overridden, legs propelling me further in, hands outstretched towards the open water.

The fin comes closer and closer until I can see a body forming beneath the dark water. Long pale limbs reach out to me, moonlight hair wrapped around a naked torso.

In the back of my mind, I hear someone crashing from the beach into the water, shouting my name. Ignoring them, I reach for the pale hand just a few feet from where my feet have cemented themselves into the sand.

"Shoo!" Nick calls, splashing at the water in front of me as he comes around, standing between me and whatever I've been interacting with. "Get out of here!"

"Avi." His dark eyes peer into mine while his wet cold hands grip my shoulders. "You need to get out of here."

I can't though. Whatever strange magic drew me out here still has me in its grasp. My free hand reaches past him and with a muffled swear, he swings me into his arms. Carrying my soaked body out of the water slows him down, footsteps sluggish in the pull of the waves.

"You're okay," he says through heavy breaths. "We're going to get you back to the beach now."

He repeats various assurances at me, but I don't take in his words. Once my body is clear of the water, I blink rapidly. My vision grows clearer, and I finally hear the cacophony of the ocean around me.

Sarah gets in my face, grasping my cheeks in shaking sandy hands. "Don't you ever do that again!"

Nick shakes his head at her and sets me down in the sand. Briefly I wonder if I'll be able to get the sand off my jeans when it's time to go before exhaustion sets in. Laying back on the beach, my hair tangles in the sand as my tight muscles begin relaxing.

Nick pushes me on my side. Staring at him with blank eyes, he presses against my back. I wonder if this is some form of CPR torture. All I want to do is lay down and stare up at the sky.

"Is she going to be okay?" Sarah asks Nick, their faces pinched.

"I think so." His curls stick up in all directions as he shakes his head. "That was a close one."

I don't quite understand what happened to me. I'm not usually quite so reckless, although the past few weeks may try to dispel that. I'm beginning to act more like my mother.

"Let's get you out of here," Nick says, his sneakers about the only part of him I can see before he scoops me in his surprisingly strong arms and lumbers up the beach to the car.

Nick lays me down on the back seat. He whispers soothing messages, mostly to himself. I block them out by staring at the moon roof window.

"Let's grab our stuff and get out of here," Sarah says, as she comes up behind Nick.

He nods and follows after her, leaving me alone in the car.

I hear Donovan's heavy breathing before I can see him. His silhouette swims into focus as he climbs into the backseat with me. He grips my limp hand tightly in his, his leather jacket more out of place than ever before.

"I thought I was going to lose you," he says, voice pitched low and haggard, the tendons in his neck popping out as he looks me over. "I thought you were going to leave just like her. Even after our unorthodox test, I never thought... I just... I didn't think it could call to you like that."

Despite everything he's done to me, I can't help but smile at him, my thoughts fuzzy. *Probably shock,* my mind whispers. He brushes back some of the limp hair stuck to the side of my face with a calloused hand. His breathing only now calming down.

"Where did you come from?" I stare at the sweat-soaked shirt peeking through his jacket.

"I've been following you of course."

The news should bother me, but I'm over it. After all, he basically said that was what he wanted to do when he asked where we were going anyway. And I *am* the one who told him where we were going. I practically invited him to follow me.

"Why do you care about me?" I ask, not sure which way I want him to answer me more. Why care about me as a person, or why as an organization do they care so much?

"You're very important to me," Donovan says as he clasps my cheek in his palm. "I thought I'd made that clear by now."

I want to ask him to explain when he looks out the

window, dark eyes alert. He releases me and disappears again. His form winking out of view.

Sarah and Nick climb into the car with Sarah taking over as copilot I focus on the dark clouds passing over the moon roof. It looks like a storm's coming in, my favorite kind of weather when I'm by the ocean. Mom used to tease me about enjoying the days that everyone else dreads, but I can't help it. Especially today, the rain just calls to me.

Sarah and Nick talk quietly in the front seat as we pull away from their attempt at being tourists. I feel a little bad it ended this way, but I hope they'll let me go straight home now. I was tired of being a tourist before the first stop.

Wishing I had Ramsey's power, I roll over to hide my face from the rear-view window where Nick keeps checking on me. I'm sure he means well, but I'm not a child.

* * *

The rest of the trip passes without further incident. The only time Nick talks directly to me is to ask which exit to take when signs for Lubec start to show up.

I sit up, eyes wide as we drive through town. We pass the store fronts of my youth, the Lubec landmarks building sitting next to the bright pink and blue Downeast Coffee. My mom and I used to get sandwiches there during the summer. That's the thing about my town, half of it is only open during the summer months. Everyone caters to the summer crowd which brings our town above its usual 1,300 odd people into a number that feels more like an actual town.

My heart tries to push its way out of my chest as we turn down my road. I shouldn't be surprised that everything still looks almost the same, after all I haven't been gone that long, but my mind can't get over the lie of five years it's been told.

Part of me wants to leap out of the car and run down my

old road, to really feel it under my feet like I used to almost every day. It just doesn't feel real enough yet. I won't actually believe that we're here until I feel it under my own two feet.

My breath stills as Nick pulls into the driveway, gaze lingering on the single turret jutting out and the bright red stairs of our front steps. I'm out of the car before he can completely pull to a stop, Sarah's shout of reason washes over me as I sprint the rest of the drive.

Smelling the salty breeze and feeling the smooth white wooden banister under my hand, I breathe in a sigh of relief. This is real. I'm really home.

Sarah runs up the gravel drive after me, shouting at me to wait. But my heart won't let me.

Pulling open the screen door, I turn the handle, letting myself into my childhood home. It smells the same as it used to, sandalwood and jasmine. I half expect Mom to come breezing down the stairs in her floral shawl with some new crazy idea or adventure for us to go on. Hands lingering lovingly on the door frame, I stare at the untouched memories of my childhood. I know it'll never be this simple again. Yearning for my old life, for the years that were stolen from me by my mother's magic, I blink back burning tears.

Never once did I see my mother practice anything I would have described as magic. Sure, she may have liked herbal remedies more than the other kids' moms but that didn't mean she liked magic.

Sarah steps into the hall behind me, her sneakers squeaking on the hardwood floor. "Nice place," she says, staring at the embossed ceiling. "If you like old homes, I guess."

I can't help but laugh. Our house was built around 1900, barely old by the standards of the town. Nick brushes past Sarah as she stares at me without comprehension, freckles standing out on her empty face. He's silent as he keeps any thoughts he might have on my home close to his narrow chest.

"So where do we start?"

I make my way to the kitchen without answering. My thoughts linger on my vision with Ramsey. Running my hand along the white countertops springs up only minimal dust reminding me once more how wrong my timeline is as my hand curls into a fist.

The drawer I remember is sitting half ajar. My heart goes still, its trembling beat filling my ears. Crossing the floor and sidling past the oversized island, I grip the handle in my shaking hand and tear the drawer out. It slams against the ground in a clatter as my numb fingers release their hold.

Nick and Sarah come running in behind me as I stare at …nothing.

"Someone's already been here," I whisper, grateful when no one asks me to repeat myself. I don't know if I could. I just feel hollow.

Nick pulls out the other drawers, inspecting the contents before closing them again. "Nothing else seems to have been touched."

"This was our junk drawer, it was never empty, not even on the day we moved in!" Bracing my face against my forearms, my fingers work themselves through my hair.

Sarah rests a slim hand on my shoulder. "Do you know what we're supposed to be looking for?"

"Yeah, I know exactly what we're looking for, that's why we had to come all the way up here and I couldn't just tell you back in New York," I snap, still reeling as my legs threaten to give out and leave me slumped on the floor.

"You don't have to be mean," Nick says with a frown. "There's only so much we can do to help you."

Gee, no pressure, I think to myself. With a sigh I remove my arms from my face and glance around my otherwise untouched kitchen.

Nick opens the refrigerator and pulls out some long-forgotten milk. "Wish they would've taken this with them."

He tilts the jug back and forth, but the milk stays in a solid clump.

"Put that back. So nasty," Sarah shrieks, covering her nose as the sour scent starts to seep out even though the top is still on.

Nick moves as if to throw it at her and she screams running out the French doors, leaving them open by the worn wooden table sagging across from the kitchen counter.

Shaking my head, I leave them to it, Sarah's playful screams echoing off the beach and against the windows. *Good, leave.* I need them gone to give me any chance to think. To find the memories I'm searching for in the house that's full of so many others.

Heading upstairs, my hand caresses the stair railing, the wood worn smooth from so many touches. So many memories in this house. My foot hits the squeaky stair halfway up the staircase and tears well up behind my eyes. *This stair gave me away so many times as a kid when I tried to escape a grounding.*

Rubbing them away with the back of my hand, I finish climbing the stairs. Mom's office was at the top of the stairs on the left, and the door hangs open letting the late afternoon sunlight streak across the floor.

Mom's desk faces me, the chair pushed away like she just left. I take off my shoes before walking across the thick piled white rug taking over most of the floor space. I'll never get used to her being gone. Even if I do, I doubt the old habits will ever leave me.

This room was one of my mom's favorite places in the

house. She loved the view of the ocean out of the rounded turret windows. She said it inspired her.

Sinking into the chair, I lose myself in the puff of air that comes out still smelling of my mom's perfume. Always unconventional, she insisted on a formal blue striped wingback chair for her desk. She hated how it didn't push in and out very well, and I told her a million times that they make office chairs for a reason. Still, the fancy chair stayed, and the small grumbles continued.

The surface of the desk is empty of any papers or pens, and I honestly can't remember if there'd been any there when I left. The front edge of the desk has a small hole in it for a tiny key, the space looking far too slim for any sort of drawer to exist. This small space is one of the only places in the house off limits to me. I run the pad of my finger over the indent from the hole while I think over what to do.

My hands tremble as I brush them across the drawer front. I've never liked breaking the rules, though it seemed to happen more than I wanted it to. And while my mom isn't here, the guilt settles on me like a wet blanket at the idea of breaking into her private drawer.

I start digging through the other drawers to find the key while I debate what to do. My decision is basically made when I realize this is the only redeemable part of our trip after the empty drawer in the kitchen.

My heart beats erratically in my chest. No one else knows about this drawer. Whatever I find in here will be all mine to puzzle over and figure out. And that alone locks in my decision to do it.

Pressed into the very back of the bottom drawer I find a key the length of my fingernail. I almost dismiss it, there's just no way it could possibly be big enough for actual use. But I don't have any more drawers to go through and I might as well try it out.

Fumbling around with the tiny key, I almost drop it several times before I can line it up with the keyhole. With delicate hands, I turn the key while listening for the telltale click. It's so quiet I almost miss it. The drawer slides open, removing any doubts.

Muffled laughter comes through the window, reassuring me that Nick and Sarah won't stumble onto my discovery. With shaking fingers, I finish pulling the shallow drawer out until its practically sitting in my lap. A few papers slide along the bottom, making my heart beat faster as I realize who ever went through the kitchen drawer definitely hasn't been in this one.

I recognize my mother's scrolling handwriting as I pull the top sheet of paper out. For a moment I can't even see the words clearly, the ink spreading and becoming fuzzy in my unfocused gaze.

"Did you find something?"

I drop the paper and slam the drawer closed. I was so worried about Nick and Sarah that I never considered having to check for Donovan. My heart pounds against my ribs, but it's too late. Donovan moves through the room and crosses behind the desk and leans against the tall back of the chair.

"Did you find something?" he repeats.

My face colors but I can't find words to brush off his curiosity.

"We came up here once before, when your mom first went missing," he explains, eyes glued to the now shut drawer as he lays a hand on my arm. "I never would've guessed there was a drawer there. I mean it has to be less than an inch deep."

I clasp my hands firmly together in my lap, swallowing around my suddenly too thick tongue. "What did you find before? Anything I might want to know about?"

He shrugs. "There wasn't really much of anything in here.

She was working for us when she left, everything we found related to the work we'd *asked* her to do."

Part of me lingers on the fact that he was part of the crew that came through here after my mom disappeared. He and however many strangers came to my house and defiled my memories. After a deep breath, I can't deny how much I appreciate having him here. Closing my eyes, I try to let go of the pain even though his work wasn't technically a betrayal. More like a white lie

"There was a note in the drawer in the kitchen downstairs that I'd really like to see," I say, trying really hard to keep my voice calm and even.

Donovan frowns. "I don't remember them finding anything in the kitchen."

"Then they were lying to you."

I slip the key into the long sleeve of the hoodie I'd thrown on in the car, praying that the drawer has relocked itself.

Donovan comes around behind me, pushing back my chair so he can get a closer look at the secret compartment. The key lies cold against my wrist where the tightened sleeve keeps it pinned against me. He runs his hands over the wood, looking for the creases hinting at where the drawer starts, crinkled eyes narrowed further in concentration. Laying back in my seat, I rest my head against the wingback.

"What are you even doing here?" I ask him, half curious and half interested in distracting him. "I thought you just wanted to protect me. I highly doubt something is waiting to jump out of that drawer to attack."

His chuckle is soft. "The longer you were in here the more curious I became with what you were finding. I want to know what's going on too."

"So, you can tell Amaro? And Patrice?" I snap.

He glances back at me, brown eyes wide with surprise. "It's not like that."

"Then what is it like?" I ask, growing bolder. "Am I not just some asset for Amaro that you'll terminate as soon as I'm not useful anymore?"

His brows crinkle with pain. "I told you I was sorry about that."

"Sorry doesn't change that it happened."

He leans against the desk, secret drawer forgotten as he stares at me, lips parted. "I wish you could remember what it was like before. This would make so much more sense and be so much easier."

I grind my teeth together. "Yes. Having my memories back would make everyone's lives so much easier."

"I'm not just talking about everyone else, or even myself. Don't you think I wish this were easier for you, too? I really do care about you." He reaches for my hand, but I pull it back.

"So far everyone I know only cares about themselves."

His face closes off to me, emotionless in an instant as he pushes himself off the desk and throws himself out the door. He stomps down the stairs and I don't hesitate to pull the key out of my sleeve and insert it into the drawer once more. Without taking the time to even try to read the contents of the letters, I shove them into the pocket of my hoodie and close the drawer again.

Hands cradling my mother's papers, I leave the office and slide the few feet down the hall to my room. This door is still closed and I grip the smooth handle for a moment before turning it, slowing my breathing down to a more reasonable speed.

It looks just as I left it, right down to the angle of the sunlight on my pale green bedspread. Plodding in, I sink into the abandoned mattress, glancing at all the belongings I had to leave behind when I was carted off to Nina's. My aunt that was never my aunt. My heart clenches. Who was she; why did

Mom pick her to care for me? What connection drew her to us? Will I ever see her again?

A flood of tears escapes before I can shove them back into their prison. At this point, I should probably be used to leaving everyone I know behind and feeling abandoned by their lack of truthfulness, but to learn that Nina and I aren't even related just feels like too much to bear. That she has no memory of me at all is unfathomable. How do you forget the pseudo daughter you've been living with for five years?

Except it hasn't been five years at all.

Chapter Nine

Heavy footsteps on the stairs announce his presence long before Nick's head pokes around my bedroom door. "What do you think about staying here tonight?"

Sarah throws herself breathlessly into the room. "We just figured it'll take all day to get back tomorrow, and we might as well just stay here and avoid any more crummy hotel rooms."

"That sounds great." I give them a surface-only smile.

"Where should we sleep then?" Nick asks. "I'm assuming you'll be sleeping in here."

His eyes travel along the walls, taking in the posters I'd hung up of faraway places and lingering on the pictures of my friends and of Mom and me stuffed into the frame of the mirror above my dresser. This room's filled with the memories of my past, and my nostrils flare as the desire to slam the door in their grinning faces grows. Can't this one part of me be protected from everyone's personal agenda?

"Maybe one of us could sleep in your mom's room and someone else could take the couch?" Sarah asks as she notices the tension lines growing across my forehead.

The smile fades from my mouth, becoming a thin line as my teeth grind together.

"That's fine," I say, after a long pause that practically screams just how not fine it is.

Sarah gives me a small hug, pressing me into her chest as she whispers in my ear. "It's going to be okay. We'll help you work this out." I give her a noncommittal grunt of acknowledgment, and her sad eyes follow me as she shuts the door behind her.

Alone, I take a deep breath and pull the papers out of my hoodie pocket. Crumpled up now, they no longer look like my mom could have just written them down this morning. Tears form in my eyes and drop onto the exposed sheets. Wiping the rest of them away, I make sure not to ruin the paper, ink already swirling in my teardrops as they sink into the paper.

I press my eyes into my sleeves until I can trust them again. Fully dry, I look over her notes once more. The words are clearer now, letting me pick up what she wrote with as much clarity as I'm capable of right now. Glancing over each page, I get the gist of what she wrote before folding the papers and putting them back in my pocket.

I barely breathe as I take in the severity of the information I possess. Laying back against my pillow, its familiarity calming me even as anxiety begins to grip my mind in its steel clutches. The realities of what I know can change the already fragile balance I've created in my shifting world.

Lying there until the moonlight streams through the lace curtains of my window, I finally decide to come to terms with what I know.

Mom worked for Amaro.

She took care of magical ancient artifacts.

We lived by the sea because Mom is a nixie.

The Trident was in Mom's care for seventeen years. Basically my whole life.

She disappeared to keep the Trident from being manipulated by Amaro and Ret.

She'd felt the beginnings of being sucked into the power of the Trident herself and knew it was time to act.

The Trident has the power to control the seas and anything within it.

She's gone to Neopolis to keep it safe.

The word rolls through my head but still doesn't make sense. *Neopolis*.

From her notes, Neopolis seems like some ancient sunken city, long abandoned by humans and lost in time. Even knowing she was a nixie, I never thought she might've gone somewhere in the sea. I almost want to smack myself in the face. All of this new magical crap being thrown around and I didn't think of the possibilities of an under-the-water city? Was the story of Atlantis a big enough hint for me at the prospect of an underwater city for magical folk? That was one of my mom's favorite stories, and now I can understand why.

A headache builds behind my eyes as I try to process the idea of secret civilizations submerged completely underwater including this one. How could we not have found this? Well, I guess what would they do if they did find it? It's already under the sea, so it's not like it'd be habitable even if we did find it.

I guess that's where nixies have the advantage. And mermaids I guess. They might want to live in a luxurious sunken city too.

Rubbing a hand across my forehead, I knead my temples and cringe at the layer of salty grease caked there. The air by the ocean is so saturated with salt that it gets everywhere, clinging to skin, hair, clothing, furniture, and just about every square inch of my house. Deep cleaning days were my least favorite growing up. I always hated scrubbing the salt out of every nook and cranny it worked its way into. Now the salt is a comfort. It's home It's familiar. Maybe the only familiar thing I know for sure now.

With a sigh, I heave myself off the bed and head into the adjacent bathroom. My towel is still hanging on the bar under the window, but I shove it in the half-full laundry basket and grab a new one out from under the sink.

My body goes through the motions of getting ready for a shower like no time has passed at all, remembering exactly how to turn the knobs to make the perfect temperature.

Climbing into the steaming stream, I look down at my own hands in wonder. If the Trident called to my mother, would it have called to me? Do I really not have any powers myself? Donovan dropped me into that tank like the stress of the experience would've jolted something out of me, but maybe there's another way to go about it. Maybe there's something I'm missing.

I sink to my knees. Why wouldn't Mom have told me about her past? About my past?

One of the notes she left outlined exactly how many memories she wanted me to lose, a methodical process that left me wondering how she could be so indifferent. Throw these memories out, keep these ones, and meld them with a fake memory; it just went completely against my experiences with her. She was a crazy, eccentric beach lover, not a calculating, calloused witch.

Stepping out of the shower, I wrench the old window open to let out the layers of steam hanging heavy in the room. Taking a gulp of the clear air, I realize how oxygen deprived I've been for the last half hour. Wrapping a towel around my chest, I head out into the hallway, soggy feet padding down the hardwood floors.

Sulfur tickles my nose, and my feet speed up until I'm securely ensconced in my room. Drying off my hair, I pull on old clothes left behind in my drawers. Sitting at the desk, I pull a brush through the tangles of my hair, but the smell is still there. It's fainter than it was in the hallway, but it's in here too. Maybe it's gas. I pull strands of hair out as I brush through the heavy mass in quick strokes and wrap it up in a bun while throwing on my hoodie.

Slipping down the hallway, I remember my bag still sitting at the foot of my bed. Doubling back, I sling my backpack over my shoulder when I hear a crash downstairs.

Heart speeding, I climb out my bedroom window to the oak tree leaning towards the house in the yard. Hopefully, I'll avoid whatever is going on downstairs. My feet hit the ground when a large *boom* rockets through the house and over the beach. The blast knocks me off my feet and I stumble through the grass until I can regain my bearing.

I stand on wobbly legs and leap over the low gate separating our yard from the untamed beach area in a fluid movement. Rippling flame cascades down my back and I glance back to see my entire house wrapped in fiery destruction. Rippling flames tear at the roof. At the walls. I fall into the weed-ridden sand. Smoke permeates the air and I choke on my breath.

Already unrecognizable, the fire makes quick work of the old wood house. Tears don't come. The house is gone. Memories gone. My last tangible connection to my mother up in flames.

I stare, transfixed in a surreal state until I remember who else was in the house.

Nick. Sarah.

Keeping my backpack securely strapped to my back, I walk on hesitant feet towards the house, pulse beating in my ears. My eyebrows singe as I get closer to the fire, peering through the exploded windows to find any evidence of them.

"Nick?! Sarah?!" I call through the increasing pain as my voice goes hoarse from the dry heat.

Flinching as I move lower to the ground, another explosion rocks the house. My ears ring from the proximity. Not willing to risk exposing myself to another one, I work my way to the front of the house, looking for Nick's car. Snapping my jaw to get hearing back in my right ear, I come around the side of the house and watch his car already pulling out, headlights blaring down the uneven driveway.

"Wait!" I call, but my voice is almost gone, the word barely perceptible to my damaged ears.

Running after them, my bare feet come down hard on the broken asphalt. "Wait!" The car doesn't slow, but I continue after it as the red of the taillight disappears around a corner.

I run until I'm a couple of blocks from town before I stop. My feet are cracked, their soft soles not ready for such extreme excursion. Blood cakes to my heels, leaving the impression of rust-colored footprints extending behind me.

My already uneven breathing leans into a sob, my jaw shaking. I slink to the ground, still in the middle of the street. It's late enough that it probably doesn't matter anyway. Curling up in the fetal position, I rest my head on my sweatpants-covered knees.

My crying grows uncontrollable, the sobs wracking my shoulders. I've been left behind after a near-death experience in a town where neither my mother nor my home are available to me. Hands grabbing at the straps to my backpack, I lay my head on my shoulder, grateful I went back for it.

Tingling numbness confirms my legs have fallen asleep when a fire truck approaches, its lights swinging with abandon and its horn blares a warning. I stand as it sweeps past, almost blowing me over in its haste.

My feet turn towards following it, but what good would it do me to watch them try to recover my home when it's long past saving?

It wasn't an ordinary fire that ripped through my home.

My nose twitches in the memory of the gas that made sure everything would go up, and quickly. It feels like a weird coincidence that it would happen the first night I'm back. The hair on the back of my neck stands up but I shake off the creepy feeling that comes with that thought.

Sitting against a tree, I stare at my ruined feet. At least Nick and Sarah are okay. Even if they did abandon me just like everyone else. It was incredibly lucky that none of us were hurt.

Then my mind skips over to Donovan.

My chest constricts, he'd been so close to us this whole time, he might have been in the house too. Should I have stayed by the house to make sure he wasn't in it? I can't see him sticking around for an explosion, but I also can't imagine him leaving without trying to make sure I was okay first. I may not trust him as much as he wants me to, but I do trust he wouldn't leave me to die.

Unless he was ordered to.

Fresh tears fill my eyes. There's really no one I can trust. Will this be the rest of my life now? No one to help me, nowhere to turn? Maybe my life won't even be long enough for that to feel like such a burden.

Stretching out my feet and wiggling my toes, I cry out with the accompanying sharp pain. With heavy, shaking fingers, I pick out some of the small rocks and leaves from the cuts in my feet. Too much of a wimp to try and walk again, I hunker down on hands and knees and crawl the rest of the way to town.

I can see the outline of main street in the early morning light when Nick's car drives past me, headed for the house. It swings back around, coming to a stop next to where I struggle. The passenger door flings open, and Sarah lands sprawled on the ground beside me.

"Avi?" she cries, her hands running over the planes of my face. "You made it out?"

I push her hands away from me, Nick's heavy footsteps running around the car to my other side. "You guys left me!"

"Not on purpose, Avi!" Nick says, his face shrouded in the darkness of early morning. "We left after the house exploded; we didn't think there was any chance of you getting out of there after that."

"Yeah, I'm sure that's what happened," I sneer, pulling my knees into my chest and resting on my tailbone to keep my feet off the ground. "I don't understand why neither of you came up to get me when you realized something was wrong."

Sarah closes her mouth, jaw tensed. "It was too late."

"But somehow you both managed to get out of the house and into the car before the explosion," I point out, refusing to back down. "Then you continued to drive away after I started chasing you."

Nick takes over for Sarah. "We didn't know you'd gotten out, so we didn't know to wait for you. As for not going back for you, we were already outside when it happened."

Even in the faint light I can see the blush growing across Sarah's cheeks. She looks away from me, but Nick grins openly. I don't bother asking what they were doing, it couldn't be any more obvious.

"We were just coming back to see if we could find you." Sarah's narrowed eyes make contact with mine once more. "We called 911 and were going to follow the fire truck and tell them we thought you were in the house."

"Why didn't you tell them I was in there when you called?" I raise my brow at him.

"She was a little stressed when she made the call, she didn't remember to tell them everything," Nick says, resting a hand on Sarah's shoulder. She looks up at him in thanks, but he doesn't return her smile. "I was really worried about you."

I shake my head. Their story doesn't make sense, but my mind is racing too quickly to clear things up. Instead, I clamp my jaw and swallow the accusing remarks bubbling their way to the surface.

Nick stands, offering a hand to me. "Let's get out of here."

I brush it away. While I may not be ready to ask questions, I already know I won't be getting back in the car with him. How could I ever trust him again? He didn't even try to see if I was okay. He just drove away. That's not what a friend would do. I wouldn't have done to either of them and I know them less than they think they know me.

"I'll get back on my own, thanks."

Sarah looks at Nick, brows drawn before glancing back at me. "We need you to come back with us."

"We're already on the way out, just come with us," Nick tries to reason with me.

I lean back on my hands. "I'm okay. I'll figure it out myself."

Sarah stands and braces her hands on her slim hips. "You're being ridiculous, just get in the car."

I shake my head, digging my fingers into the damp earth, letting it press painfully under my nails.

"Get in the car," Nick says, voice tense.

I don't respond and he comes closer to me, hands outstretched. Immediately I start to scream. He backs up, eyes widening as he pulls his hands away from me.

"Get away from me!" I continue, hoping someone is close enough to hear me and force Nick away.

I haven't made it close enough to town to attract very many people. Even so, Nick's head whips back and forth as he checks the street for anyone who may have heard me. Sarah backs up too, staring at me like I'm a stranger to her. I'm glad we've both finally realized that. We don't really know each other, and I'm tired of everyone acting like they do, tired of trying to act like I do. Just because I've lost memories doesn't mean I don't know who I am anymore.

"Avi," Nick says quietly, his voice pleading with me. "Please get back in the car with us. We're not going to hurt you."

He doesn't look me in my eyes though, his gaze focused on the spot between them on my forehead. He may have been my friend for years, which I realize is something that only took place in my own planted memories, but too much has happened between us for me to trust him.

"I'll come back to Ret," I promise even as the words fill my mouth with bile. I'll tell him anything to get him to leave. "But I'm coming back in my own way."

Sarah and Nick glance at each other, Sarah submitting to Nick for guidance. Waiting for their silent exchange to end, I keep my hands clenched, ready for a fight.

"Will you let us follow you?" Nick asks, trying to bargain with me.

"No!"

Sarah runs a hand through her curly red hair, fae-tipped ears peeking out. Nick looks from me to the closed door of the car and back to me, chewing his cheek.

"I don't understand what's happening," he says, still not moving towards the car. "Why won't you come with us?"

"My house just blew up, my life is a lie and I'd really appreciate some time to myself." It's not like it's a lie, and my chest feels lighter with the admission. I really need some time for myself. Near-death experiences kind of make me want to reevaluate my life. If only I could tell him how much I don't trust him, how sometimes the sight of him makes me want to punch a hole through the wall.

Sarah leans over Nick, her chest pressing into his shoulder. "Everyone is feeling pretty heated right now. Let's just take some space, breathe a minute and meet up before we get to

New York. How about we get together in Providence? Can we do that?"

Agreeing with her is the easiest way I can think of to get rid of them. My small nod brings the smile back to Nick's face.

"We're going back, all of us. If I don't see you in Providence, I'm coming right back here, okay?" Nick reaches for my arm but I step out of his reach.

"I'll be there," I whisper, just wishing he would leave.

He nods and hops back into the car without another word to me. The car turns around and speeds off toward town, probably headed toward the highway.

I tenderly press my hand against the bottoms of my feet. They're still not in a good way, but at least all the bleeding has stopped. Pulling out a pair of socks from my crumpled backpack and slip my wounded feet into them. I pray this small level of protection will help me on my way back to the house.

The peeling white garage wasn't attached to the house, something Mom always complained about on days when it snowed, which felt like half the year sometimes. I'm so grateful she didn't ever get around to building the garage addition onto the house because it's the only thing that might have saved her car from the explosion.

I didn't want to go back to the house before, but now the need to see the level of destruction the explosion caused is overwhelming. With the fire put out, now is the best time to go.

Getting up is harder than I thought it would be, beads of sweat break out across my forehead as I use the tree trunk as a crutch. My legs shake from the pain caused by all the pressure, but I force them to steady enough to start down the road. Every step is a small agony, but I force myself to keep going. It's this or ask the people in town for help. I've already made a big enough spectacle of myself and have proven I'm not a good judge of who to trust. Why should I add any more people to this sorry equation?

The walk back takes three times as long as the walk out here did, my body swaying from fatigue and the searing pain coming from my feet. The fire truck passes me when I'm halfway there, the sirens turned off now that the emergency is over.

As I turn up the drive and catch a view of my home from behind the trees, my breath catches, heart sinking and taking my body with it. My knees hit the pavement, not even registering the pain anymore.

The fire and the explosion have been so complete that my home stands like a two-hundred-year-old ruin. Walls sink in, the second floor missing completely, and black scorch marks cover everything. Even the red steps have been obliterated.

Tears cascade over my cheeks until I have nothing left, too dehydrated to make anymore. I rub the back of my hand over my cheeks. They come back dry. I kneel in the front yard so long that what tears I once had are now completely evaporated in the still heat of the dead fire.

Standing up, I walk over to the garage and pull the warped door open. The garage only has a little scorching on the outside of the building to show any sign of the explosion. Swallowing the lump in my throat, I walk to the driver's side of her old sedan. The white door is covered in a layer of grime, its teal bench seats stiff with dust.

Mom always left her keys in the ignition, she said she liked to be able to leave quickly and didn't want to worry about lost keys. She's lucky no one ever thought to check our garage for a car to steal, although I doubt they would've wanted what they found anyway.

The key sticks as I turn it, but the car starts with a slow chug when I give it some gas. Relieved my plan will work, I turn off the car and head back up towards the house. I'll head down, but whether I make it to Ret or not remains to be seen.

I got the information I was looking for, I don't need them anymore.

Tripping over the debris of my home, I stumble up to the damaged front steps. Stepping on the porch it creaks under my weight but surprisingly holds steady, the warmth of the wood burning into my damaged soles.

Standing before the blown out front door, a mewling sound pushes past my lips. Where my kitchen once stood is now just a hole all the way down to the foundation. That would explain the gas smell. Mom loved our old gas stove even though I was always afraid one day she would leave it on and blow us up.

Looks like I wasn't that crazy after all. The victory is hollow in the face of the explosion.

Backing off the porch, I walk the perimeter of the house. I don't know what I'm looking for. Clues? A reason for why my house would spontaneously explode while I was in it? I don't see anything, which doesn't surprise me. The back of my mind whispers it was Nick. How easy it would've been from his position on the couch to turn the gas on, light a match, and get away. Although it's probably more complicated than that. I'm not an arsonist, so I wouldn't know.

A broken piece of a robin egg blue mug sits in the yard. Picking it up, I cradle it to my chest, lost in memories that will never happen again.

"Want some company?"

I glance up sharply, my hand bringing up the broken mug like a weapon. Donovan's form is outlined against the glare off the ocean. He walks closer, face coming into focus as he gets farther from the beach. His leather jacket covered in dust; his face smeared with ashes.

"Where have you been?" I refuse to wait politely through small talk.

He pulls his hands out of his pockets. They're almost completely black. "Looking for you."

I drop the cup and reach out to him, needing someone after everything I've been through. The cup smashes against the cement as he cradles me in his firm grip. He holds me tight against him, heartbeat erratic in his chest. Reaching my arms around his torso, I secure him to me as he breathes heavy in my hair.

"I didn't realize you'd gotten away," he whispers in my ear. "I've been looking everywhere for something that would tell me where you were. I couldn't leave without knowing what had happened to you."

My stomach heaves. I can't find the words to speak, and he doesn't try to make me. If Nick knew what I was doing, he might try to finish the job he started last night and murder me where I stand.

"Let's get out of here." I release him from the hug, but keep a hand laced in his.

He nods mutely, following me as I lead him to the garage. Walking him over to the passenger seat, he barks out a rough laugh but doesn't complain. I check the mirrors as I pull out of the garage, my feet aching against the pedals, I get one last look at what remains of my home before speeding off towards the highway with the only person left I might be able to trust.

Chapter Ten

I pull off at the first rest stop, my body sore, my feet in too much pain to continue, and my soul exhausted. Leaning the seat back for a much-needed nap, the events of the day settle deep into my bones. Donovan is silent beside me, his glazed dark eyes still living through the shock of the night.

"You want anything?" I ask with a pointed look toward the faded blue vending machine leaning against the side of the cement block restrooms.

He shakes his head, reclining his seat to match mine.

"I'm sorry I scared you," I whisper. His eyes, mid-flutter, peek open at my own. "I didn't know if you were there or not. I... I wondered if you were okay too."

He closes his eyes again, eyelashes dark against his pale skin. "Aside from some minor burns I got rummaging around in the ashes, I'm perfect."

"I can relate to that, although I don't know that I'll ever feel perfect again." I glance down at his hands. They're folded on top of his jacket, soot streaks hiding the burns he's referring to. "All right, out of the car," I say.

Donovan blinks up at me from his reclined position.

"You heard me. Get out of the car and up to the bathroom. I want those hands cleaned up so I can check your burns." I shoo him out, but he doesn't budge.

"We have to take care of you first," he says, gesturing toward my feet. "let me look at *your* burns."

I hesitate but I know it's a fight I'm going to lose. I shift my feet towards him, wincing as they hit the gear shift. Donovan's mouth draws into a tight line as he looks at the damage.

"You drove all this way like this?"

I shrug. "I couldn't feel it for a while."

He curses under his breath and takes a small bottle of out his pocket. He squeezes out some liquid and rubs it on my feet. The liquid burns like ice, but as that sensation dies, I find the pain has too.

"*Now*, I'll get cleaned up," he says with a small smile as he moves my feet back into my side of the car.

He climbs out and I follow his weary steps up to the bathroom, my own feeling much more buoyant than before.

Taking a deep breath of the comparatively clean bathroom air, I can't believe how easy it was to get used to the smell of soot and burning still coming out of the open windows of the car. We're completely permeated by the smell. It's soaked into us.

There's a drinking fountain in front that Donovan points to with a nod toward me, but I shake my head and push against his back until he goes into the men's room. I'd love to clean him up myself, the rising blush on my cheeks a statement to just how much, but I don't want to make a mess of the drinking fountain either. Plus, if Nick didn't set that fire, I'd hate to leave a trail for some mystery arsonist to follow.

Slumping down on a metal bench outside the restrooms, I let my head hang between my knees. Even though I'm not alone and am over-exhausted after the explosion, I feel freer. My mouth pricks up in a small smile. I'm free to do anything

I want, including not following Nick back like I said I would. Warmth blooms through my chest as I dream of driving off in the opposite direction, leaving all this mess behind.

Those hopes come to a jarring halt as Donovan comes back out of the bathroom with his hands scrubbed pink.

I sigh. I'll never really be free of them, not that I think Donovan would make me go back to Ret. I'm too entangled in this mess than I'd like to admit. I just want to find Mom and get out.

"You were right, cleaning up feels great. I'll probably get a better nap now that I don't have to worry about leaving a mess on the seats," he says, plopping next to me on the bench.

His wet black hair drips onto his jacket, each drop making an audible plop against the leather. He looks down at the rivulets of water running off his jacket and laughs. "Maybe I shouldn't have tried to wash my hair out though."

I can't help but laugh at his accurate drowned rat impression. Donovan laughs with me, everything about him feeling lighter than when we were in the car. But my smile grows weak as I look over Donovan's hands. The skin is pink and tender, not just because of his recent wash. There are a few spots where the tiny bubbles of blisters have already started to form.

"We need to do something about this. Your skin is still burning up which will only make these burns worse."

He pulls his hands back out of my grip, shoving them into his jacket pockets. "I'll be fine."

"No really, can we use that stuff you just used on my feet? This is really bad," I insist.

"I used the last of it on you," he says with a shrug. "Don't worry. I don't need it."

I haven't had to doctor many people before, and I curse my lack of information. Ordinarily, I'd just look something like this up on my phone but now I'm stuck floundering around and racking my brain for any hint of knowledge about burns.

"It's fine. Let's just go, do you want to nap while I drive?" Donovan gets off the bench and walks toward the car, his spine straight.

"Is there something you want to tell me?" I ask, following him but not getting into the car. "Is there a reason why you don't want medical attention?"

He doesn't answer, sitting in the driver's seat and drumming his hands on the steering wheel. "You're worried about me?"

"Of course, I am," I say with a laugh. "You burned your hands while digging through the rubble of *my* house looking for *me*. I feel pretty responsible, crazy as that sounds."

Donovan stares back out through the windshield, eyes vacant. "You don't have to worry about me, I know how to take care of myself."

"Just because you *can* take care of yourself doesn't mean that other people *won't* worry about you." A smile tugs at my lips. "I'm sure your parents worry about you."

His eyes practically disappear as he scrunches them up. "My parents are dead."

Well, that explains why he gets to traipse around the country without checking in with anyone. I put my hand on his broad shoulder, squeezing it to convey my apologies. I've felt that pain, even if I never fully believed Mom was dead.

"No matter what anyone else does, I'll still worry. Now tell me."

He pulls his hands out of his pocket, revealing the burn-shiny palm. Already, the pink is starting to fade, the bubbles I noticed earlier sinking until they're flush with his healthy skin. Running my hands over his, the pads of my fingers slide from healthy to burned skin almost imperceptibly. Even without being burned myself, a tingle spreads up my arm as my hand lingers on his.

"You don't have to worry about it because it won't be an issue for long." His voice is sullen as he gazes out the dusty windshield.

My mouth hangs open, not believing what's happening before my eyes. If his hands look this way now and are healing at such a rapid rate, I shudder to think what they must have looked like when we first got in the car. Did I see bone and mistake it for his pale skin?

Donovan yanks his hands back, gripping the steering wheel until his knuckles turn white.

"Why didn't you just say that before?" There's no reason for him to have gotten such an attitude. I only want to help him. "It's not a big deal."

He hunkers down inside his jacket, face hidden behind the steering wheel. Slamming the door closed, I walk around to the passenger side, throwing myself into the seat with a huff.

Donovan starts the car, staring out the rear windshield as he backs out of my parking spot. He gets onto Interstate 1 headed towards I95, and I stare out the window with a cranky resolve to be upset with him. However, as we pass mile marker after mile marker, I feel my eyelids drooping, my head growing heavy.

He braces a hand on my shoulder. "Just relax and take a nap. I'll get you there okay, I promise."

He went back for me. That's more than I can say about anyone else in my life right now. My head lulls forward until it hits the window and I lose myself in sleep.

I trust him. I have to.

* * *

"Avi?" Donovan asks, his hand shaking my shoulder. "You should get up and eat something."

Blearily, I blink at the dashboard clock, the hazy *1:00pm* finally coming into focus. We've been driving a long time, an exit for Portland coming up on the right.

"I figured we should stop and get some food. Have you eaten anything today?"

I shake my head, finger-combing my hair after I catch a reflection of myself in the side mirror. I look like a feral child. Soot still clings to my skin and my hair sticks up in all directions.

"Well good. There's a great place up here that I think you'll like. You in the mood for burgers?" He gives me a side-long glance.

"I'm always in the mood for burgers." I laugh, my throat even more sore after my rest as breathing in the smoke catches up with me.

Donovan makes me feel comfortable in a way Nick was never able to. At least not since I found out about our secret lives.

Thinking back to our first encounter, it doesn't make sense that I would be drawn to him like this. Just some rough boy chasing me through the streets of New York? Not all that appealing typically.

I glance back at him, hiding a smile behind my hand. I can't help it. He's been there for me since all of this started and never tried to hide our history together. I have to admire his candor in the face of my rejection. Nick certainly didn't do that.

Just thinking his name puts a sour taste in my mouth. He must have been involved in the attack on my house last night. There just doesn't seem to be a way around it. He and Sarah would've driven off into the night together while I burned to a raging crisp in my bed. My mouth thins, hands turning to fists. Donovan glances toward me while turning off the highway.

"You okay?"

"Bad dream," I say through clenched teeth. When I see Nick again, I just want to give him a good slug in the face. He deserves it after everything I've been through because of his lies.

Donovan pulls up to a quaint little burger shop in one of the bordering towns of Portland. Its red and white awning leans to the right, and more than a few roof tiles have started to peel up, but the smell of sizzling meat wafting in through the air vents has me salivating before he can even park the car.

He locks the doors as he gets out, making me stress for a moment before remembering I can unlock them from the inside. A big grin grows across his face as he comes around and opens the door for me.

"What was that for?"

"My mom always taught me to open the door for ladies," he says, linking his arm with mine. "I just didn't think you'd wait long enough to let me."

"You're right, I wouldn't have." A warm blush spreads over my cheeks as we walk arm-in-arm up to the window to order.

"I hope you don't mind; I was just going to order for both of us," he says, not waiting for my response as he steps up to the window and rattles off a long order. The woman behind the window smiles, takes his card, and tells us to wait about five minutes.

Donovan leads me over to a wooden picnic table, sitting me down before heading back to the window to grab two large cups.

"Here," he says, pushing one across to me.

I stare dubiously into the creamy depths of the cup but am pleasantly surprised when I take a sip. It's a vanilla milkshake, one of my favorite things to eat. I haven't been able to find a good one since I moved to New York, and the thick shake slides across my tongue like heaven.

Donovan sits across from me, arms crossed on the table as he slurps from his own cup. At some point in our drive, he changed his clothes, exchanging the ashy shirt and pants for a new combination of dark colors. The jacket is still firmly in place.

"What do you think?" he asks with a smile that says he already knows the answer.

"It's amazing!" I don't bother holding back my enthusiasm, making his shoulders shake with laughter. "How did you know?"

The smile fades away. "This isn't our first time here."

My response is cut short as the woman from the window returns with our food, laying out trays of thick greasy burgers, onion rings, and curly fries.

Donovan grabs one of the burgers, a slice of bacon sliding out of the end, and chomps down. I follow suit. He obviously isn't waiting for my response.

It's so easy to forget I had a life before. The forgotten five years. I can't imagine how hard it must be for him, not that he's really made me feel bad about it.

I start in on the fries, dipping them in a complete coating of ketchup. Donovan's too focused on his food to pay much attention to me, and I'm too caught up in my thoughts to eat very fast.

Finally, I excuse myself to the restroom, needing a moment away from him and genuinely just needing to pee. When I get a look at myself in the mirror, I can't help but grimace. My hair is a flyaway mess, my skin darkened by a fine layer of soot. I wet a paper towel and rub it across my face, my skin brightening with each swipe.

Pulling a hair tie off my wrist, I wrap my hair up in a messy bun. It's not a typical look for me, but I want the level of grunge I'm sporting to look more on purpose than like the actual mess it is.

When I come back out, Donovan's gone through all the burgers but one, leaving it sitting fat and lonely in my abandoned spot.

"Feeling better?" he asks through a mouthful of onion rings.

"Yeah, I just couldn't handle feeling so gross anymore." I stick to the truth, not bothering to mention that his comment drove me to seek the solitude of the rest stop bathroom.

He nods, eyes glued to the food. "Yeah, you looked pretty bad."

"Hey!" I smack him across the shoulder. "A girl can say that about herself, but you're never allowed to agree with her!"

He grins unapologetically. "You should eat that before I do."

I pick up the burger he ordered, still warning him with my eyes to keep his comments to himself. The taste of meat and cheese fills my mouth, and I sigh. Small town food is so much better than anything you can get from a chain.

"Any idea when you need to be back?" he asks. "Wouldn't want you to be late."

I grimace. "I don't know. I'm supposed to meet back up with Nick in Providence, but..."

I let my sentence hang. I may trust Donovan, but that doesn't mean I feel right telling him how uncomfortable Ret makes me. How uncomfortable Nick makes me.

"I promised I'd go back," I say instead. "I just didn't say when. Although I'm sure Nick expects me to just drive right back down there."

"That doesn't sound like any fun." Donovan leans back in his seat now that his tray is empty.

"Yeah, not really. I'm not even sure what they'll want to do with me once we get there," I say, licking the grease off my fingers before wiping the rest off on a crumpled napkin.

"We should do something with your temporary freedom then. Let's make the most of it." His brow quirks suggestively, making me laugh. "No, but really, what do you want to do before we have to meet up with Mr. Boring?"

I can't think of much I want to do along our drive. It's one I've taken before, and the usual tourist pits just don't appeal to me.

"If you can't think of anything, I'll just have to surprise you," he says, loading the trash back on our trays to dump before escorting me to the car.

"You think you could surprise me with another shake?"

He gives me a grin. "I think I could arrange something like that."

We load back in, my stomach as heavy as my heart is full. Donovan turns up the stereo, singing along with some 80s rock band. I can't help but laugh as he mock plays the guitar along with it, completely in his element.

"Let's put something good on," I interrupt, pressing the seek button despite his protests.

I push it again and again, stopping at some sappy love ballad my mother used to listen to. I sing along, but my mind is far away, not even hearing Donovan as he teases my atrocious music sense.

"I can't believe you switched it to this! This isn't even music, just some woman crying into a microphone," he says with a smile, hands relaxed on the wheel.

Memories swirl through my distracted mind, all of them of Mom. Her long blonde hair flies around her face, her brows tense, her mouth tight as she speaks to me. I can't remember the words she's saying, my mind muting all sound but the radio. She grips my shoulders, forcing me to investigate the wild depths of her fluid brown eyes as she tells me the same thing over and over again.

"Avi?!"

I jolt back to the present with a rough shove against the window. Donovan glances over at me, face twisted as he tries to pull off the highway. He swerves through traffic, stopping us on a small ledge of grass off the side of the highway.

Unbuckling, he crawls across the middle seat, holding my face in his large palms. "Are you okay?"

I brush his hands aside, heat flaming across my cheeks. "I'm fine. What's the big deal?"

"You went completely unresponsive," he says, scooting back into his own seat. His hands still reach for me, but my reaction was enough to keep him from trying to touch me.

"Well, I'm fine." I shove him back into his seat with hard hands. I'm not sure what I just saw, and I don't want to tell him about it. Can't anything just be mine to think about? Can't I ever try to figure out my past alone?

He lowers one brow, eyeing me with a critical gaze. "Are you sure? You were pretty out of it for a minute there."

I watch the cars on the highway speed by, ignoring his stare like he ignored mine earlier.

Finally, he pulls back onto the road, our car being passed repeatedly as he picks up speed. The silence between us is tense, Donovan's knuckles standing out in white points again.

"I'm not trying to be difficult," I say after a few miles. The distance between us feels like it's literally pulling at my chest.

"We all have our secrets."

His words are chaffing; striking against my heart. I hate being reminded of the secrets he keeps from me, of his involvement in an organization I don't understand. One that's willing to hurt me to get my secrets.

"I'm trying to figure things out," I tell him after a long pause.

He smiles at me, but it doesn't reach his eyes. I reach my hand out and lay it on his tense leather-clad arm. Donovan looks away from me, but I catch the narrowed eyes before his face has completely turned.

"Is everything okay?" I remove my hand.

He shrugs. "Just trying not to worry about you, since you're okay and all."

"'Okay', that seems like such a relative word. I'm okay compared to how I've been, but I'm nowhere near actually being 'okay'." I stare at my reflection in the window, a streak of soot I missed curving across my throat.

"I get that. You've been going through a lot lately. It'd make sense that you'd still feel a little jumbled up inside."

I rotate my body, so Donovan's broad form fills my view. "Why did you think I would know you when you came to collect me back in New York? Had we not been talking for months? Is that how you didn't know my mind had been wiped out? Because that doesn't sound like the kind of relationship you've told me we had."

"Woah, that's a lot of questions." He holds his hands up in mock surrender.

"It's just one of the things that hasn't made sense to me. You looked so familiar in my kitchen, and I don't have any memories of you there," I say with a small shrug. This is one of the few things I can get an answer for, and I'm not going to let him off the hook.

He runs a rough hand through his dark hair. "I hadn't talked to you for a few months because you'd asked me not to talk to you anymore."

His confession fills the void between us. "Why wouldn't I want you to talk to me?"

"You thought we should break up. You knew your mom was moving you to New York and you felt like we should be free to pursue people geographically closer to us. Plus," he says with a pause. "I think you were already talking to Nick at this point."

"Nick?" I ask, completely flabbergasted.

Donovan sighs. "Nick had started talking to you after you joined some Facebook group for your new school. I recall you saying he was really cool, and you thought you guys'd be friends after you got to Brooklyn."

I twist in my seat, my back flat against the sagging cushion. "I don't get it."

"Yeah, I never really got it either," he says, still not looking at me. "I figured I'd give you a few months to cool off and then get back in touch and see where we were at. I did send you a few texts though."

My mouth puckers in a frown. I don't remember getting any texts from numbers I didn't know, and I know that Donovan's name wasn't in my contacts. I feel pretty confident his name would've stood out among the other more conservatively named friends in my contacts.

"I don't think I ever got any of them."

"Or someone made sure you never saw them," he says, mouth pulled down to his chin. "I can think of a few people who could've helped you out with that. Wouldn't want anyone from your past to interrupt the new little life they'd set up for you."

He's back to brooding. Question and answer time is over. I lean my head back against the headrest, trying to work free any memories that could validate Donovan's thoughts. Without my memories, I'm left feeling lost with only a headache to show for my efforts.

Chapter Eleven

The sun sinks low in the sky, but the tree line blocks the fading light long before it can set.

"Are we stopping anywhere for the night?" A change of subject might clear his conversational pipes.

He gives me a sidelong glance. "I've got a place in mind already, we're about ten minutes away."

"You made some secret reservations, did you?" I ask with a grin.

"I just thought we'd need somewhere to stay and thought we might make it this far south. Didn't do too bad, did I?" His self-satisfied smile transforms his face back into someone who might be my friend.

"Yeah. It's almost like you've done this before." I watch to see if my comment triggers any further memories in his beleaguered mind.

He rubs the back of his neck. "I may have done this a few times. Although I prefer to travel in a different way."

"What's up with that?" I ask him. "Why is it that you and Ramsey can do that weird magic disappearing act? Can anyone else do that? Can I do it?"

Donovan gives me an unhappy laugh. "It's not for everyone. It's actually one of my family traits."

His face grows dark, mirroring the way he looked when talking about his burns.

"Where's your family?" I clean out my fingernails, trying to look as nonchalant as possible. "Do they live in New York?"

Donovan shakes his head. "I don't want to talk about them."

His brows are drawn, and the back of his neck has a splotchy crimson stain. Chewing on my bottom lip, I think about Sarah's parents. She didn't want to talk about them either. I wonder if that's part of the job description of working with these people, 'must have missing or disappointed parents.'

We slip off the highway, driving to a motel across from the main exit. He doesn't say a word to me when we get out, just grabs my backpack and heads up the front steps. Face burning, I wish I could take back the last five minutes.

He checks in at the reception desk, grabbing the card key from her outstretched hand, with only a backward glance to show he cares about my existence at all. It's his casual look that gets my blood boiling. Following behind him, a blush permanently stains my face.

I hesitate as he ushers me into our nondescript but clean room, the door clicking shut behind him. He sets the backpack down on one of the two double beds, still not looking at me.

"Are you finished with your tantrum yet?" I set my hands on my hips. "Because I'm done with this attitude."

His head jolts up, wide brown eyes meeting mine. "What are you talking about?"

"I'm talking about this attitude you've gotten since I asked about your parents, which you brought up in the first place, by the way." I poke him in the chest. "You don't have to punish me because your home life is a mess. You think I don't know what that feels like?"

Donovan rubs the back of his neck with an open hand, looking at his feet for a moment.

"I've never made you feel bad for asking about my home life, even though that's all anyone wants to talk to me about."

"I'm not trying to punish you," he says, slumping onto the mattress, pale face tight. "I just don't like thinking about them."

I stand in front of him, hands anchored to my side. "Well, you need to get over it, because you're punishing everyone who has the displeasure to be around you. Something that I don't even have a choice about right now. We're stuck together, so be considerate, otherwise I'll start wishing I was back in the car with Nick and Sarah."

His mouth twists to the side, staring at me sardonically. "I highly doubt they can offer you any better company than I am, even at my worst."

"I'm just saying, make me enjoy our time together." I smile, shoving him in the shoulder.

"I'm sure I can make this trip worth your while," he says, standing in a fluid movement.

I rock back on my heels, Donovan's chest suddenly filling my vision. He grins at me until I take a few steps back. I pull my backpack onto my lap to hide my face which has somehow managed to turn even redder. I poke through its contents, pretending this had always been my intention. Donovan is still laughing when the door to the bathroom closes behind him.

Left alone in the room, I turn on the television and flip through the few offered channels. There's not much on tonight, but I leave the news on for background noise, so I don't have to be alone with the sound of Donovan's shower. I'm confident he'll be in the bathroom for a while, so I feel like I have enough privacy to put on my pajamas. Without Sarah and Nick here, I'm glad for the nicer pajamas in my bag to replace the worn-out sweatpants I feel like I've been living in for ages.

Remembering the fire sends a chill through my body and I grab at my sweatshirt as it slips off the edge of the bed. Mom's notes fall out of the pocket. I'd almost forgotten about them in the chaos of the day.

Sitting cross-legged, I wince from the pain in my feet and grip the notes tightly. Reading over everything with a critical eye, I look for any clues I may have missed.

One of the pages has her specific recipe for me. My gaze follows the words even though I don't completely understand them, my head starts to pound.

The bathroom door clicks open and my body jerks. Shoving the papers under my pillow, I keep my eyes glued to the less-than-entertaining news. Donovan towels off his hair as he comes in the room, jeans slung low on his hips and a wrinkled shirt tight over his chest.

He glances at me, the screen, then back to me. "Anything good?"

"Not really." I try to shrug to get the lines of tension out of my shoulders.

Donovan looks me over, gaze lingering on my feet. "When did this happen?"

"After the fire."

I haven't had shoes all day, but he hasn't commented on my lack of appropriate footwear. I'd almost forgotten about my feet too, but the pain of walking on them again as we moved from the car to the hotel room pushed them back to the forefront of my mind.

"That doesn't look so good." He comes closer to me, his gaze never leaving my ruined feet. "Would you let me clean them?"

My hands shake and I shove them behind my back.

Somehow my head nods despite the alarms going off in my head, and in a reversal of roles, Donovan grabs an unblemished washcloth from the bathroom, wets it, and starts rubbing the grime off my feet. His hands are gentle on my wounds, the warm washcloth a sweet relief after the day we've had. His almost black eyes narrowed in concentration as he works.

"Thank you," I mumble after his second trip to the bathroom to wash out the cloth. Its once pristine white is now streaked brown.

"No problem." He stays fixated, getting right back to work. "I'd hate for these to get infected. You're lucky they're not already."

He keeps rubbing the cloth in circular motions, my feet becoming the cleanest part of my body.

"I don't get you," I say at last. "You're so hot and cold. One minute you're cranky and quiet, the next you're cleaning off my feet like it's your only care in the world. I can't figure you out."

Donovan doesn't answer me right away. Instead, he gives my feet a final wipe and throws the washcloth into the bathroom sink. "I don't know that there's much to figure out."

"I think you like having this bad boy persona but don't know how to keep it up." My eyes go wide as he stands, my hands clenching the comforter.

He laughs. "Is that so?"

"Yeah."

Donovan pulls off his jacket and slings it on the back of the chair by the desk. I'm still waiting for his answer when he pulls off his navy V-neck and tosses it on the floor. Barechested, he stands before me grinning, watching the inexperienced blush creep across my face.

"You don't think I'm really all bad?" he asks, walking

closer to me, his narrow hips accented by the low-hung pants. "I can be bad."

I push myself farther against the headboard, pulling my legs in toward me as he braces his hands on the foot of the bed. My pulse skyrockets as I wait for the grin that tells me he's joking, but it doesn't come. He creeps up the bed, dark narrow eyes serious.

"You're not like this," I tell him, my voice too quiet and cracking halfway through. "You wouldn't do this."

He runs a hand down my leg. "I might if I felt I had to prove a point."

"I'm not afraid of you," I whisper.

Donovan smirks, cupping my face in his rough palms. He tilts my face up to his, minty breath filling my nostrils. My lips part—in anticipation or fear? I can't tell. My heart beats too fast for me to make sense of anything happening right now.

His face lowers to mine, our lips millimeters apart. I stop breathing altogether.

"Nah, you're right. This isn't me," he says into my mouth. My jaw grinds closed, and he laughs at my red cheeks and heaving chest as he crawls back off the bed. Hiding my face, I crawl into the plush covers, turning my body to face the sliding glass door in the back wall of the room. Donovan keeps laughing, but the springs in the mattress shift as he gets into his bed too.

"I didn't mean to scare you," he says to my tense back.

"You didn't scare me." I'm not sure how much of that statement is a lie.

He shifts in the bed. "Don't be mad at me."

"I'm not mad," I mumble.

"Then turn and face me."

Rubbing my hands against my face to clear away any evidence of embarrassment, I roll over. Donovan lays on his side, eyes peering into mine in the near darkness of the hotel room. He reaches a hand across the way between our beds, pouting mouth pleading with me to forgive him. Sighing, I reach over and grasp it, his hand dwarfing mine.

"I'm sorry about before," he says, voice so quiet the news almost drowns him out.

"It's not a big deal." I lie about the odd sense of rejection I have from our embarrassing encounter.

He squeezes my hand. "I'm glad we're here together."

I bury my face in my pillow to hide the smile I can't keep from growing.

"I didn't know if we'd get another opportunity to be alone," he continues. "I followed you the last few days just praying we would get another chance to be together before Ret got you in their clutches again. I know you didn't like your time with Amaro, but I really didn't mean to hurt you. Patrice just wants what's best for everyone."

"I don't want to talk about her." I clench my eyes closed, remembering her name printed out in Mom's loopy hand-writing.

Donovan nods. "You're right, she's not important right now."

Except that he still works for her. Studying his relaxed face, I don't get it. "Why do you work with them?"

"I have to. They're going to save the world, and I'm going to help them do it," he says, face still relaxed but eyes watching something distant.

"A little melodramatic don't you think?" I tease, squeezing his hand.

"I'm serious," he says, pulling his hand out of mine and leaning on his elbow. "The world is going to change, and we need to be ready for it. All that stuff I showed you before, I did for a reason. Without us, without Amaro, all that will cease to exist. Magical creatures won't be able to find employment anymore, won't be able to live in their own homes anymore.

Ret's king wants to close everyone down, send us back into hiding."

I lean up and mirror his position. "What are you talking about?"

"He wants to send us all back into the Dark Ages, hiding out from any threats of witch hunts. They say it's not because they're afraid of humans. Ret thinks we need to protect humans from us!" Donovan says with a disbelieving laugh. "Apparently, we need to go into hiding to save the humans' delicate minds from finding out more powerful beings than them exist. It boggles my mind! Anyway, we're not going to let a stuffy king ruin things for everyone else. We're going to liberate them! We shouldn't have to hide who we are anymore."

Donovan grows more and more impassioned as he finishes. He sits up completely, throwing the blanket off his bare torso, the muscles across his chest shaded from the television's blue light.

"Why would they want that?" I'm still trying to reconcile the image of Ret he's created with a medieval old king ruling over all with the Ret I know from my time with them.

He swings his legs over the side of the bed, reaching out for my hand again. "They're more worried about keeping bloodlines pure and humans safe than they are with any progress we could be creating."

He's too excited; I can't show him the growing doubt in my mind. Donovan might believe what he's telling me, but I still can't get it to click.

"We don't have to talk about this anymore if you don't want to." His face grows less tight as he reads my face. "I just didn't want you to go back without knowing."

"I appreciate that," I say, laying back on the bed.

His knees thump onto the carpeted floor between our beds. "Could I...do you think it would be okay... could I?"

I'm still not quite sure what he's asking, but a splotchy blush has risen across his throat and into the lower reaches of his cheeks, his face not quite meeting mine.

"Do you think it would be okay if I laid next to you? No funny business," he says in a rush as he sees the skepticism on my face. "I want to be close to you for as long as we have left."

While my head is certain the question is innocent, my heart skips several beats in reply and I nod to him as he leaps into the bed next to me. His cold feet brush against mine, the air from where he pulled up the covers sending a chill into my bones. He pulls me back against him so that we're spooning when I shudder, one of his arms wrapped around my stomach.

He breathes deep and even in my hair. I reach out to the remote and turn the television off, plunging us into complete darkness. Donovan doesn't move, not even as I wiggle around to get comfortable, my butt pressing into him momentarily. My face flushes in mortification, and I lay as still as possible, not wanting to disturb or inconvenience him with my presence even though he's asked to lay with me. Clenching my eyes closed, I breathe him in, the smell of cheap hotel soap coating the air between us.

My heart beats fast and I can't get it to calm down. Even as crazy as things have been, I can't help but focus on the attractive boy laying in my bed with his arm around me. Nothing like this has ever happened to me before. At least not that I can remember.

"Donovan?"

"Hmm?" His voice is already low and sleepy.

I sigh, building up the courage to keep talking to him despite every warning bell in my head telling me to shut up. "Why are you so nice to me?"

He chuckles into my hair. "Because I like you, of course."

"Oh." I lick my suddenly dry lips. "You're all over the

place all the time, I never know what you're thinking or what I actually mean to you."

"I wouldn't want you to get too comfortable with me." He pulls me closer, and I can feel him smiling.

"It'd be nicer for me if you would be clear about what you want. Everyone wants something from me, and I'd just rather know what you want so it doesn't take me by surprise again." My words came out in a gushing flood.

Donovan's hands tighten on me, turning me by the shoulders to face him. We stare at each other in the darkness, his dark eyes giving off a light shine. "I don't want anything from you. I just want to be *with* you."

Staring at him, I chew my lip as I try to find a lie to tell him, cursing the lack of light for hiding so much of him from me.

Donovan sighs, running a hand down the side of my face and tucking a length of hair back behind my ear. "I'll get you to believe me someday."

My laugh is low and unconvincing. "I hope I have enough time for somedays. I might not have enough time even for next week to get here."

"What makes you think that?" he asks, fingernails digging into my skin through my nightshirt.

"Well, how long before someone else decides it's easier to get the information I have without dealing with the collateral? I'm pretty sure no one on either side wants much to do with me aside from the information I represent. Patrice made that perfectly clear. Plus, I'm not sure how much my Mom ever told me. It's not like I knew everything about this world, and she simply wiped away traces of the Trident. She never told me anything about any of this." I sigh, disgruntled once again by Mom's lack of trust in me.

"I'm sure she took the last five years for a reason,"

Donovan says, trying to reassure me. "You'll figure out why soon enough."

I don't tell him about the small flashbacks I've been getting. As much as I trust him, I feel better keeping this information to myself. "I hope you're right."

He presses a kiss into my forehead, our chests temporarily touching and sending tingles through my skin. "Things will get better, I promise."

He turns me back around and wraps a muscled arm around me. I count my breaths to calm down until I slowly drift to sleep.

* * *

The alarm goes off in the weak morning light, I blink blearily and slap a hand at it. Its shrill bleat stops, and I sit up and look over the bed next to me. Donovan's already gone, his side made up in neat lines.

Stretching, I wake up much slower than normal under the circumstances. With a barely suppressed yawn, I finally get up and make my way into the bathroom.

Turning on the water, I wonder what could've happened to Donovan. I know he'll come back, and I hope against hope that he'll bring some donuts with him when he does.

The shower wipes away all lingering traces of sleep by the time I shut the water off. Pulling on clean clothes, my spirits sink at the thought of meeting up with Nick today and going back to Ret with him. I still have too many unresolved thoughts from the other night swirling around my head for me to trust him, and going back to Ret like this feels like a bad idea.

Brushing out my tangled hair, I pull it into a ponytail and step into the main room. Donovan sits on his bed, pulling pastries out of a brown paper bag.

"I wasn't sure what you wanted," he says, his face a wrinkled apology as he crunches the paper bag in his hand. "So I got a little bit of everything."

"Everything sounds good," I tell him with a wide smile.

Grabbing a chocolate donut from the top, I take a large bite out of it, watching his face as it slowly relaxes. He picks up a matching donut and salutes me with it before chomping down.

We finish off his bag in companionable silence, having a couple donuts each. A few times he looks at me as though he wants to say something, but I give him a small shake of my head. I'm not ready for words right now, especially not serious words.

"I have a surprise for you today," Donovan says, rubbing the crumbs of breakfast off on his pants.

"And it wasn't breakfast?" I ask with a laugh, gesturing to the empty wax-paper wrappers around us.

He grins back at me. "This is going to be much better than donuts."

"I don't even know how that could be possible," I shriek as he grabs my bag and ushers me out the door.

A complete gentleman, he opens the car door for me and sees me carefully buckled into the old bench seat before climbing around to the other side. The early morning light filters through the car, highlighting his black hair with blue streaks, his pale skin bright against dark narrowed eyes.

The longer I watch him, the more I can't help but smile. He backs out of our parking spot and I take his hand in mine, not wanting to be further away than necessary.

He looks at me with wide eyes but doesn't pull his hand out of mine. Instead, he gives it a squeeze and continues out of the parking lot.

"So, what do you have planned for today?" I can't help but

hope he's come up with some way to avoid meeting with Nick.

Donovan smiles. "You're going to have to be willing to show up a little late to that meet-up with your Ret pals."

My grin grows, stretching from ear to ear. "I'm more than okay with that."

He passes the on-ramp to the highway, setting off on a western route instead of the southern one Nick'd be expecting. My smile burns brighter the farther away we get from my expected future. I don't have much to rely on anymore, but in the back of my mind, I really did think I'd end up in Providence with Nick by noon today. Now I don't have to worry about that little annoyance.

"I'm glad you had an alternate route in mind. I'm so not ready to get back to the sterile Ret offices." I throw my head against the worn headrest as I resist the urge to shudder.

"Amaro's not looking so bad right now, is it?" he says, glancing at the side mirror as he switches lanes.

I push against his shoulder with my free hand. "Yeah, I just love dark prisons that try to suck my conscious mind away."

Donovan gives me a sly side grin, my smile fixing itself into a permanent fixture. Somehow, against all odds, I've been able to forgive him, at least for this moment. Maybe I do believe he called in Ret to save me. I don't know if it's something he'd really do, betraying Amaro like that, but I like believing that story. I like believing he didn't want to hurt me.

He lifts our joined hands and places a dry kiss against my knuckles. Sparks fly from my hand into my stomach, and I bite my bottom lip.

"I know I can't convince you to leave Ret and be with me again, but I'm glad you're taking this trip with me. It'll be a good farewell. You know, give you a little something to remember me by," he says, eyes glued to the road as a small blush creeps up his neck.

"It's not like I'm dying or anything." I raise my brows at him, missing his point on purpose. I'm not ready to deal with absolutes right now. "I'm sure we'll see each other again."

Donovan shakes his head. "They won't let you see me again. Seeing you within Ret is hard enough, but when you get back without the information you left for, they're going to freak out."

My heart sinks. Of course, they will. I've been so caught up in the papers I *did* find that I haven't spared much thought to what Ret will think about the empty kitchen drawer.

Even though it wasn't my fault, guilt nags at my stomach. The information I found in Mom's desk would be beneficial to their investigation, if I had the decency to share it. I probably won't.

"Yeah, I guess you're right," I say, voice small. "They'll be pretty mad about the time we've wasted."

"Hey!" Donovan squeezes my hand. "These may be our last moments together, let's just be happy."

He gives me a pointed smile, my answering one weak and timid. I squeeze his hand back, and he places another kiss against my fingers. Looking down at my one lonely hand sitting in my lap makes me smile in earnest.

I lean onto Donovan's shoulder as he takes a sharp right turn and leave my head resting there. He releases my hand and wraps his arm around me, weaving his fingers through my hair. Unbidden, a sigh rises out of my throat, making Donovan chuckle.

Pulling to the side of the road, he parks the car in the stretch of grass bordering the thick tree growth. He turns down the radio while my pulse spikes. Taking his hand off the steering wheel he trails his fingers along my jawline. My breath hitches and he grins at me.

"Relax," he breathes. "We've done this before."

He leans into me, time slowing down as his lips brush

against mine. His breath is cool against my cheek, filling the air with the smell of mint and musk. My face melds with his, his hands moving through my hair to keep me fused to him. I grip his forearms with trembling fingers in an attempt to keep me grounded as my mind attempts to fly away.

Releasing me, his brown eyes sparkle as they meet mine. "Not bad, huh? Just like riding a bike."

I bite my lower lip while a smile tugs at the side of my mouth. "Definitely not bad."

Donovan twists a lock of hair between his fingers. I reach up and still his hand beneath mine. He presses a hand against my cheek, and I lean my face into his palm, breathing deep.

"Thanks."

"For what?" His eyes crinkle like he's laughing at me.

"I'm not used to people sticking around once I've outlived my usefulness." I shrug.

"That's not true," Donovan says, face brightening up. "I think you have more of a problem with too many people coming to help. It's getting a little crowded around you."

I laugh, shoulders rocking with the genuine reaction. "It doesn't feel that crowded right now," I point out. We're still blissfully alone on the side of the road.

"No," he says, face smoothed by seriousness. "It doesn't."

Donovan pulls me back into him, our lips crashing together as he directs my head with his hand. His fingers twist in my hair as he pulls my face up farther, giving him better access to my mouth.

Fingers tap on the window, jolting us apart before it can get any further, although Donovan leaves one of his hands where it's climbed up my leg. I glance up, expecting to see a cop, but instead find a black-outfitted man glaring through the window at us as he rests his hand on a belt holding a dark handled weapon.

Donovan curses while climbing out of the car. He offers

me an apologetic smile before he shuts the door. I don't follow him, fingering the twist in my seatbelt. He walks around to where the intruder stands leaning against my window.

"Donovan," the man says in a deep muffled voice. "What're you doing out here? You know where you're supposed to take the girl and I'm pretty sure Patrice won't appreciate the delay."

Donovan scowls. "What I choose to do while I'm with her is none of your business. I'm not hurting anyone, and Patrice will get what she's looking for," he says, voice low so that it's hard to hear through the glass.

"Just see that you get her back quickly. We don't want to have to instigate another explosion to get her on her own," the man says, muscles flexing in intimidation.

Donovan's mouth pulls into a frown. "That was you?"

"Of course," he says with a laugh. "We couldn't let them snoop around too closely. We don't need Ret finding out *all* our secrets."

My heart free falls. This has just been a game to him. My emotions are toys these boys keep playing with, keeping me purposefully in the dark to further their own agenda.

Raging, I want to punch something. Instead, I clench my fists and try to think.

Mind working faster than I can keep up with, I crawl across the bench and into Donovan's abandoned driver's side.

Nick didn't blow up my house. Donovan's people did. They did it to get me on my own. To get me here, alone with Donovan.

The engine's still running, so I buckle with shaking hands and shift the car into drive. Donovan looks up at the sound, eyes panicking as he sees my new position. The man beside him grips the passenger handle, wrenching it open as I hit the gas.

I floor it, tires sending gravel flying while he attempts to throw himself through the open door, but the bump of joining back with the road throws him off, leaving him in a crumpled heap on the asphalt. Donovan stands next to him, shoulders slumped, and hands left open at his side.

Blazing down the road, the adrenaline surge ebbs away, leaving me hollow. All this time I blamed Nick for the fire, but it was really Donovan who bore the responsibility.

Maybe not completely, I mentally amend, but Amaro did it. The people he's so proud of representing blew my childhood home into a pile of fiery ash.

Tears course down my cheeks as I come to terms with what feels in the moment like my worst betrayal yet. At least my mom never lied to me about what she was or what was going on, she just didn't tell me. She picked her team, and Donovan has too. Neither of them was willing to pick me.

I take a few left turns until I'm running parallel to where I left him, hoping to make it back to the highway without having to see his stupid face again. Wiping my running nose off on the back of my hand, I merge onto the on-ramp and away from what was almost a huge mistake.

If I hurry, I can meet up with Nick without him ever being the wiser of my little detour.

Chapter Twelve

Keeping an eye on the exit signs, a big one for Haverhill flashes by, putting me just an hour and a half away. The small digital clock in the dashboard blinks 10:11, I have more than enough time to get there before Nick gets worried.

Looking back, I'm surprised he left me in Lubec in the first place. It's so unlike him to just leave me stranded. Maybe he thought I was taking everything better than at first, and he trusted me? My feet cramp up from driving, reminding me of the care that Donovan put into them to fix the cuts and burns from the explosion.. Wincing, I push through, wanting to get as far away from Donovan as possible. Even though I know he can blink and appear next to me, I feel comfort in the distance. Plus, if he were to show up in my car again, I think I'd honestly just punch him right in the nose.

The thought brings a smile to my face, and I clench my fist to mimic the daydream of smashing the cartilage in his nose.

Staying on the 95, I creep around the heart of Boston and all the craziness that would probably be awaiting me there. Living in the country hasn't made me familiar with driving through big cities, and Boston can be one of the worst to drive in. At least that's what Mom taught me. Frowning, I wonder if I should be looking for lies in her well-meaning advice after the revelation of her double life.

Still, going through Boston wouldn't be a good idea. I don't need my mom here to know that.

I'm just passing Waltham when it occurs to me that I don't have to go back at all. I have no loyalties to Nick, not after everything he's put me through.

I'm alone in the car, no Nick, no Sarah, no Donovan, no reason to stick around any of this craziness anymore. Gritting my teeth, my knuckles grow white on the steering wheel. I don't have to do any of this. Let them find me again if they're so desperate, but I won't be headed to them like a lamb to the slaughter.

It's an easy thing to pull over at the next exit. It's time to figure out what my real options are.

Going back to Ret means more demeaning behavior, people who don't trust me, and Nick and Sarah pretending to be my friends. If I go back, I'll be expected to hand over any information I've gathered from my house. My hand clenches the bundle of paper in my hoodie pocket, whispers of Neopolis traveling up my spine. Those pages outline just how little I know, which won't help me establish myself in Ret. If anything, it'll probably kick me out. 'Thanks for your contribution. Now leave'.

Ret's given me protection though. Staying with them means staying away from Amaro's unethical behavior and keeping my mind intact. It'll also keep me away from Donovan. If I leave their protection, he's free to track me down any time he feels like it as long as Patrice says it's okay. He's still her lackey no matter what he says.

Honestly, I can't believe it's taken me this long to realize I could just leave. Why should my promise to Nick mean anything when his promises have meant nothing to me? I can't keep holding myself to a higher standard than everyone else. It's exhausting and hasn't been helping me any.

Mom's papers crinkle in my grip, ensnaring my attention as I get an idea. I'm the only one who knows where my mother is. I could go after her right now and neither group would ever find me. I'd be safe in Neopolis with Mom. Anxious excitement blooms in my chest as I commit to this plan.

Driving through town looking for the 2, I decide to head away from the coast to do my research on Neopolis. I just want to be sure Nick and Donovan can't find me before I find Mom. The 2 crosses the state and will get me far away from Providence and Lubec. Turning on the ramp headed west towards Leominster, the tension rimming my body relaxes. I'm more comfortable now than I've been since all of this started. *More comfortable on my own than I was with Donovan,* I remind myself.

My eyes threaten to fill with tears thinking of his last betrayal, and my fingers dig into the cushion on the steering wheel. He held me and comforted me all while being involved in the explosion. Is that why his hands were burned? I can't even begin to imagine his thought process. What would make him think I'd forgive him for that? Surely, he didn't think Ret would keep Amaro's involvement a secret.

He'd been trying to say goodbye though, a small part of me whispers from the darkness in my mind. It's true. He told me that after I returned to Ret that he wouldn't see me anymore, he just didn't mention it would be of my own choosing.

I rub the remnants of betrayal from my face and narrow my brows. I've been soft and manipulated until this point, and I won't let it happen again.

* * *

The miles melt away under my tires. I'd probably never stop driving if not for the E light blinking on the dash. Pulling over at a large gas station nestled in the trees right off the highway, I fill up the tank with what little cash I have left.

The smell of fresh baked donuts and strong coffee wafts through my nostrils and directly into my brain. It's a call I can't avoid, my stomach responding without my consent. The rumbling sounds of hunger drive me into the convenience store before my mind can tell it to back off. Breakfast with Donovan was too long ago for me to avoid the siren song of hot donuts.

I'm far enough away from the 95 that I don't have to worry about running into anyone I know. There's no reason why they would've driven this way. The anonymity rests well with me and I decide to buy one donut and a bottle of water. Coffee isn't a luxury I can afford at this point.

I hand over the wadded dollar bills to pay for my Boston cream, a flash of neon green in my peripheral vision catches my attention.

"Having a rough day?" the cashier asks, a perky smile on her face.

"A little." I glance around for the green I saw before, trying not to think about how I probably still carry some of the fire smell with me.

"I'm sure you'll feel much better with a little treat," she says with a wink.

I don't respond as I back away through the motion sensor doors, heart pounding in my ears. My body feels tight as I wait for that flash to come back.

There's no one waiting for me outside on the pavement and I allow myself a sigh of relief. Even this far away I'm a little paranoid.

It's just that I'd never seen a color green like that before until I saw Ramsey's glowing head...

Shaking my head, I climb into Mom's old car and buckle up.

"Headed anywhere interesting?"

Ramsey's voice cuts through me.

"What are you doing here?" My heart is beating a mile a minute as she leans over my seat from her spot in the back.

"I thought you might need a little persuasion in coming back, especially after Sarah called me and told me what happened back at your house. I'm so sorry," she says this last bit with genuine sadness reflecting in her eyes as I stare at her in the rearview mirror.

"Get out of my car!" I can't force even a hint of kindness into my voice. "I'm not going back with you!"

She places a tapered hand on my shoulder. "I'm afraid it really isn't your choice anymore."

I slam my hands into the steering wheel as my chest heaves.

"You can't make me go back there." I meet her eyes through the mirror as I grip the steering wheel with bone-white hands. "I just want my life back."

"And you think driving off to Leominster will help you do that?" she asks sardonically, one of her neon brows raised. "There's nothing for you out there."

"There's nothing for me anywhere." I look away from the mirror before I can see her all too sympathetic face.

Ramsey sighs. "You're wanted in Ret. Don't let anyone tell you you're not."

I lean back against my seat. So much for my new adventure. So much for getting away from Ret and the people so bent on ruining all the normal aspects of my life.

"Are you ready to come back with me now?" she asks, squeezing my shoulder in what I'm sure she thinks is reassurance. Instead, I feel more trapped than ever.

I shrug, mostly in an attempt to knock her hand away, which it does.

"You have a couple of choices," she says, climbing awkwardly over the console with her lanky body so she can sit in the passenger seat. "We can go meet up with Nick in Providence, or I can take you right back to headquarters. It all depends on what you want. I mean it. Let's do what you want."

She's leaning over me, making it impossible to look away from her intent face. "I don't know what I want."

"That's not uncommon at your age," Ramsey says with a laugh. "I know you don't want to go back, but how you go back can be all up to you."

Previously, Ramsey's presence and calming tone would have been enough to relax me, but I'm learning not to trust anyone, especially not those I think have earned it. It's not like I've been able to rely on my intuition before now. It's this lack of trust that sets me adrift on an island of my own. No matter how many people tell me I'm wanted or that I'm not alone, I know the truth.

Starting the car, I exit the gas station. This exit didn't give me the option to change direction, it's a gas station only for westbound traffic. So, I keep heading toward Leominster. Ramsey buckles her seatbelt without comment.

"Why don't you get off at the next exit and turn around?" She keeps her voice calm and soothing.

"Because I couldn't think of that myself," I snap, fed up with everyone thinking they know what's best for me.

Ramsey lets it go, not encouraging my aggressive streak or even trying to defuse it. This only makes me more irritated. "Are you ignoring me now?"

She looks up with startled eyes. "Of course not."

"Then what? Too good to argue with me?" I know I'm being irrational, but I can't hold back. Too much stress has turned me into a bomb ready to go off at any moment, and apparently, that moment is now. They won't make me cry again, so this is what they get.

"What are you looking for from this? Do you really think it will make you feel better?" she asks, her calm voice grating on me.

"You don't get to decide what makes me feel better and what doesn't!" Angry tears obscure my vision as I take the next exit. "If I want to argue, then I'm going to argue!"

Ramsey folds her arms over her chest. "You're arguing with the wrong person."

"You don't know anything," I grumble.

We stop at a light, waiting to turn onto the eastbound ramp. She doesn't say anything further and I don't have anything else to say to her. She's right. I'm not really mad at her. What did Ramsey do to me besides give me glimpses of memories no one else could without disassembling my fragile mind? She's just the only one here with me. The only one who hasn't made an emotional connection with me to protect him from my emotional outburst. That's really her only fault.

"You really think I should go back?" I whisper.

Ramsey nods. "I think you should. I think it's the best way to find your mom."

I try not to think about the note I found. I try not to think about what was written there, the places I don't recognize.

"Ret isn't the only one who can help me find my mom."

"No, that's true." Ramsey taps a finger against her chin. "But they're the only ones with the power to find her. Between you and me, I'm not sure what they'll do with her without you. I know they're getting close to finding her; if she doesn't give them the trident..."

My chest grows tight. "Are you saying they want to hurt her?"

"Absolutely they'll hurt her." Ramsey grabs my hand. "She needs you. You have to come with me to keep her safe."

I hate this. I hate that no matter what I do Ret is right there to keep me trapped. They didn't need to send Nick with me to make sure I came back. All they have to do is threaten my mother.

"Fine." The word comes out tight, my body not wanting to do what my mind requires of it.

Ramsey nods.

"Did you want to eat your donut?" she asks, her voice quiet.

It sits on the seat between us, forgotten in its crumpled brown bag. All the excitement I felt while buying it ebbed away. My stomach is a hard rock in my gut. "I don't think so."

She shrugs her slender shoulders, staring out the window as I merge with the midday traffic.

"Did Sarah really tell you to come after me?" I finally ask, voice small.

"She called to tell me what happened," Ramsey says, hair catching the glints of sunlight coming in through the windows. "She was worried about you, despite what you may think, she actually does care about you. I thought it might be best if I met up with you to see where you were at and how you were feeling. I figured since I wasn't as close to you, you might not be *too* upset to see me." She chuckles under her breath. "Guess I was wrong."

I give her a wry smile. "Sorry about that."

"It's not the first time a pretty girl has yelled at me, and I'm sure it won't be the last. I'm just glad I caught you before you were too far established in your new life," Ramsey says with a slightly mocking smile. "I'd have hated to uproot you again. What was your plan, anyway?"

I shrug, tucking away my dreams of meeting up with Mom. "I'm not sure that I had a plan," I lie. "I just knew I wanted to get away. I still do, but you won't let me go. Why does Ret need me so much anyway? I don't have any information for you, I'm just a drain on your resources. There has to be a better way to find out what my mom was up to than by interrogating her teenage daughter."

"I'm not involved in their decision making, I'm just here to give them magical assistance when they come knocking," she says, delicate fingers picking lint off her suit jacket.

"Aren't you curious though?"

"I'm sure I was in the beginning, but I've learned not to ask questions," she says with a sardonic smile.

"I just don't get you. I don't get any of you. Everyone is so invested in this 'cause' they seem to know nothing about. You're all just a bunch of grunts doing your higher-up's bidding. Doesn't that bother you?" I ask, glancing at Ramsey's pensive face.

She braces her arm against the door and rests her head in her hand. "When you've been around as long as I have, you learn to accept that there are things out of your control. I work for them because it gives me security. I like security, as crazy as that may seem."

I focus on the road before me, blocking out Ramsey's body splayed out on the seat next to mine while I try to process everything. I don't trust her. I've promised myself I won't. So, if I can't trust what Ramsey is saying to me, what do I do with her?

Obviously, I have to let her continue on this journey with me. She wouldn't leave even if I asked. Ramsey caught me in a runaway plan, she wouldn't be as naive as Nick to think I'd come back on my own.

Still, for someone as powerful as Ramsey to be working with Ret for their protection says something. What on earth could be out there that would scare her enough to work for them? What else don't I know about? My mother has left me at a serious disadvantage.

"What will they do with me when we get back?" I ask,

nervousness itching into my voice. "Are you going to tell them I tried to run away?"

"I'll only tell them what I feel like they need to know, and at this point, I think it's best they don't know about your little side venture. That can stay between you and me," she says, flashing me an unnaturally white smile.

My shoulders relax a little. "Thank you."

"Like I said, I've been working with them for a while. What they don't know can't hurt them as far as you're concerned." She reaches out to take my hand. "We really are just trying to help you, all of us. Even Nick, as misguided as he may be. Just remember he's young and doesn't understand everything yet. Give him a little slack. He's still working things out too."

"I just wish he'd figure things out far away from me."

Ramsey laughs. "I'm sure you do. He's too caught up in you right now to make that kind of self-sacrificing decision."

"Self-sacrificing?" I ask, mouth screwed up and genuinely lost.

"He likes you too much to stay away. It's clouding his thoughts and giving you all that trouble with Sarah. Teenage boys can be thoughtless," Ramsey says, eyes lost in memory.

I shake my head. "That can't be true. He likes Sarah, not me. We're just friends."

"No boy knows how to be just friends," Ramsey says with a sly smile.

My brows pull down low over my eyes. I've got enough problems right now without adding Nick's feelings into the mix. We're just friends, and even that is iffy. I haven't been feeling charitable enough to give him that distinction lately.

"I don't care about what he might be feeling," I tell Ramsey honestly as my gut twists.

"And that, my dear, is the problem," she says, pulling a pair of large black sunglasses out of her jacket pocket to block the bright rays of afternoon sun.

A sigh of exasperation escapes me. I'm done talking about it, there's nothing Ramsey can tell me that will change my mind or make anything better. I'm going to have to deal with Nick on my own.

My mind drifts as I continue south on the highway, the music on the radio comforting in its generic beat. Glancing over at Ramsey, her head still resting in her hand, she appears to have gone to sleep. Is she in some wort of witchy meditative state? I'm kind of on my own again.

Reaching over for the brown paper bag, I pull out the donut from earlier. I'm finally relaxed enough to enjoy this treat, and I'm glad not to have to talk to Ramsey about it.

I take a big bite out of the pastry, cream and chocolate frosting exploding across my tongue. And something else. The sharp taste of something unusual has me peering into the donut. There's a thin line of purple between the brown layer of frosting and the light crust of the pastry. As I stare at it, confused frustration filling me as I am reminded of just one more thing outside of my control, I start to feel a tingling in my limbs.

At once, my mood takes a drastic shift. Glancing back at the road, my shoulders lift, my mouth turning up into a crazy smile. I'm not mad about the change in my donut anymore, not irritated by Nick's involvement, and most of all, I don't care that I'm essentially being kidnapped for the third time in so many days. Feeling light, I speed down the highway. I'm smiling, I'm happy, I'm more carefree than I've been in years.

We're cruising at least fifteen miles over the speed limit when Ramsey shakes herself back to life. "What the heck is going on?"

"Just feeling good," I tell her, leaning over and bushing her shoulder with a smile. "Just driving back and feeling so, so good."

Ramsey whips her sunglasses off, eyes wide as she stares at me. "What happened to you? How long have I been out?"

"Nothing happened. Can't I just feel good?" I tell her, not even upset by her confused irritation. "I'm just happy."

Ramsey stares at me for a moment, eyes glancing from my face to the lingering traces of chocolate on my fingertips. Reaching out, she grabs the now empty paper bag, rubbing her fingers along the inside of it and bringing them to her face. She breathes in deeply, her mouth quirking into a smile. "So that's it."

"What's it?" I ask her, face beaming as I glance over at Ramsey's smug face.

"You've had a little help today, haven't you?" she asks rhetorically. "Did you know what you were getting in that donut, or was it a surprise?"

I shrug, practically bouncing with exuberance. "I just ordered my favorite. I was hoping for a pick-me-up after everything that happened. I don't know why it's such a big deal."

"Consider yourself hopped up on the magical equivalent of anti-anxiety meds," she says with a laugh. "Someone else must have thought you needed a pick me up. You really should be more careful. There are more witches out there than you realize."

"Well consider me picked up!" I say, waving one hand in the air with enthusiasm.

Ramsey laughs, running her hand through her neon green hair before replacing her sunglasses. "I guess I'll just have to keep an eye on you. Wouldn't want you happily speeding into oncoming traffic or anything."

I laugh with her. Why wouldn't I? Everything is right in the world, everything is beautiful, and I am so, so happy as I speed back to Ret.

Chapter Thirteen

The potion wears off just outside Bridgeport. I feel it in my shoulders first. They sag low, my head drooping in their place. Ramsey's been quietly observing me and leans forward to place a slender hand on my shoulder.

"It's all right. You're going to be okay. Coming down off this stuff can be a little rough," she says, face tensed as she takes off her glasses and puts them back in her pocket.

Not completely sure what she's talking about, I continue to melt under the pressures of my life as they come crashing back down.

"I'm sure that witch was just trying to be nice, but I've never felt better after having one of those potions. An hour of good feelings doesn't usually negate what made you so upset in the first place," she says, squeezing my shoulder before releasing it. "Would you like me to drive?"

I nod, tears leaking down my face. Without the potion to keep me together, an hour's worth of fear for my mom is all coming out. Pulling over, she gets out and I slide across the bench. Reaching the other side, I curl up in a ball. Ramsey gets into the driver's seat and adjusts all the settings for her lanky figure. Seeing my position, she takes off her jacket and tosses it over me. I appreciate the gesture even though a dress suit jacket isn't exactly the same as a comfort blanket.

"We'll be home soon," she says, voice calm and soothing. If I didn't know better, I'd say she was trying to use magic on me right now to try and counteract the potion's effects. "We've just got about an hour left."

"I don't want to go back to that place." I hide my face in her jacket. I know I must go back for my mom, but I can't stomach the idea of being trapped in that place.

She sighs, fingers tight on the wheel. "I've been thinking about that. I thought if you were interested you might come stay at my place. Don't get too comfortable there, I don't usually let people live with me. I just thought you might like a break from being surrounded by so many professionals."

I know what she's really saying. She's giving me the opportunity to get away from Nick without putting Ret on edge. "That would be so great."

"Good. I'll get you set up in the guest room when we get back then," she tells me, a smile thinning her lips into a hard line.

With that promise, I'm finally able to relax. I'm not going back to an interrogation room, I'm going to stay in a real home.

The next hour passes quickly as I doze in and out of sleep. Ramsey navigates the crazy New York roads with ease, Mom's white sedan is farther away from home than it's ever been. Not that it matters I guess, I'll probably never go back to Lubec. There's nothing there for me now.

Shaking my head back and forth, I try and throw off the growing sadness threatening to overwhelm me. My hair flies around my face but I'm still nostalgically low.

We drive over a bridge and the sounds and smells feel a little more like home with my five formulated years of memories. The smell of sewer and seawater mix into a less-than-delightful cacophony that relaxes my anxiety with its familiarity. Even Ramsey's more relaxed, one hand stretched out over the wheel while she leans back into her seat.

"Happy to be back?" I watch her with a small smile.

"You have no idea," she says with a grin.

She's wearing her black button-down shirt folded up to the elbows, a look more casual than I've seen her in before. It makes me smile to think of this ridiculously tall woman hanging out in one of the many cyber cafes throughout New York with a latte just chilling. In fact, it makes me smile to think of her doing any normal behavior. I can't even imagine all the looks she must get when she goes grocery shopping. This last thought has me laughing, causing Ramsey to look over with a bemused smile, though she doesn't ask what I'm laughing about.

She's not like the rest of them. A loner as much as I am with her solitary house and lack of interest in Ret's agenda.

She feels like one of the few people it's safe to be around. I already know why she's here. Her job has her coming after me, and that's it. She doesn't want anything else. It's too easy to relax around her when she's this transparent.

"Do you think they'll be okay with me staying with you?" I pick lint and the odd green hair off her jacket.

"I'm sure they won't like it very much, but I actually have a lot of sway within Ret. They pretty much let me do what I want."

"That must be nice for you," I grumble.

Ramsey laughs. "You have to work with them for a long time to get those kinds of privileges. It's also important to give them something they're looking for."

She gives me a pointed look, and I clench at my hoodie pocket. Nodding, she turns back to the road.

"You'll figure out things in your own way, I'm sure. Just don't expect all of what you want all at once."

"It's like you haven't been watching my life at all," I tell her, mouth pulled down.

She looks at me in surprise. "Did you want me to be watching your life? I didn't realize or I would have gotten a front-row seat."

Put off by her sarcasm, I sit back as we putter through New York and into the parking lot at Ret's headquarters. I half expect Ramsey to take me right into the building, but instead, she offers me her arm and leads me around the blocky industrial building and towards the back green where her little townhouse sits.

Ramsey opens the door with a flick of her wrist, ushering me into the room as lights flicker on in the deserted darkness.

"Not worried about being robbed?" I can't believe she wouldn't lock her door in the middle of New York City.

"There are other security measures I have in place which would make stealing from me a most uncomfortable proposition," she says with a wide smile.

Ramsey walks down the dark hallway, waving for me to follow. Even with lights on, the dark stained panels make the walls feel like they're pressing in on me.

There's a small twisting stairwell towards the back of the house starting in her pristine kitchen. We traipse up, backpack clenched firm in my shaking hands as my feet tap against the metal stairs.

"I thought you might like this room. It has a great view of New York," she says, waving a hand toward the door right off the stairs that slowly opens on its own accord..

Walking in I understand immediately what she really means. The room's one small window looks away from headquarters, my only view being the actual city. Thankful for her thoughtfulness, I turn to tell her so, but she's already gone, the hallway empty behind me.

Closing the heavy wood door, I lean against its paneled surface. It was so generous of Ramsey to open her home to me. I know she didn't have to. I don't know when I'll have to face everyone again, but at least it won't be today. Already the tall buildings are blocking out the sun, leaving the townhouse in a mild state of twilight even in the late afternoon. I'm sure Nick has found other 'important' jobs to do that don't involve interrogating me.

Putting my backpack down on the end of the bed, I pull out the papers from my pocket. My eyes glaze as I go over their contents, hitting on all of the inconsistencies. I'm not sure what it all means, but I know this is my only chance to understand what Ret wants me for. The answer to what my mother was up to has to be located on these pages.

I shuffle aside the papers dealing with my particular potion. Why didn't it work out exactly as she specified? They don't say anything about Nick or Ret or any of the major factors of the last five made-up years. Instead, the notes go into other details, like how many memories of her need to be erased and that I'll go live with Nina. In fact...I look over the page, holding it closer to my face. She's written Nina's name differently from the rest of her instructions. It doesn't look entirely purposeful, instead maybe ... affectionate? Nina's name has the same slant to it as mine does.

Confused, I run my fingers over the indentation from her pen. I don't have any memories of Aunt Nina before my mom's disappearance. No mention of her in my questions of Mom's childhood, no Christmas cards or birthday wishes.

My forehead wrinkles. Why haven't I noticed this before? If she isn't really my aunt, as memories would confirm, who is she? Why was she important to my mom?

Shaking my head, I put the pages down. This is a mystery

that only pertains to me, not one that will help me figure out Ret.

Next, I pick up the pages mentioning the Trident. She was obviously afraid of its power. There are quite a few mentions of what could happen if the Trident ended up in the wrong hands. Whose hands is she thinking about when she says that? Ret? Amaro? She never mentions anyone by name, but her hand wavers where she's written down her concerns. *Was she being threatened? Were they already after her? Is that why she sent me away?*

On the last page, she talks about taking the Trident somewhere safe. She doesn't even finish writing this page, one sentence just hanging without an ending.

It must be taken away from land, away from-

It just cuts off. I wonder what distracted her. Was it me? I can just imagine how hard this secret would have been to keep with me around all the time.

Still, away from who? Should I show this last page to Ret's officials? It doesn't have any real information in it, and then I can keep the other pages without having to look over my shoulder all the time wondering when Ramsey will tell them I have something. How does she even know? I wonder briefly if she was following me around in my house too, just her and Donovan watching me like sneaky sneaks, but I brush the thought away. She doesn't seem to care enough to do that. Plus, that would mean having to hide herself, and she seems to like how she looks way too much to keep her presence a secret.

The last thought makes me chuckle. I can just imagine Ramsey hiding around corners, her neon hair poking out and her suit wrinkling in the process.

Gazing out the window, I take some deep breaths and take in New York. It does feel good to be back. It's not the same kind of release that being back in Maine gave me, but it does feel good. My memories of the last five years may be fake, but they still *feel* real, which makes New York feel like a real part of my history, a real home.

Turning back to the room, I sit down on the mattress of the four-poster bed, sinking as it cradles me. The room is small but clean, containing the same old-timey decor as downstairs. I've always enjoyed studying history and visiting historic homes, but I never thought I'd get the opportunity to actually stay in one.

I just wish I'd known I'd be coming here so that I could've packed appropriate costumes. Not that I think Ramsey would've appreciated my efforts. She's easygoing, but I think dressing up in 1800s clothing might push her over the edge. I'm sure she'd think I was mocking her.

Laying down against the embroidered maroon bedspread, I throw my arms over my head. It's still early in the evening, but I don't know what else to do. Ramsey didn't say whether or not she was going to feed me or if she had anything planned tonight. There's no way I'm going to the little cafeteria. I can't face all the stares, the questions, and most of all the possibility of running into Nick.

With the safety of being alone in the room, my thoughts drift toward Donovan. I don't know what he was thinking. Did he really think I'd never find out he was responsible for the fire? Did he think I forgive him? Or was he okay with spending a few days with me and then saying goodbye forever? I just don't like to think of him reasoning out how much of me he could have. I bet he'd have tried for more last night if I'd been even moderately willing.

My face burns and I put my hands over my face as though that will hide me from myself. I can't believe that I'm still this easily manipulated. How many people have to disappoint me before I cut them loose from my emotions? Even now, I'm laying on Ramsey's bed, trusting her not to hurt me. It doesn't make sense, and logically I know that, but emotionally I can't stop myself.

Stomach grumbling, I roll onto my side, facing the oak door. Logically I want that door to stay closed, to block me off from everyone else, but my emotional side begs for someone to come in. For someone to care about me. It doesn't have to be Ramsey either, that's how pathetic I am.

Maybe *I* need the Trident. Something that powerful would be able to keep my emotions at bay, and anyone else I didn't want around too. I wonder what Ret's king would do if I told him I had an idea of where the Trident might be.

Mom's notes combined with a few comments from Donovan created an image in my mind that I can't shake. All I can think about is my mother, Trident in hand, walking out into the waves, until the ocean absorbed her. She was going to Neopolis, that much is clear from her notes. Mom knew where the Trident needed to be and knew that I couldn't go with her.

That's the part that really gets me. Why couldn't I come? I'd much rather be in hiding with her than being appropriated by Ret.

Whatever.

I think the word, but it doesn't take away the tightness in my chest. With a sigh, I push myself off the bed and head back to the window, pulling it open and leaning my head out. I breathe deep, really expanding my lungs.

My life is not that bad. I repeat it in my mind over and over again. If I tell myself that enough, then maybe it will start to feel true.

"Avi?" Ramsey's voice on the other side of the door breaks my concentration. "Are you hungry?"

I nod before remembering she can't see me. "Yeah."

"Well, if you want to come down, I've ordered some Chinese food. I hope you like beef and broccoli."

I laugh with a grin only I can see, swinging the door open. Ramsey steps further into the hallway. I follow her down the stairs and into the kitchen where a pizza sits on the wood block island. The delicious aroma of rice and soy sauce sweeps through the room, bringing with it memories of of Aunt Nina and late-night study sessions with Nick.

"Thanks for dinner." I scoop some of the rice on one of the laid-out China plates.

Ramsey nods and dishes herself up a full plate. We eat over the counter together, not getting comfortable on the couch or even in the fancy dining room I'm convinced she has even though I haven't seen it yet.

She doesn't say anything to me through dinner, checking a tablet with her clean hand while we eat. We're too far apart for me to see what she's doing, but my curiosity is piqued.

"What're you reading?" I ask, tapping my fork against the plate.

Ramsey shakes her head. "Just work stuff."

"Oh really?" I lean over the island to get closer. "That's interesting. What does Ret want you to do now? Any other girls they need you to pick up?"

She just laughs, closing the tablet and washing her hands in the industrial sink. "You're my only ward tonight."

"Bummer, I could've used the company."

Ramsey looks at me with a raised brow and I give her a playful wink, surprising even myself. This isn't the distance I promised myself, but I can't seem to help it. She's always been straight with me, and I appreciate it.

"What do you want to do tonight?" She wipes her hands off on a towel hanging from the gas stove. "Any big plans now that you're back in New York?"

"Seeing as how you've brought me here against my will, I can't say that I've made any plans. What about you?" I can't help but hope I won't be spending the remainder of the evening sequestered in my room with only my thoughts for company.

She shrugs. "I don't really have much I want to do right now. What makes you so curious, Avi?"

"Boredom will do that to you," I say, only half truthful. What does Ramsey do? What is her purpose for Ret and why is she still here?

"I might go for a walk. I find evenings to be rather pleasant for mild exercise, plus it usually makes sure that I get out of the house every once and a while," she says with a sly smile. "I don't tend to leave very often, just when Sarah comes over to drag me out and make me do odd jobs for her."

"Are you guys friends then?"

She slips on a sleek black sneaker, still wearing her expensive-looking suit. "I guess you might say that. Friends against my will."

Thinking back on our first encounter, which feels farther away than just the few days it's been, I realize we never accomplished what she first offered me.

"Have you thought any more about testing my blood to find out my genetics?" I ask, sitting on a barstool while I wait. I never took off my shoes when I came in the house, something my mother would've never allowed me to do in her own home.

She looks up at me from where she's stumped over lacing her shoes. "Not really. Is there something you'd like to know?"

"I know who my mom is. I know she was a nixie. I just don't get *me*. Where do I come into all of this?" My face betrays more of my confusion and intensity than I'd like.

Ramsey looks me over as she stands. "Let's take our walk and see what we can work out."

She guides me out the back door into a small alley behind the row of townhomes. We walk out into the crisp New York night and Ramsey holds out her arm to me, which I take. I'm not sure how much I can lean on her or what the proper etiquette for this stuff is, so I stand awkwardly away from her side and hope she doesn't notice the nervous sweat quickly drenching my underarms.

"Of all the places I've lived, I think I like New York the best," Ramsey comments to me, her eyes turned up toward the city around us.

"Where else could you have lived that makes New York look that great?" I ask with a strangled laugh. I slap my other hand over my mouth, wishing I could just die.

Ramsey has been so nice to me and has helped me avoid Nick at any turn. She's what I imagine a cool older sister would be like. I know she probably doesn't see me that way in return. Maybe I'm just a charity project to her, but it's nice to pretend.

She ignores my teenage weirdness. "I've spent a lot of time in Asia actually."

"Is that where the," I point to my own head. "Comes from?"

"Nope, this is all mine. A genetic anomaly that I've come to embrace," she says, fingering a few strands of vibrant hair.

I wonder what her ancestry is that would give her such crazy traits. I mean, don't get me wrong, some of them are pretty great. She's built like a dancer and is well over six feet. I know lots of girls that would kill for Ramsey's figure. There are just a few things about her that feel off that I can't quite put my finger on.

"I hope that screwed-up face isn't on my account." She turns to meet my eyes.

My face burns but don't look away. "You're a very interesting person."

"I could say the same about you," she says.

Her comment makes me laugh. "There's nothing interesting about me. My mom couldn't even pass down a few decent traits to make me stand out around here."

"You're just a normal girl who has everyone teetering on edge to find out her darkest secrets," she says, face turning serious while her tone remains light.

I shake my head, burnished bronze hair landing on my mouth before I can brush it away. "That's just the thing. I don't have any secrets. I don't know what you're looking for."

From the back of my mind comes a reminder of Mom's pages, left vulnerable on my bed. My legs twitch to run back and put them in a more responsible place, but I don't want Ramsey to be on alert.

"I think you probably know more than what you're telling me. There was something waiting for you in Maine, wasn't there?"

"It was cleared out by the time we got there. Someone else knew where to look." I sigh.

Ramsey just chuckles. "You can tell me the truth whenever you feel like it. I won't turn you in to Ret."

"Wouldn't you have to do that? You do work for them," I remind her, studying the sidewalk to hide my apparent guilt.

She pats my hand where it rests on her arm. "Like I told you earlier, I tend to do what I want, regardless of what Ret says."

I can't even imagine what that freedom must be like.

"I don't think Ret would like it very much if they knew you felt this way," I comment.

She just shrugs, the fabric of her jacket scraping against my shoulder. "They need me too much for it to be any other way."

We've been down this road before, so I know she won't answer any specific questions about her job, but my mind brims with them anyway.

"Let's talk about you," Ramsey says to me. "What is it that makes you want to discover more about your genetics? That doesn't seem like a normal interest for a teenage girl."

"I just feel like my family history could have something to

do with why my mom left me, why everyone is so interested in me."

Ramsey frowns, "But no one even knows your family history outside of your mother. Why would we care about it?"

I pull my arm out of hers and increase my pace to walk in front, darkness descending upon us more rapidly now, the last light of sunset winking off the high-rise windows. "You may not know it, but I can just feel that it has something to do with all of this."

"Why can't you just accept that you *personally* might be exceptional?"

I turn to face her. "Don't you understand how ludicrous that sounds? No one has any interest in me personally, it's all about what I might be able to tell them. That doesn't exactly make me feel warm and tingly inside."

Ramsey places her hands on either side of my shoulders. "You're involved here for a reason; something that has nothing to do with your mom."

Her swirling eyes pierce through mine, searching for something in my gaze. My body feels weaker the longer she stares at me. I swallow a few times before I feel like I'm in any way on the road to recovery.

"If it's that important to you, then I'll take you somewhere, but I need you to think long and hard about your own self-worth. Despite what you may think, you mean something to us. We need you here. Otherwise, I wouldn't have gone all over the east coast looking for you," she tells me with a wry smile.

My mouth turns into a sulky frown, but she leads me into a tiny clinic perched under a lopsided sign. A bell rings as we walk through the glass door, my sneakers sticking to the floor, making a sucking sound with every step across the faded white linoleum.

"How can I help you?" a woman behind the counter

asks. She eyes Ramsey curiously and overlooks me completely. She's wearing an old-fashioned nursing uniform, complete with a hat that has me hiding a grin behind my hand.

Ramsey pushes me forward. "We're here to get a full run-up."

"Oh really?" she asks, her gaze finally meeting mine.

"We just want a basic genetic history. Let's not make this into any big deal," she says, still standing by the door at least two feet away from me.

The woman's fingers click across the keys as types something up on her computer. "Is this going on your tab?"

Ramsey nods and my eyebrows shoot up. What could possibly make it so Ramsey would need to have a tab at a blood clinic?

"If you'll just come right this way," she says, coming around the corner and sweeping me up with an outstretched arm.

"Aren't you coming with me?" I ask Ramsey as the nurse pushes me through the back door, but she's standing cemented to where we first came in together.

She shakes her head. "Go along without me. I'll be waiting here when you come back."

"She never comes in the back," the nurse whispers in my ear as the door closes behind us.

I guess that clears one question up, Ramsey never comes here for herself. So how many other sad orphans has she ushered through these doors?

The nurse sits me down on a plastic chair, rubbing an anti-septic patch against my throat. "This will only hurt for a moment and then you'll have the answers you're looking for."

Her heels click as she turns back down the hallway and through the door where Ramsey is waiting. As soon as she's gone, a man enters from the door across from me. My pulse skyrockets, but I keep my sweat-drenched hands clasped in my lap.

He's wearing a grungy lab coat, but the rest of him is pristine, beautiful, as he looks over the paper the nurse brought in with me.

"Just a basic genetic profile?" he asks me, gaze still on the paper.

"Ye-yes," I say, cheeks heating with my stutter. He's the most beautiful man I've ever seen. Even more than Donovan whose strong body and well-structured face have left me weak more than once.

He sits on the seat next to me, using his hands to lift the crook of my elbow to his face.

"You're not going to draw it first?" I ask with a swallow; this is not at all like what Donovan showed me.

"I find it dilutes the material and I don't get as many results that way," he says, breath warm as it caresses my skin.

I squeeze my eyes shut and wait for it to happen, my whole body tensing.

"Relax," he says, running a hand down my arm. "This will be so much nicer for both of us if you enjoy the experience."

I can't imagine enjoying what he's about to do to me, but I take a few deep breaths and try to relax anyway. He waits patiently, then with a sigh of relief locks his mouth against my arm.

My eyes fly open as I feel the sharp prick of his fangs. He's got me locked in his grip; a hand wrapped around my waist to keep me close. Trying to relax like he told me to, I close my eyes again.

A cool tingle like mint in my mouth, spreads from my throat, coursing through my bloodstream. My eyes snap back open, but they glaze over and I'm thrown into darkness. The man attached to me groans before pulling away. I realize that it must be difficult for people like him to stop once they start.

There must be a great deal of self-control required to do what he does. Sinking into my chair, he releases me from his solid grip. He gets up and makes a few notes in my chart, his gaze flicking back and forth from me to the paper.

"Well, that was a new experience," he finally says, placing my chart down on the counter next to our seats. "One that I'm very grateful to have been able to try. Thank you for choosing our clinic for your bloodwork needs."

"I...is there anything you can tell me now?" I feel unsteady on my feet, but I want to get what I came here for, I don't want to wait another second.

He taps a finger against his chin and I try not to notice the fleck of blood on his lip. "You need more Vitamin D. I would also be wary of your iron counts. The really interesting thing is the level of salt I could taste in your blood. I wish I could tell you more about it, but like I said, I've never had anything like it before."

"Oh." My arm falls to my side.

"If that is all?"

I nod and he flashes me a stunning smile, winks, and walks back through the door he came out of. I sit, shocked into numbness until the nurse comes back and picks up my chart.

"You ready to get your results? Ramsey is waiting for you," she says, gripping me under the arm and lifting me back on my feet.

I follow her unsteadily, my knees not up to holding the weight of my body just yet. When she takes us back into the main lobby, I almost open my mouth in protest. This open space seems too insecure to divulge the information Mom kept secret from me my whole life. Ramsey's seated on one of the plastic chairs, her back at least a foot from the edge of the seat, making me clamp my jaw shut. I can handle a little more discomfort to keep her from having to go any further into the belly of the beast, although why she can't stand the clinic is beyond me. Especially if she's been here several times before.

"If you'd just take a seat," the nurse says gesturing to the cracked greying chair beside Ramsey. "We'll read you your results."

It boggles my mind they have this kind of power here. I can't imagine how incredible it would be in a real medical setting. It could really change lives if they became more open.

Maybe I agree with Amaro more than I thought I did.

Plopping down into the seat by Ramsey, she takes one of my hands in hers. Her fingers are cool, her palm clammy as it closes over mine.

"Okay," the nurse says, eyes widening as she skims the vampire's notes. "Your parents were nixie and fae, a very uncommon combination. In fact, I don't think I've ever met someone with your mixed blood. Congratulations."

I bite my lower lip as it wobbles. Apparently, none of me is human at all.

"He says he didn't find any latent powers from either parent. You're 100% normal."

My teeth dig into my lip further as I keep back a hysterical laugh. Half-fae and half-nixie couldn't be any further from normal in my sheltered opinion.

"Could I see that?" Ramsey asks, extending her hand for my chart.

The nurse hands it over with a shrug and saunters back behind her desk, fingers once again clicking away on the keyboard. I wonder if she's writing about me.

"Let's get out of here," Ramsey says quietly, using our linked hands to pull me to my feet and out the door.

I stumble back towards Ret when Ramsey releases me to press my paper against her eager eyes in her haste to read over all the notes herself.

"This is very interesting," she mutters. "I didn't even know it was possible."

My forehead wrinkles and my eyes narrow. I rework my long blond ponytail to keep myself from ripping the paper out of her hands to read it myself.

"What does it say?" I ask when it becomes obvious she's not going to share what's caught her attention.

Ramsey's swirling blue eyes widen as she looks over the paper at me like she'd forgotten I was even here. "I just can't get over who your parents are."

"It says who my parents are?" I've obviously known my whole life who my mom was, but she always said I wasn't old enough to find out who my dad was. Since she's been gone I've had to resign myself with never knowing.

"Yes, he has your mother down as Minna, which we already knew, and your father as Bracken Bitterleaf. Now *that* is the real surprise," she says, her focus going back to the notes.

"Why is that so surprising?" I smooth down my t-shirt with sweaty, shaking hands. She's just read aloud the answer to so many of my childhood questions like it meant nothing. *Bracken*, I mouth, feeling his name on my tongue.

Ramsey folds up the paper and puts it in her jacket pocket. "It's surprising because Bracken's been working for us for about fifteen years."

My mouth goes dry. "Work-working with you?" I ask, mouth sticking as I try to get over my shock.

"Yeah, he's working in security, I think. You may have even already met," she realizes, her long index finger pressed into her chin. "If you haven't then it would be a simple thing to remedy. We could do it right now if you'd like?"

I shake my head in jerky movements. I don't think I'm ready to meet my dad yet. I don't even know what I would say to him. *'Hey, it's your daughter that you abandoned or never knew about, I'm not sure which. How's it going? Yeah, I don't think so.*

"Suit yourself," Ramsey says as we reach the back door of her brick townhome. "Off to bed then?"

I nod and dash up the stairs, eager for a moment alone to breathe, or die, whichever comes first. Closing the bedroom door behind me, I sink to the floor and wrap my arms around my raised knees.

No wonder she never said anything. Mom obviously wasn't ready to talk to me about her own background, let alone some stranger's I'd have to call 'dad.'

Resting my head on my knees, I take a few breaths to try and calm myself. Do I want to meet my dad? It's not like it'd really make a difference. The pressure I once felt to figure out who he was died a long time ago, and I don't know what to do with the information I've been given. I don't know how to feel about the fact that I'm not even a small part human. How has that never come up? What made Mom think I would be fine never knowing that little piece of information?

I stand up and sit back down, my breath coming heavy. What was her grand plan? We live in Maine forever, completely secluded from the world until even she forgets who she is? It just doesn't make sense. Would she have told me when I was older? Or would she have let me go on throughout life, just living and getting married and having more half-breed babies without even realizing it?

I pull myself off the floor and onto the bed, kicking off my sneakers as I go. The comforter is thick and warm, and I wrap myself up in it, content to find any comfort I can right now.

What does it mean that my particular breed is interesting? Is that why people want me in their organizations? That still doesn't make a lot of sense, because I don't have any of the powers of either of my parents. I'm just a dud; a mule.

The thought makes me giggle, the sound muffled in the

blanket. I'm sure I was just an accident. Especially if nixies can't usually have children. I must have been quite the surprise. Maybe that's why she ended up in Maine. I knew she hadn't always lived there. She'd said she wanted a more quality childhood for me. Maybe she was just hiding me, her embarrassing half-breed mistake.

My thoughts are uncharitable, and in the back of my mind, I know that my mother loved...loves me. I just don't understand anything right now and can't deal with it.

My mind goes around and around in unhelpful circles as I stare up at the ceiling, but there's no answers there and I'm only left with my own thoughts.

Chapter Fourteen

"Avi?" Ramsey's muffled voice jolts me from my dreams as she taps on the door. "I thought you might want to get up and get ready. Ryul Valmaris wants to see you this morning."

"Is that name supposed to mean anything to me?" I push myself out of the safety of my blanket cocoon and into the chill morning air. My hair sticks up in all directions while the ends hang limply in my face.

She cracks the door open but doesn't come in. "He's the king, you know, the one in charge of Ret. He'd like to know what information you have, and I hope you're willing to share something."

I know what she's really saying: *give them some information if you want to protect your mom.*

My mind instantly takes me to where the Trident and my mom are before I can shut down that train of thought. "Do I have to go right now?" I ask instead.

"I don't understand why you wouldn't."

Of course, she wouldn't. She wasn't there when I met Patrice. The leaders of these crazy organizations are just not the kind of people I'd like to have anything to do with. Not that I get a choice in it.

After waiting for me to answer her, Ramsey finally gives up. "Just get ready and come downstairs. There's a bathroom next door to you if you want to use it."

Her footsteps drift down the stairs and I grab my backpack and head towards the bathroom in a hurry. I might not have felt it last night, but my bladder is sure letting me know this morning that I went to bed without taking care of it.

Once in the bathroom, I consider taking another shower. My reflection looks drab, with dark circles sitting under my eyes even after going to bed so early, not exactly the best way to make a good impression on someone. Deciding on a quick shower to clear my mind, I quickly prepare and jump in.

The tub is of the claw foot variety, matching the rest of Ramsey's antique style. It takes me a couple of tries to get into it. I'm not exactly short, but even my 5'5" frame has a hard time and I'd need a stool to do it with any dignity. *Not that it matters I guess, no one is here to see me.*

The warm water does a great job of clearing my thoughts as it flows in a solid stream down my back. I think I'd like to meet my father; I just don't want him to know who I am when I do. I'd like to know some basic information. Mom was always so light and beautiful, while I existed as her faded counterpart. *Do I resemble him at all?*

It won't change any of the decisions I've made, and I don't really want it to. He can't tell me whether to tattle on my mom or not. He may not even remember her enough to give me any guidance.

While I lather the shampoo into my hair, nose filling with the scent of violets, I decide there's some information I can give Ret that won't hurt Mom and won't really help them either. I see no reason why I can't tell him that my mother simply walked into the ocean when she left me. Just walked in, never to be seen again. At least that's what some of her papers imply. *I* know there was something waiting for her down there, but on the surface, it looks like she just swam away. Especially to anyone who knows that she's a nixie.

If I'd gone with her though, it would have been a murder.

I know that now that I've had some time to think about it. There was no way for her to take me when she left. She had to make other arrangements. I just wish she hadn't felt like she had to lie to me. I would have felt so much better knowing she was still alive all this time.

I mean, is common courtesy dead? My life experiences lately would imply that's the case. I just can't imagine letting the people I love think I was dead or kidnapping someone for my job for that matter. It just isn't me. Not that that's important, there are plenty of people I know who *are* that way, and they're already more than enough.

Turning off the water does little to curb this train of thought. I rub a towel vigorously through my hair to try and scrub away the feelings of doubt that creep into my mind.

Pulling on my clothes, I let them hang on my skinny frame which has only gotten smaller from stress and run a brush through my hair before pulling it back into another pony. I don't have anyone to impress. King Ryul wants to see me, so he'll just have to live with what I look like.

Ramsey is passing through the kitchen when I come down the stairs. "I thought you'd move a little quicker. You don't want to make the king upset."

"I don't really care who I upset," I tell Ramsey with a bravado that's only skin deep. I don't need any more trouble, but I also don't want to come off too eager. I'm anything but eager about this encounter.

"I'm sure that isn't true." She looks me over, her face tight. "Let me just help you out here."

She touches my hair and it feels like a ripple of electricity runs through me. I shake my head, my hair falling in perfect waves.

"You're welcome," she says with a wink.

I try not to gawk at her. "That's a pretty impressive trick."

Ramsey runs a hand through her neon locks before gripping me by the shoulder. "So much of magic is inherently selfish. Now come on," she says as she leads me through the front of her house and out the door, cutting across the grass to Ret headquarters.

She uses a key card to get the heavy metal door to open, almost flinging me through in her attempt to pick up the pace. We sprint down the sterile hallways, but there's no one around to notice. I've never seen the place so bare. *Not that I come here often or anything.*

Ramsey mutters under her breath, but I can't hear her words over my own heavy breathing. I've been too sedentary lately to match her pace with any grace. She pushes open a metal door and reveals a hallway I've never been in before. This space already stands apart from the rest of the building, the lighting less glaring, the walls warmer. Even the metal, nondescript doors have been replaced by wood ones.

Opening my mouth to make a crack about it to Ramsey, I stop short as she abruptly changes directions.

"Oh good, we're not too late," she says, not looking at me as she raps smartly on the door.

"Come in," a cool voice responds.

Ramsey turns the doorknob and swings it open, revealing a wallpapered room with a Persian rug spread across the floor. There's a warm wood bookcase running along one wall with a matching expansive desk filling the remainder of the space. I draw my eyes back to the desk, noticing the man watching us behind it.

"So good of you to join us," he says. Ramsey flinches despite the lack of inflection in his tone.

I wait for Ramsey to respond, but she keeps her head down, standing in the doorway with limp shoulders. Stepping forward, my feet sink into the plush rug, I settle myself into the chair across from this imposing stranger.

"I would've come earlier if I'd had more notice." I cross my arms to hide the shaking of my body. I have to be here, I know I have to be here for my mom, but I don't want anyone else to push me around. I may be here because I'm out of choices, but this is something that can be my choice.

He leans over the top of the desk, silver hair gleaming against the thin circlet of gold playing as a crown in the over-head light. "You would've had more notice if you'd stayed in the building."

"Forgive me, but I didn't find your staff very accommodating."

He gives me a smile that reveals far too many teeth, his pale lips thinning as they turn up. "You didn't tell me she was this lively, Ramsey."

"I didn't realize she was," Ramsey replies. I can practically feel her eyes boring into the back of my head.

"Most of your people don't actually know me very well," I tell King Ryul. "They haven't spent much time with me when they aren't trying to dig through my head to find information about my mom. Rather rude if you ask me."

"Rude indeed," King Ryul says, silver eyes trained on me over his thin nose, pointed ears poking out through the length of his hair.

Inside I'm a mess, even as I stare him down with my own blue gaze. I'm never this forward. At least I'm not usually this way outside of conversations with Mom or close friends. Fading into the background has always been more appealing to me than dealing with the more aggressive people in my life. Too bad these people are quickly swamping me.

"So if you could just tell me what you want so I can get

back to what I was doing, or...?" I ask him with arms extended to either side.

King Ryul laughs aloud at this. "I like this one," he says, speaking over me to Ramsey.

I glance back at Ramsey as she gives the king a weak smile. "I'm glad."

I stand with weak knees and take a step towards the door. "If you're just going to waste my time, then I'm out of here."

"Come back." King Ryul motions me back while still laughing. "Let's talk."

I plop back into the chair. "I'm listening."

Years of watching teen dramas have finally paid off, I think, wishing for a pair of aviators.

"I won't bother playing coy with you, we don't have time for that thanks to your fiery little escapade with Amaro," King Ryul says, leaning back in his chair. "You have some information and I want it."

"That's a common misconception," I tell him, irritated once more that this is all anyone ever wants from me. "My mother didn't share any of her life with me beyond what was necessary."

King Ryul sighs. "I was hoping you would be willing to cooperate with us. Especially after all of our help when you were with Amaro."

"I never asked for your help."

Ramsey's hand clenches the back of my chair. "I don't think she's trying to make this harder. She genuinely doesn't know much."

The King's elegant brows crash down over his forehead as he leans forward. "I'm not talking to you, am I, Ramsey? You're here for unknown reasons and should consider yourself lucky I haven't kicked you out yet."

Ramsey releases my chair and moves back to hover in the doorway, effectively cowled.

"Now," King Ryul says, turning his built torso to face me. "Let's talk about what you know."

My fingernails dig into my arms as I clench impossibly tighter. "I already told you; I don't know anything."

His face grows dark. "I thought you didn't want to play any games."

"So, are you saying that anything I say that doesn't match with what you're looking for means I'm playing a game?"

King Ryul takes a deep breath, closes his eyes, and removes his hands from the desk. "I know there was something waiting for you in that house. If I hadn't thought you were going after something, I'd never have let you go. Now I just want you to share what you found with me."

I bite my top lip as I digest this new revelation. "I'm sorry, but since when are you in charge of my life decisions? I can go where I please regardless of what your particular wishes are."

"That's where you're wrong." King Ryul stands at an impressive height. "You're our property now. When you came with my men, you became indebted to me. You'll remain with us until you can pay back that debt. Now, you can do that through information, and share what you found out about your mother, or you can start working for us and repay our efforts through labor."

"I didn't ask anyone to rescue me," I tell him, hands fisted at my side.

He smooths back his platinum hair with thin hands. "Be that as it may, the fact remains that because of you, my men were taken away from their other projects and that must be accounted for."

Gritting my teeth, I rise to face him. "I won't be punished for circumstances that are so obviously outside of my control."

"That's not your decision to make," he says with a side smile.

"What's with you people? You think you're better than

everyone else? That your mission is more important than any individual life you may tread all over? This is my life, and I will not stand idly by anymore," I tell him, spit flying in my passion. "If you want something from me, you can ask nicely. I refuse to be dictated. Call off your henchmen and treat me like a human being."

I realize I've slipped up when King Ryul gives me a thin-lipped smile. "But you're not a human being, my dear. You belong with us, which does put you under my jurisdiction. You need to let me help you before you inadvertently destroy yourself with all of your stumbling around."

I sit with a huff. Not sure what to say next, I just glare at King Ryul as he sits again. He's got a small point. I don't know what I'm doing. I don't know what it means to be a nixie or fae. All I know about nixies is their propensity for water. I don't even know what talents Donovan was looking for when he dumped me into that tub. Should I have sprouted gills or something?

"Now," King Ryul says, addressing Ramsey. "You told me you thought she had something from the house I might be interested in?"

Ramsey doesn't look at me as she approaches the desk. From her jacket, she pulls out papers I recognize and my stomach sinks. I knew I should have put those in a safer place.

"She gathered these from Minna's office. I looked at them myself a little, and I'm pretty sure I've narrowed down where the Trident is," she says while the King looks over my mother's notes.

"Very promising," he murmurs, long fingers still going through my private things. "Anything you'd like to add, Avi?"

My mouth pulls into a frown, and I shake my head. "There's nothing there."

Sweat trickles down my back as King Ryul smiles at me. He knows I'm lying. I don't know what to say. I'm not going to give anything away that he won't already know just from reading those notes. Anything I add now could be a hint he needs to decipher her clues.

"I see what you're talking about Ramsey, there are quite a few indicators here," he says, putting the papers down. "I think we're going to have to take a trip to Neopolis."

My eyes go wide. He didn't need my help after all. Ramsey was right, he was already close by himself. It's a good thing I came back with Ramsey.

"That's precisely what I was thinking," Ramsey says, voice cool. "It would make sense that Minna would flee to her own people. I just think you should be cautious about going to Neopolis. There are many dangers there."

King Ryul dismisses Ramsey's warning with a wave of his hand. "We've dealt with them before, and we don't have any time to waste. We must get there before Amaro. Plus, the nixie's powers are made for men, which I am not. They won't prove to be a distraction to me."

"I don't think you should discredit human men; the nixie's powers have been known to affect males of all races. Even fae have been subject to their overwhelming attraction."

I grip the arm of my chair, brushing off the implication that Mom is some kind of siren. A supposedly barren siren. A barren siren who could have seduced my father. "Take me with you."

The King glances up at me with raised brows. "After all your lying, you really think I'd take you on such a dangerous journey?"

"You just said it wasn't dangerous, and I didn't mean to lie to you. How was I supposed to know Neopolis was a real place?" I keep my voice earnest even through my little lie.

I have to go to Neopolis to see Mom. No matter what she's done, I have to see her face-to-face and get answers for myself. I could've been with her right now if Ramsey hadn't stopped me earlier.

"She'd be a great bargaining chip," Ramsey tells King Ryul, a finger stroking her chin. "Minna will have to listen to you if you have her daughter."

"Wait a second!" I turn to Ramsey, her eyes narrowing, telling me to stop. But I can't. "I'm not going to go anywhere as someone's captive! I'm a free person! I have rights!"

King Ryul laughs. "While we may have residence in the United States, we are above them as a nation of our own. We do not follow their laws, which means you don't really have any rights but the ones we grant you. You're not a human being, remember?"

His smile is cruel as he watches my face fall. The reminder of my family origins is uncomfortable at best, but now it hits me in the chest like a knife.

"You make an excellent point Ramsey," King Ryul says, ignoring me now that I've been effectively crushed. "Maybe I *should* consider bringing the girl along as incentive."

I'm pinned, stuck between a rock and a hard place as I'm made more aware of my lack of options. As long as I'm here with Ret, I have no options, no choices. I glare at Ramsey as she purposefully looks away from me. Wishing for laser eyes or some useful way to attack my enemies, I keep staring at her as she and King Ryul make plans around me.

"We'll get ready to go then," he says, placing his hands flat on the desk and standing up slowly with a wide grin. "I can't wait for our little reunion. We leave in an hour."

Ramsey gives him a tilted head nod, then grips me by the shoulder and manually drags me from the room. The door clicks closed behind us and her hand digs into what little meat lines my shoulder, making me wince with the pain. As soon as we're through the heavy doors partitioning this wing from the others, she whirls me around to face her.

"What were you thinking?" Her voice is low and hissing as flecks of spit hit me in the face. "That is the last man you should ever antagonize! Do you want to make life harder for yourself? Do you like living this way?"

I wrench my shoulder out of her grip with a scowl, marching past her and out of the building. Her feet pound the pavement behind me, but I don't turn around. I have nothing to say to her. Of course she would betray me. *They all betray me eventually.* I want to hit my head against the wall for being so stupid. After everything that's happened to me, I should have known that no one would be genuinely nice to me. Everyone has an angle to exploit.

"Avi, wait!" Ramsey calls behind me, her lanky legs make it easy to keep up but she stays just behind anyway. "Slow down!"

I don't answer her. There's nothing I want to say. She's betrayed me and I can't take it anymore. I *refuse* to take it anymore.

Opening Ramsey's front door, I fling it wide in my anger. Running through the rooms and up the stairs, I slam my bedroom door closed and lock it behind me. Ramsey stops outside my door, her polished shoes padding through the carpet.

"Come out and talk to me," she says through the door, the irritation in her voice giving way to desperation.

"No!" I kick the door for good measure.

Ramsey's back hits the door, the wrinkle of her pants showing through the crack as she thumps her large body down. She knocks her head against the door a few times. "Please talk to me."

"There's nothing you could possibly say to me that could make this right." My voice is low as the adrenaline drains from my body in slow waves.

"It's the only way I could get him to even consider letting

you go, don't you realize that?" she asks, voice cracking. "I suggested it for you."

I shake my head and run my fingers through my hair, dragging out long pieces from my ponytail in the process. "I can't trust you." It feels good to be completely honest.

She sighs. "I know."

Sinking into the bed, I keep an eye on the door where I know Ramsey is still waiting for me. I'm completely adrift. Alone without allies, I know it'll be near to impossible to make it out of this unscathed. From the back of my mind comes the reminder that I've already been scathed by this process. There's no way for things to go back to normal. This is my life now.

"We'll be leaving in an hour," Ramsey says after a long pause. "I know you don't have much, but you should probably pack up what you do have and be ready to go. I'm not sure what the King will do if he finds you unprepared. He's not a patient man."

"Big surprise," I mutter under my breath, but Ramsey gives a quiet chuckle.

The muffled sounds of movement alert me to Ramsey getting up from her spot on the ground. "I know you don't believe me, and I don't necessarily blame you, but I did that for you. Maybe someday you'll be able to appreciate that."

Fat chance, I think as her feet pad across the hallway and down the stairs. That's like thinking I'd thank Donovan for blowing up my house, or Nick for leaving me behind during the fire. These people are insane to think their actions are in any way something I'd want to thank them for.

Mostly I just want to give them a good punch in the nose.

Rolling over, I clutch the thick comforter to my chest and bury my face in it. My backpack still sits at the foot of the bed, its back sloping over from the lack of items inside. It's almost laughable to think I'd have anything to pack. My childhood home's been destroyed, my aunt isn't really my aunt and doesn't remember me, and I'm not allowed back in her home. This is it now. All my possessions can be contained within half the space of a ragged backpack.

My mind won't slow down. Even though I'm being taken as a prisoner, I'm still about to see my mom. At some point in the near future, I'll be able to face her and demand answers. My heart pounds and my body quivers with anticipation. If I can keep ahold of my mouth in front of King Ryul then I'll be able to do this.

I have to do this.

Chapter Fifteen

I wait until I can breathe steadily again before grabbing my bag and heading downstairs. Ramsey waits for me on one of the kitchen stools, fingers tapping against the counter. Paper cranes fly around the kitchen in a swirl. The stairs squeak under my feet and the birds hit the floor as she looks at me.

"Good, let's go."

She doesn't wait for me to fully come down the stairs as I sling my backpack over my shoulder before she's out the front door. I struggle after her, my backpack making me too wide to fit comfortably through the hallway, but I don't ask her to stop. Pride keeps me silent as I stomp across the wet grass toward the parking lot where my mom's car sits. A large black van sits running in one of the parking stalls and I watch the neon tips of Ramsey's hair as she flings herself into the backseat.

Assuming this is where I should be heading too, I jog over and climb in after her, pushing myself into the far back row. Looking up as I pull my backpack off, I make uncomfortable eye contact with Nick, who's pressed into the far-left seat in the same row as me.

He looks away from me in a jerky motion, just as unhappy to see me as I am to see him. *It would've been nice to be warned about Nick coming*, I think at the back of Ramsey's head while a faint blush creeps up my neck.

"Everyone ready?" King Ryul asks, thin crown sparkling from his position in the front seat, his designer leather jacket making me think of Donovan as he turns to face us. No one says a word. "Good." He nods to the driver, and we rumble out of the parking lot and head toward the bay.

Besides the King, Ramsey, Nick, and myself, the van's filled up with a few other men. Each one is large and built, their heads partially stooped to avoid hitting the van's ceiling. The slight tilt of their ears tells me a little about their heritage, but I've never seen fae like this before. Patrice and Ryul have slender bird-like figures, more similar to my own when I think about it. These men are built like beasts, muscles bulging out of every available space. *Are they here for security?*

As we get closer to the dock, the van makes a sharp left and takes us to a secluded stretch of sand where a sleek black boat is perched next to a metal dock. We tromp across the sand and the extra men filter in between us, confirming my theory.

"All right, let's get moving. We've got a lot of ground to cover," King Ryul says, lowering himself into the boat through a circular opening.

I follow the line, looking at the boat in front of us with wide eyes. I've never really been on a boat before, even though I've lived by the water my whole life. Still, this one is not like any of the others I've seen out on the water or in pictures. It doesn't have a sail and I think that's what throws me off the most. *Still*, I shrug, *I'm no expert on anything nautical so what would I know?*

The inside of the ship is quite luxurious, nothing like the clinical setting of the Ret building. Instead, it reminds me more of King Ryul's office, warm tones and soft fabrics, a circle of plush couches filling the room for a comfortable journey. Maybe this is his version of Air Force 1.

The large men file in last, filling the space by the door as the rest of us spread out and away from each other. It's a relief not to have to sit so close to Nick, but I can feel his presence in the room like a tingle across my skin. There are conversations we should have, but this is neither the time nor the place. Plus, I'm more concerned with what I'm going to say to my mother than what I'm going to say to Nick. He's low on my priority list, only his proximity brings him to mind at all.

King Ryul spreads out over a couch, his long legs filling enough space for three people. This boat could hold at least three times the number of people we've loaded into it, but I've yet to see any more ready to come in behind us. This is it.

"Ready for your adventure?" King Ryul asks me with a sly smile.

I nod, keeping my hands in fists in my lap to keep me from lashing out. He leans back against the couch with an easy grin, thin lips pulled tight, shirt taut across his toned chest. I look down at my lap, to keep him from seeing my narrowed eyes. His low chuckle says I haven't adequately hidden the tight pulsing of my chest with each breath as I try to calm down.

There's a clunk from the door closing and a shudder as the boat pushes away from the dock. I look around in mild panic, hands reaching for safety restraints that aren't there. Nick laughs under his breath, and I glance up in time to see Ramsey giving him a sharp look from her own place adjacent to me.

The room we're in is oval-shaped, with small couches filling the space while keeping the center open for a round table with a vase filled with ivory flowers placed atop. It is only partially lit, with the warm accents of the room adding to the dark atmosphere. I almost feel like I'm in some sort of evil lair and find I'm half expecting the King to lean forward and describe the diabolical plan we're about to undertake. Although, if he were being honest, that *is* what we're about to do.

We're about to enter Neopolis without permission, which is something I understand is very frowned upon by their government. Will they attack us? Or will King Ryul try to find a way for us to enter the city without detection? Will this create a magical international war?

Honestly, while I may wonder, I don't actually care. My concern lies with my mother. He knows that too. There's plenty of space on this boat, his lack of desire to include me on this trip had nothing to do with causing an inconvenience. It's because I'm a risk.

King Ryul knows my loyalties aren't with him. I don't care about his goal. I don't care about the Trident. It makes me a liability. When it really comes down to it, he doesn't know what my reaction will be to any situation we find ourselves in, other than that it won't be with him in mind.

I'm not sure what my reactions will be either.

Despite my age, I do understand why he wouldn't want that. I know Ramsey found a great way to convince King Ryul to bring me, and I know he probably wouldn't have let me come without him. But, it doesn't make me any less angry with Ramsey for suggesting that I act as a hostage.

The way King Ryul has looked at me before tells me he wouldn't mind if I were tied up like a genuine hostage. Something that he could probably order without blinking if I became the kind of trouble he suspects.

The low to nonexistent hum of the motor reveals the expense of the boat we're in. Turning around, I try to find a window in the wall behind me. Shocked, I sit back heavily when there aren't any, and there aren't any in the wall across from me either.

Pride wars within me as a million questions bubble up my throat. I want to try and figure out what kind of boat we're in, but I refuse to talk to any of my betrayers.

Fidgeting, heart hurting, I yearn for my Aunt Nina. I know I'll get Mom back, but Nina's been lost to me. No more late-night Chinese runs. No more cups of hot chocolate in the window seat on rainy days. My aunt never felt overly warm to me, but I know she loved me in her own way. Maybe she always knew we weren't really related.

If I could have one more conversation with her, I would've asked her how I came to live with her in New York. Did she really know my mom? What did she say to my mom about taking me in?

I sigh, mentally brushing those thoughts away. They won't help me to linger on.

Ramsey makes eye contact with me, her head tilted in a question. I shake my head at her, twisting in my seat to take her out my peripheral vision. Unfortunately, I'm now in a great place to see the glare of King Ryul's twisting gold crown and one of his many goons. I decide to pass the time studying this guard as the others participate in soft conversation and elevator music pumps out of the ceiling speakers.

Originally, I thought these men were almost exactly the same, but further focus on this guard proves this theory to be wrong. His head is squarer than the others, a detail I missed before because of how they all wear their long hair slung in low ponytails. I can't be held responsible for how much of their face is hidden by hair, I think with a shrug. His head is different though, the grey eyes staring across the room at me also making him stand out from the others that came in with us.

We study each other, his mouth quirked up to the right, arms crossed over a broad chest. I wonder how long it took for him to get that buff. Is he a gym rat at home? Thinking of him kissing his flexed arms makes me laugh out loud, and he raises a brow at me as he smirks.

Ramsey said my dad worked for Ret. Could he be here in this room? I look around, taking in each of the potential candidates. If any of them contributed to my genes I'm just upset that I'm not taller or buffer.

Mom and I didn't really look much alike. She had slender curves, long legs, and shiny blonde hair. I, on the other hand, am adequately tall, completely shapeless, and have dull blonde hair. I glance back over at my study subject from before. If I let myself believe it, we could have some similarities. Starting with his grey eyes, the mirror of mine.

Stomach twisting at the thought, I see King Ryul smiling darkly at me. I'm sure he doesn't know what I'm thinking. At most, he probably just thinks I'm checking out the hired help. That's a teenage girl thing to do, right?

That's only if Ramsey hasn't told him about my heritage though, and I wouldn't put it past her. Why would Ramsey keep my parents a secret if she didn't have to? She has no loyalty to me, and I never asked her not to tell anyway.

Shifting in my seat, I hate the position I've put myself in to hide Ramsey from my view. King Ryul takes out a book, not interested in talking with the rest of us. I don't care, it makes it easier for me to watch his cronies.

I'm not the only one interested in watching either, I realize when I look back at the grey-eyed guard and see him watching me with his head tilted. Has he been watching me this whole time, even after I looked away from him? Or did he turn back when I did? It shouldn't matter, but I can't help the chill that travels up my spine. *I'm surprised they haven't put me in a magical zoo or something.* Wouldn't they do that for a rare creature just like we would? Isn't that what I am? Probably not because I didn't inherit any of my parents' magical capabilities. My teeth grind together at the thought. I can imagine a few tricks I wouldn't mind having right about now. Even just the ability to grow gills and swim away like my mother did. At least I think that's how being a nixie works. No one's actually given me a rundown on how they work yet. Or fae for that matter. For all I know all the fae are just pointy-eared humans.

A giggle escapes my lips at the thought of someone telling the King he's just a pointed-eared human. King Ryul glances at me over his book as if he knows I'm thinking about him.

"Something funny over there?" he asks me in clipped tones, the guard behind him still eyeing me over his shoulder.

I bite my lip, smile spreading across my cheeks. King Ryul shakes his head and goes back to his book, turning a page with a slender finger. His guard hasn't dismissed me so easily though, one brow raised in question.

I shake my head at him. Does he think I could actually tell him anything from over here without King Ryul hearing? Yeah right.

Time starts to lose meaning the longer we're down in the depths of the ship. The light doesn't change and there are no clocks to tell me what time it is. I'm only completely sure time has passed at all when my stomach starts to rumble. I didn't even think about grabbing any food at Ramsey's for later, didn't even grab breakfast now that I think about it.

Glancing around, I'm more tempted than ever to finally say something to Ramsey, when the panel in the wall next to me slides open to reveal a small woman pushing a silver cart heavy with covered trays. My mouth starts to salivate as she brings it around, starting with the King and going down in rank.

The cart is almost empty and there are still a few people left, my stomach cramps up in desire. King Ryul opens his tray to reveal pasta in a white cream sauce, scallops delicately placed around the plate. It's almost more than I can bear.

She comes my way, the cart no longer sinking into the plush carpet, the wheels rotating unencumbered. Eyes squeezed shut in a quick prayer of gratitude, I miss her walking right past me and back through the door. The panel closes on silent hinges behind her, and I long to throw myself against it.

"Something wrong?" King Ryul asks, his fork held suspended in the air with a scallop speared to it.

Looking around for help, my eyes land on Ramsey, her eyes crinkled at me.

"No, nothing's wrong," I whisper.

He leans back and continues eating. "Good. I'd *hate* it if this trip was uncomfortable for you."

Sure, you would. I turn my attention to the other members of his party. There's obviously a rank here, with not every tray holding the same contents. No one else has the same meal as the King, which I'm sure he did to make himself feel special, but even Ramsey has a plate with steamed vegetables and a slice of what looks like lasagna on it. She doesn't look at me as she eats it, and I glance around at the others. Nick got a burger, and the guards are all chomping down on some unrecognizable slop. In fact, it almost looks like an old MRE I had on a school trip. Tasty, but the aesthetics left something to be desired.

That guy probably is a gym rat if he needs that many calories, I think bitterly as I watch the King's guard spoon bite after bite into his waiting mouth. My ears ring with the sounds of utensils hitting plates and scraping against teeth.

"Are you sure I can't help you with something?" King Ryul asks me, a half-smile on his face.

He's waiting for me to beg; I just know it. He'll be waiting a long time for that. I've decided to be stronger. I won't break this time. I clench my hands into fists once more, the nails biting into my palms. "I don't know what you could possibly be talking about."

If he's going to play stupid, then so am I. It'll be a good game to play to pass the time anyway.

"Are you sure there's nothing you want? Nothing I could tempt you with?" he presses, voice like molasses.

They're not making it easy to like them. Which doesn't really make sense to me. I scratch the side of my head. Ret should want me to join up with them. Don't I represent some value to their organization? Apparently not. Ramsey should take note.

"If there's something you want to say, just say it. I'm not playing your little game." I keep my voice in flat tones.

He eyes me appraisingly but doesn't comment on my passive-aggressive behavior. On the other hand, I can practically feel Ramsey twitching across the room. It's funny really. She told me she was so valued she could do whatever she wanted but once in the King's vicinity, Ramsey's nothing but a wilting flower.

"Something you'd like to add, Ramsey?" King Ryul asks with a thin smile, picking up Ramsey's tension too. Ramsey shakes her head and stuffs her mouth, the less-than-delicate move decidedly unlike her.

A rumble in my belly spoils my minor victory. The sound echoes against the empty walls of my stomach and rumbles through my throat amplifying it through the room. Ramsey's eyes flick back up to mine, the smile a permanent fixture on King Ryul's face. I'm pinned in the middle of a power struggle I'm not strong enough to be the winner of.

With a sigh, the guard I've been watching walks around the back of the King's couch and plods heavily in front of me. "Take it, I'm done," he says, voice low and smooth.

I glance up at him with wide eyes, not able to keep the surprise off my face.

A thump comes from King Ryul's direction. "Now you've gone and ruined all the fun."

The King crosses his arms over his chest like a petulant child, his bottom lip sticking out to complete the picture.

The guard goes back to his place behind the King. "I'm sorry sir, I just didn't think we should let food go to waste if people were still hungry." His eyes are clear and vacant as he stares across to where I'm sitting stunned with his tray across my lap.

King Ryul huffs but doesn't say anything further about it. I pick up the spoon and fill it with mush. I think I can make out some macaroni noodles and hamburger pieces, but other than that it's still a mystery, even this close to my face. I can feel him staring at me as I lift a bite to my mouth. Warmth fills me almost immediately and I swallow the stuff down before it can touch my tongue. I'm sure the taste is fine, but I'm just not risking it right now. I don't know when I'll be fed again, so this stuff needs to stay down. My lips tip into a smile as I begin shoveling food down.

The plate was half full when he gave it to me, and in what feels like seconds I clean it down to the porcelain. A crusty piece of garlic bread sits to the left of the mush and I take the time to really savor it, completely sure what it's supposed to be. There's something so satisfying about bread, it always hits the spot for me, and my eyes close in bliss.

Picking up the glass of water, I drain it in quick gulps. The tray now empty, I let it sit on my lap. I'm not sure what else to do with it. While I've been eating the other trays have all been taken away, so I'm the only one left with the remnants of lunch.

King Ryul pulls his book out, but his gaze stays glued to my face. His mouth pulls into a thin line, but behind him, my guard is openly grinning. I feel pretty confident calling him mine. I'm not sure what's between us, but he pays attention and seems willing to protect me. Glancing back to my lap, I don't return his smile. Maybe I would have just a few days ago, but not anymore.

I'm going to make it on my own. I don't need any more backstabbing allies.

Chapter Sixteen

"Is there a bathroom I can use?" The water has hit my bladder and my legs long to move around.

The King smirks at me, but the guard cuts off whatever insult he's about to deliver. "Through the door behind you and straight down the hall on the right."

Placing the tray back in my seat as I stand up, I walk towards the wall behind me. I looked it over before for windows but never noticed a door. It looks like a blank piece of wall with a few paintings of mermaids spread across its tasteful forest green wallpaper.

My face burns as I run my hands along the wall's face, hoping to find a chink or something that will tell me there's a door here.

"Just walk in front of it," the guard says, his voice gentle.

I walk across the floor in front of the wall, feeling sillier and sillier as nothing happens. I'm about three-quarters of the way across when a panel slides open. Motion activated maybe?

It's a long narrow tunnel through the boat, but there is a door about halfway across it on the right. Thankfully it has a handle and I'm able to quickly get inside before I embarrass myself again.

"Jeez, I thought you'd never get away."

My body feels stiff as I slowly turn. I expect to see a cramped bathroom like on an airplane, but I'm surprised by the amount of space it's been afforded. There's a full vanity, complete with sconces on either side of the mirror and a stand-up shower. There's even enough room for a small chair in one corner, where Donovan is currently perched. He gives me a weak smile and a wave while I close the door behind me.

"What are you doing here?" I hiss, stomping over, hand raised and ready for a slap.

He holds up his hands in a pathetic defense. "I wanted to make sure you were okay."

"Do you hear yourself? You've snuck onto Ret's ship just because you wanted to make sure I was okay? Give me a break." My mouth twists in a snarl.

Donovan starts to stand, and I hold up a hand in warning. "You need to leave."

"Would you hear me out? It's not like I can just walk out the door and be gone. I came at great risk to myself because I was worried about you," he says, face screwed up and eyes pleading. "It's not like this is easy for me."

My hands turn into fists. "I don't care whether it's easy or not for you. You've done this to yourself. I didn't ask you to come after me, and I sure as heck didn't ask you to blow up my house. You've done this to yourself and I'm over it," I whisper-yell to him.

If I wanted to, all I'd have to do is scream and he'd quickly be discovered. For reasons I can't quite understand, I'm just not ready to do that to him yet.

"Can you just stop for a minute?" Donovan stands in a swift movement and grips my hands in his. "I don't think you really understand what's happening here. This is bigger than just your house, and I promise you I'm the only one on this stupid ship that genuinely cares about what happens to you!"

Wrenching my hands out of his, I press myself against the back of the door. "I don't know how you got here, but you need to leave."

Donovan's face falls and he doesn't try to argue with me again. With one last forlorn look, he pushes his hands into his jacket pockets and disappears in front of me.

Chest heaving, I walk to the sink and brace my hands against the side. Peering at my reflection shows nothing but a small, disheveled girl in an old band t-shirt, blonde tendrils of hair escaping my ponytail and obscuring parts of my face. I don't belong here. Everyone else knows it. I haven't tried to hide the fact that I know nothing about anything that we're doing. So why do I feel so alone now?

Splashing some water on my face, I double check my face isn't red before making my way back to the fancy sitting room. It's kind of an exquisite torture. All of us sitting, staring at each other, and unable to go anywhere else until the King says so.

* * *

I resume my place on the couch. My tray is gone. Other than that the room remains identical to how it was when I left. Nick glances up at me as I come in, eyes narrowed, but he says nothing. No one says anything. The only sound in the room is the crisp movement of paper as King Ryul turns the pages in his books and the soft classical music playing on the speakers.

Leaning my head back against the couch, I'm tempted to bash it against the wood backing a few times just for something to do. Don't these people get bored? Or is that just another special power I didn't get from my parents?

When dinner comes, I'm not denied a tray this time. King

Ryul must have gotten enough of the satisfaction he was looking for last time, so I'm presented with a turkey sandwich on white bread. It's by far the simplest meal here, but I'm past caring. Especially when it comes with a bag of potato chips. They're just classic, but still.

The hours of sitting begin to get to me after our trays are taken away. Covering a large yawn behind my hand, I use the movement to peek around at the others. Surely one of them wants to lie down somewhere too. Aside from a few of the men shifting their position, everyone else seems to be holding steady where they are.

Irritation ripples down my spine, but I rub it away by getting more comfortable in my seat. I slump down, letting my tailbone rest against the cushions and put my feet up on the seat. I haven't done it before now because I was worried about getting my dirty feet on the nice cream cushions. At this point though, I just have to find a way to get comfortable, even if it messes up the couch a little. Whatever, by the looks of this place they can afford a little extra cleaning.

My eyes drift closed, the boredom lulling me into sleep whether I like it or not.

"Are you hoping for different accommodations?" King Ryul asks, causing me to blink in surprise as I bring myself back to consciousness.

"What are you talking about?" I sit up and rub my eyes. This is the nightmare that will never end.

"You're settling down to sleep in here? This is a living room." Condescension drips from his voice.

I wrinkle my nose. "I'm not asking to go somewhere else. I will, however, make myself as comfortable as I can since I don't know how long we'll be here. It's not like you've told me how long this trip is."

"I didn't think it was pertinent information for a captive," King Ryul says, eyes gleaming.

I grind my teeth until my jaw hurts. "I am no one's prisoner."

"Your place in my sub says otherwise."

Without even thinking about it, I stand to confront him but Ramsey heads me off before I can do anything, meager as my skills are.

"Do you have to antagonize her all the time?" she asks. "She's just a child."

My neck cracks as I whip around to glare at Ramsey. "I'm not a child."

Neither of them recognizes my interruption. Instead, the King speaks directly to Ramsey. "If she wants to be in our world, she'll need to learn how to act in it. It's not my fault Minna was so inept in her education."

My focus on the conversation is shattered when I see the guard behind King Ryul flinch at my mother's name. I tilt my head at him in a question, but he's not looking at me. He's watching the King while his neck slowly turns red. My mouth opens in a small o.

Searching his face, I find the answer to his concern as his eyes immediately flick over to me before returning to King Ryul. Every emotion is written in the lines of his face, and I'm worried he's going to attack the King.

Ramsey notices the guard's attention too and immediately tries to defuse the situation. "Regardless of what her past was, it doesn't mean that you can't be a little more considerate in your dealings with her," she says slowly. "At the very least maybe we should all just leave her alone. She's been through a lot."

"Fine. Go sit down. You'd think I was actually hurting her with your crazy reaction," he says, flicking his fingers at Ramsey in dismissal.

Ramsey meets the eyes of the guard and gives a subtle shake of her head which King Ryul misses because he's gone back to his book. I see it, though. I can't take my eyes off him after what I've noticed. It was there in his eyes this whole time. After hours of considering him, why did it take my mother's name to make me see myself in him? Looking in his eyes is seeing a mirror image of myself.

This man is my father.

His shock at King Ryul's casual remark shows just how little he knew of my existence too. I feel a little bit relieved at the thought that he hasn't just abandoned me my whole life. He literally didn't know I was around. Why would my mother keep that from him? Just because of my unusual origins? Or was there more to it? Because he worked for Ret, and she worked against him at Amaro? That seems like something that could've been easily remedied.

"I'm bored," King Ryul announces from his place on the couch, sprawled out like the royalty he is. "Let's retire. For those of you who don't know, we should reach Neopolis sometime tomorrow morning."

His look is pointed at me, and he doesn't say anything further, but I know it's not because he wants to avoid irritating Ramsey, he could care less about other people's emotions.

The panel door where I left for the bathroom opens again and the inhabitants of the room begin filing out. I linger in the room, not knowing where I'm supposed to go. King Ryul strides past me with a self-satisfied grin. I don't pay him any mind.

My guard follows behind him, his emotions better controlled now, and his eyes trained directly on the King's back. I reach out a hand to stop him as he walks past but hang back instead, so my hand just hangs in the open space between us.

"You okay?" Nick asks as he starts toward the door.

"Fine." The word comes out short and sharp.

He runs a hand through his thick curls. "You want me to show you where to go?"

"Sure." I let out a tired exhalation. I don't really want his help, or really anything to do with him at all, but I do need someone to tell me where to go and it's not going to be my dad.

Nick nods towards the doorway and I walk through just in front of him, my backpack slung across my back. His feet fall heavily behind me. We pass the door to the bathroom, and I'm distracted out of my stupor long enough to wonder where Donovan went. I don't know much about these things, but I know that Ramsey is pretty powerful and even she can't reappear that far from her current position. That knowledge, combined with the fact that we've been at sea for a full day at least, makes me think Donovan is hiding out somewhere around here. He'll end up at Neopolis with us whether I like it or not.

The hallway twists to the left and doors line the walls. The muffled sounds of talking reveal where all my day companions have disappeared to, although I don't understand how they knew where to go. There aren't any labels on the doors we pass, and each dark wood door-front looks exactly the same. Nick seems to know though too, and he takes me almost to the hallway's dead end before swinging one of the last doors on the right open.

"This will be you for the night," Nick says, leaning against the doorframe. "I'm really sorry about earlier you know. I never meant to hurt you like that."

"I'm sure you didn't," I tell him with a sigh while walking into my room and closing the door behind me. I just don't have the emotional energy to try and deal with his feelings of guilt. All I can do is cut him off right now and see if I feel differently about him later. Sarah can have him.

Honestly, I feel worse for Sarah than I do for Nick. She

didn't know me well enough to know how her actions would affect me. Nick knew and did it anyway. But Sarah's not here, so I can't make-up with her.

The room has motion sensor lights that slowly flicker to life as I enter. It's a small room, an airplane-sized bathroom through one small door which is currently open, and a military-grade bunk set against the wall. No windows or pictures to break up the monotony here. I guess the help isn't as special as the leaders. We should just be counting our blessings that King Ryul decided to share his living space with us for so long, though I could've done without it.

I lay on the bed and wrap a scratchy grey blanket around my shoulders, head resting on the almost flat pillow. But I can't fall asleep. My mind is too busy for that. My thoughts just keep spinning in circles.

My father is here.

My father is on the sub with us.

My father exists.

I don't know what to do with this information.

There's probably not much I *can* do with that information. I'm in a confined space with King Ryul, and the last thing I want to do is give him an edge over me.

I rack my brain for the name Ramsey gave me to match the face I've now seen. *Something with a B I think. Brayden, Brandon, something like that maybe? No, no, it's Bracken!*

Bracken something. Whatever, the last name doesn't really matter. What matters is that he's here, he knows about me now, and we can make decisions on our own about what that means to us. Especially because we can't talk to each other about it. Now that I think about it, he might not even know that I know. My brain hurts just thinking about how complicated this still is.

Chapter Seventeen

The room is pitch dark without any ambient light from the hall when I sit up. Rubbing the back of my neck, I thrust the thin blanket off my legs, too hot despite the climate-controlled room. The anxiety about my father is still going strong, but now I have to think about my mom too. In just a few hours I'll get to see her again after wondering for so long what actually happened to her. I don't kid myself into thinking I'll get an opportunity to confront her, that'll have to happen in a more private setting. Still, I'll get to see her.

Washing up in the small bathroom, I pull on the few clothes I've packed. Another pair of jeans and a T-shirt, hardly the type of clothing that will make a good impression on this underground world, but I don't have much of a choice. The jeans hang loose over my hips, and I get a flush of early embarrassment. This isn't how I would've chosen to present myself to a foreign dignitary.

A knock raps at the door, and I smooth back my ponytail before swinging the door open so fast that Ramsey's knuckles hover braced for another knock.

"Yes?"

"We're there," she says, brushing off her jacket with the raised hand to avoid any embarrassment on her part. "We've been asked to meet back in the King's living quarters."

"Joy." I roll my eyes.

She gives me a sidelong smile. The wall I've been building back up is slowly crumbling. I'm too positive to hold a grudge today, especially when I know the grudge was partially unwarranted. Not that I'll ever admit that to Ramsey.

My anticipation makes the walk back take forever.

Bracken stands in the same place as yesterday, his eyes following me as I enter the room. I give him a little smile, not big enough for anyone else but him to notice, but his eyes narrow at me almost imperceptibly.

"Good of you to join us." King Ryul looks crisp in a black three-piece suit.

I plop down on the couch and give him a shrug. "Had to make sure I looked my best."

His gaze travels down my body with a smile that doesn't reach his eyes. He's more stressed than he's trying to let on. I wait for him to give me a talking-to about my outfit, but it never comes.

"We are connecting with their port now," one of the guards says to the King as the ship stops suddenly, throwing me from my seat.

My head hits the decorative table and instant blinding pain wraps around my temples. I fall back on my butt on the carpet. Bracken twitches in the corner of my eye. He shifts like he wants to come to me, but I know he doesn't dare under King Ryul's watchful gaze.

Instead, it's Nick that comes to my side. "Are you okay?"

He wraps his arms around my shoulders and pulls me to standing. I rock for a second, the pain making it hard to breathe. His fingertips graze where my head hit the table.

My cheeks redden and I wrench myself out of his grip.

Everyone else has already headed out the open door behind Ramsey's seat. This must have been the way we came in because it opens directly to the outside. I wonder briefly how something so unfortified could have been capable of keeping us safe before tossing the thought away. Magic, I remind myself. These people have magic. They don't need to worry about such trivial things as physics.

I trail behind the group with the last of the guards and Nick. I hate that I'm going to be associated with that traitor, but there's nothing I can do about it unless I want to sprint to the front of the group. I'd rather not be seen as that undignified, especially as a foreign guest. Let me clarify that, a foreign uninvited guest.

Ahead, King Ryul is already deep in conversation with a man that looks like he's just come from a costume party. Even with the small differences, I don't think turquoise bottoms would be allowed and I doubt they used tridents, but the man in front of us could easily pass for Egyptian with his white skirt with a long triangle pleat and straight black hair that comes across his shoulders.

The Egyptian's thick dark brows bunch up, creases growing deeper between them in as our group reaches his post and King Ryul won't take no for an answer. The King doesn't seem to care though about the obvious agitation our presence has caused, his body relaxed in his suit like he's having a conversation at a picnic.

King Ryul may be a jerk to me, but being king has taught him lessons I'll never understand in how to deal with people. His skills have us quickly walking past the guard before I can even reach them. The guard gives me a raised brow as I hurry past him, speaking into an intercom set in the coral arch we walk through.

My mouth drops and I'm suddenly breathless as we enter Neopolis. The city is ensconced in a bright bubble, with the ocean completely viewable through its clear wall. A school of shining silver fish flit by the city before detouring in another direction.

It's so bright down here, even though I know we're sitting on the bottom of the ocean. I'd imagined something dark and crumbling, but the bright sunshine filling the bowl fills me with wonder.

The buildings aren't quite what I thought they'd be either. Instead of the ruins of a fallen civilization, we walk through architecture that feels like I should be in ancient Egypt or even Greece even though it's brand new. The few people on the street are dressed like the person who met us off the boat with white short skirts and no shirts on the men and long pleated dresses on the women. The columns and the pyramid that I can see blend together beautifully. Egypt has always been on my bucket list, so I'm not overly disappointed, just curious as to how this could've happened.

My skin tingles as we move further into the city. There's a confidence, a peace to my movements that wasn't there before. Magic feels like it's tingling around me. The colors here are deeper than any I've ever seen before. It's like the magic keeping this place together is rushing through me, pushing its way into my blood. The men around me walk silently, their muscles tense through the thin material of their shirts. I'm too far away from the King to determine how he must feel, but I can't imagine he's immune to the anxiety everyone else is filled with.

Even Nick's shoulders slump, although his back remains straight. He's been warring with the need to be a man and feeling like a boy in a way that I almost feel bad for. He catches me staring at him and gives me a side smile and a wink. That move alone immediately puts me off from him and I keep my eyes on the city instead.

The buildings we pass have been inspired by their

surroundings, which reminds me once more that we're not in Egypt. Beautiful seahorses stand guard over the many homes we walk past, the carvings in the white stone showing immense skill and time.

I've never been to a city whose main architecture goal was beauty. In New York, there are many beautiful buildings, but no sense of cohesiveness, and many more functional buildings in between. The effect of all the similar building styles and colors has me feeling small and out of place.

We walk a mile into the city before we start to run into more people, and I can get a better feel for the city itself.

Large fountains set every fifty feet in the road fill the air with the patter of water and children running around in them as they play with leather balls, their wide smiles putting me more at ease. Tension drains from my body, leaving me feeling light even as my group moves closer together in defense. My feet move quicker, meeting up with the main group as we reach a gated wall in front of a massive white stone open-air pyramid with columns at least three stories tall.

A guard walks into my back as I stop short to crane my head up at the pyramid. Its top reaches high enough to almost puncture the bubble protecting Neopolis from the ocean. There are a few other tall structures in the city, but none of them are half as tall as the pyramid.

The guard gives me a shove to get me moving again, the gates swinging open to admit us onto the immaculately curated grounds. Under the bright blue of the bubbled sky, the green of the grass looks even more vibrant. Not a single blade is out of place as we shuffle across a white rock path towards the giant pale stone stingray spreading out over the end of the walk, the shade from it providing the only difference in color throughout the space.

"It should go without saying that you are not to speak while we're here," King Ryul's voice drifts back to me, and I know without him explicitly saying it that he's only talking to me. The rest of his group already knows the routine.

I don't think he'd appreciate me yelling back to him that I get it, so I keep my mouth closed and keeping my irritation on the inside.

We march up the steps, the hard soles of our shoes clacking against the smooth stone. We're quite a party, six guards, two teenagers, a witch, and a king. I can't imagine how King Ryul talked his way in here like this, especially without using me as a hostage. What was his bargaining chip?

There's no door to go into, we just transition from outside to inside seamlessly. The biggest difference being that instead of walking on a path with manicured grass on either side, we're now walking on a rug with straight-lined furniture on either side. Stone pillars hold up the frame of the pyramid, without walls or even glass to close off the inside of the structure.

Keeping my hands close to my sides, I follow single file behind Nick. A thin line of sweat works its way down his spine despite the perfectly moderated temperature, after all, there must be some mechanical aspect to this place to make it so bright and perfect. I should be freezing and it should be dark down here, yet I'm as comfortable as I'd be in any air-conditioned building at home.

"Ryul," a tall man says, drawing out the name as he steps into the room. "What are you doing here?"

He's a perfect inverted triangle, his shoulders almost three times as broad as his waist. I catch my mouth falling open but can't find the strength to pull it back up as he walks toward us.

"Is that all?" King Ryul asks. "You can't even pretend to be happy to see me?"

"Let's not act like we're anything that we're not. I know you wouldn't be down here if there wasn't something you needed. You'd be back on land pretending you're a king."

He crosses his hands over his bare chest and raises a brow

at King Ryul. I openly grin. Anyone who can put the King in his place is a friend of mine.

"Calm down Kai, I'm not even technically here for you," King Ryul says, collapsing into one of the very uncomfortable-looking chairs. "Plus, do I need to remind you of the power being king affords me? I know you weren't so appreciative the last time I stepped in."

Kai hides behind a look of disdain, but the muscles in his jaw flex as he grinds his teeth. "Why do I not believe you?"

Ryul crosses one leg over the other, a finger at his temple. "I don't pretend to know what goes on behind that beautiful face. So regardless of what you may believe, I'm really not here to talk to you. I wouldn't even be in your home at all if not for the necessity of my task."

"And here it comes," Kai says, voice pitched in disgust.

"I need your help. I'm looking for someone who's taken something that belongs to me. I thought you might be useful in finding her," King Ryul says, keeping his voice slow and bored despite the excitement I can only imagine growing within him.

"You can't just come down here without invitation and then make demands of me. I'm a very busy man."

King Ryul sits up. "I'm not making demands. I'm coming to you as a friend looking for a favor."

Kai scoffs. "After what you did, we're anything but friends."

The King's face tightens. "Fine. Let's not play games then."

Silence meets his statement. I shift from one foot to the other, not sure what to do with myself. The guards around me are stoic, this isn't new to them. My father gives me a sidelong glance, his lips twitching in a small smile.

"Are you going to help me or not?" King Ryul finally asks, giving up the high ground in favor of information.

Kai braces large hands on his hips. "I don't understand what you're looking for me to say here. You've given me almost no information at all. You've marched yourself right in, despite what my security attempted to tell you, and made yourself at home. We're not friends and I do not consider this to be a friendly visit."

Even *I'm* feeling the burn of that one, and I'm not sure what King Ryul will do. Even he looks a little stumped. This isn't a man used to hearing the word no, let alone get a lecture on his poor behavior.

"Kai, calm down. I'll give you information and be out of your hair in no time. You don't have to be so dramatic," King Ryul tells him with a feline smile. "We're looking for a woman named Minna. Tall, blonde, aquatic like the rest of you. She should've arrived sometime in the last three months."

Kai's elegant brow furrows. "What do you want with her?"

My heart stops.

"As I said before, she has something that belongs to me. All I want is to get it back and get out of here."

Kai's face doesn't soften, if anything it just grows more contorted. "What makes you think she has something of yours?"

"She was entrusted with something that she decided to take with her when she left the mainland," King Ryul tells him, his voice slow like he's talking to a child, something Kai doesn't fail to notice as his hands tighten on his hips.

"She has amnesty here. I don't think I have to remind you of that."

"Why else do you think I'm here?" he asks. "If it weren't for that clause, I'd be sleuthing her out myself instead of having this pleasant conversation."

Kai shakes his head. "I don't know that there's anything I can do to help you. You know the laws here. She's protected, regardless of what she did before coming."

The desire to physically back away from this argument is overwhelming, but I force my feet to stay still. Drawing attention to myself right now would not be wise.

"Are you telling me I came all this way for nothing?"

"Maybe you should call first next time," Kai tells him, a self-satisfied smile growing over his perfectly contoured face. "Would you like an escort on your way out?"

I can hear King Ryul grinding his teeth from where I stand two feet behind him. "Are you kicking us out? I didn't think you'd need another reminder of the power I wield, even here. How long did it take you to rebuild after our last visit?"

Kai's smile stretches across his face while his eyes stay narrowed at the King. "I just thought you'd like the added protection. My people really aren't used to visitors and things can sometimes get a little out of hand."

I glance behind me at the gates we came through. A group of men stand crowded around it, although none of them are trying to get in.

"I think we might just have to trespass on your hospitality a little longer," King Ryul says, causing Kai's mouth to snap into a frown. "You see, I have something of Minna's that I think she'll want. I'd hate for it to get damaged or lost on the way home."

King Ryul's eyes flit over to me, that smug smile back in place. This is a game he's played before.

Kai follows his gaze, his brows shooting up into his hairline as he slowly takes me in. His kohl-lined eyes widen the longer he looks at me. "But that's not possible!"

I don't know how he could possibly understand that she was my mother from that small interaction. It's not like we look very much alike. Nick could pass for her kid just as easily as I could. Yet, Kai's black gaze rakes over my body, exposing me in a way I haven't been even with all the other chaos in my life the last few weeks.

"I'll have some rooms made up," he finally says, making his face blank once more.

"I knew you'd see it my way." King Ryul grins while he rises to stand.

Kai snaps his fingers and two of his own guards appear in the aisle with us. I'm sure they've been here protecting Kai all this time, but their sudden appearance makes me start.

"Take this gentleman and his companions to our guest suite," Kai tells them, voice low. "Are you sure you won't just leave her with me?" he asks, turning to King Ryul but keeping his gaze on me.

"I really don't think that would be a good idea. She's rather attached to me you know," he says, the tension of his body coiled like a serpent.

It takes every ounce of willpower I have to remember what King Ryul told me earlier and not say anything. Attachment is the last feeling I use to describe to my relationship with him. Okay, maybe affection is the last feeling I'd give him with attachment a close second.

"I see. Well, in that case, you'd best make sure no harm comes to her while she remains in your possession, no matter how temporary the time frame," Kai says, and I catch the small elements of defeat in his voice.

King Ryul just smiles, the look of it wicked on his pale face. "I don't foresee that being a problem, especially now that we'll be working together."

The guards lead us away from Kai, and I glance back to see him staring at me, face unguarded and vulnerable. The sight makes my knees weak, and I quickly shift my eyes forward, keeping them on the line of sweat running down Nick's back. My stomach sits like a rock as we're led to a door that looks like the heavy stone architecture around us. Kai's guard pushes it open with little effort, the exposed muscles in his arm barely flexing, making me wonder what it's truly made of. I don't get an opportunity to touch it myself before we're whisked through the doorway and into our suite.

"Try not to get too comfortable," King Ryul tells us. "We've made our stance perfectly clear. They'll do just about anything to make sure Avi doesn't fall into the wrong hands, which puts us in a perfect position for bargaining. Great call, Ramsey."

"I'm glad you think so," she says, keeping her face turned away from me.

I blow out an exasperated sigh and march as far away from the two smug jerks as I can get.

Our group starts to spread out, and I put aside my anger long enough to be curious about exploring the little piece of the city we've been given.

King Ryul's watchful eye catches me before I get the chance to move. Immediately I pull back the hand I'd been reaching out with to caress one of the two-foot-tall decorative vases sitting on a side table. His thin lips twist into a snide smile, but I turn away from him and walk slowly through the rest of the suite.

The colors are bright and clean like a beach resort. Lots of whites, aquas, and soft corals fill my senses and soothe my nerves. Coastal Maine may not look like a tropical resort, but the beach makes me feel more at home, nonetheless.

The area of the palace we've been given is larger than my entire house back home, room after room of soft inviting beds and low couches make this place more luxurious than any retreat. I wonder which room will be mine, but don't feel up to the fight with the King to ask.

A shadow follows me through the cool rooms as I peel off from the others, trying to put a little distance between the King and me. My shadow hangs back and waits for me to acknowledge him. Regardless, my father's presence brings my stress back to the surface.

"Yes?" I ask when we're far enough removed from the others that I don't have to worry about being overheard.

He steps out from behind a white pillar, coming into the room with me. "I thought you might want to talk."

"Is there a particular topic you wanted me to talk about?" I ask with a tired smile. I know he wants to talk about our relationship, but I'm not in the mood right now to hear questions I don't have the answers to.

Bracken shrugs and slips his hands into the pockets of his dark cargo pants while taking a deep breath. "I'm your father."

"I know."

He clears his throat. "Isn't there anything you'd like to know then?"

"You could tell me what happened if you want." I pretend to clean dirt out from under my nails, the slight smile twitching at the edges of my mouth the only evidence of my enjoyment of the flipped situation.

"Your mother and I were in a relationship a long time ago. She broke things off when she decided to work for Amaro, and I never saw her again. I guess I just wanted you to know that I didn't...I didn't know about you."

I glance up with narrowed eyes. "Convenient."

"I didn't know you were possible. If I had, I would've been in your life, and now that I know about you, I'd like to be a part of your life now." He pauses and takes in my less-than-friendly pose, arms crossed over my chest, before adding, "if you'd let me."

He waits and watches me with open, clear eyes. He's waiting for a response, but I don't know what to say. I never really thought I'd get a chance to meet my father, let alone dictate his involvement in my life.

"How could you not know about me?" The question is out of my mouth before I have a chance to stop it. I know it's not fair and that pregnancy is an easy enough thing to hide when you want to, but it's something I've been wondering about, nonetheless.

Bracken's mouth pinches smaller with pain. "She never even hinted at a pregnancy, and I'd never heard of a nixie having a baby before, so I didn't know to look for any signs. Since I found out about you on that sub, I've just been reliving that last day with her over and over again, wondering if anything she said was a hint or a clue that I missed. But there's nothing I can think of. She really didn't want me to know."

My mother was a very independent woman, and I can imagine she faced the idea of having a child as her next great adventure, something she was more than happy to jump into alone. She was never big on listening to other people's opinions when it came to what to do with her life, and having a child with someone would have meant having to listen to his opinions for the rest of my childhood. The pressure must have been overwhelming.

"I'm sorry for not being there," Bracken says, pulling his hands out of his pockets and wringing them in front of his thick chest. "I know me saying that means nothing, but I really would've been involved. I'd still like to be involved."

I shake my head, loose hair coming out of my ponytail in thin wisps. "I don't really need a father right now."

"I think you might be surprised," he says to me, backing into a respectful distance as more of our group comes around the corner.

They call out to him, and Bracken gives me one last look before joining in as they walk away, an easy smile painted across his face.

My chest feels empty as I realize what he was trying to say. Without my father, I don't have anyone to watch my back, but just because he's my father doesn't mean I can trust him. Family relations mean nothing if you don't have an actual relationship.

Still, there was a genuine pain in his eyes when he asked to be involved in my life, a pain I couldn't deny even if I wanted to.

I thump down into one of the smooth stone chairs, bruising my butt against its surface. With no one left in the room, I take a moment to just sit and stare out at the exposed wall of the pyramid. There haven't been any outer walls in this place, and my room is no different. I could just walk off the edge of the room and be in the garden outside. It's both awesome and intimidating. There won't be find any real privacy here. I wonder if that's what Kai was going for in the pyramid's design.

The city sprawls out before me, dappled sunlight shining brightly against the white stone buildings. We're up just high enough that I can only see the roofs of the buildings, making me unsure which are businesses, and which are homes, with the exception of the skyrises that may not be as tall as the pyramid but are still at least ten stories high. The only reason for buildings like that that I can imagine is business, although what business they have to do here escapes me. It's not like they're doing any trade with humans or anything. I'm not sure what they have to do, or how they're surviving down here at all.

"What do you think?" Nick asks, coming around the same corner where Bracken and his friends went.

I look up, eyes hooded. "It's pretty crazy."

He sits on the chair next to me, his body laid out in strange angles as he attempts to make himself comfortable on the hard furniture. "Yeah, I don't know that anyone truly believes something like this could exist down here until they see it themselves. Kai does a good job of keeping it together, which hasn't been easy. Any water creature around would kill for the opportunity to live in this place and get away from the rest of us."

"Why is that?" I ask, leaning towards him. This is the first bit of information he's had that I truly want.

He leans back in his chair, bony shoulders pressing against the stone. "Well, wouldn't you?"

"Why would I?" I retort, not finding his coyness funny at all.

"Well, wouldn't you love to live in a place where almost everyone is like you? Wouldn't it make you feel so much more comfortable to never have to explain some of your more questionable aquatic tendencies?"

I open my mouth to contradict him before slowly closing it again. The idea of a place where I could be less confused and less guarded is appealing to me. I'd love to be able to talk to someone about how I got none of my mother or father's abilities or how I just found out I wasn't human at all and have them understand. There's no place like that for me though, not when I'm the first of my kind.

"Yeah," Nick says with a knowing smile. "Next thing you know, you'll be asking to live here too."

"I hardly think they'd want to take me," I say with a self-deprecating laugh.

"Family gets priority and they took your mom no problem," Nick reminds me.

It's true. From what I understand from her papers, they'd been seeking her out. They wanted her here, for what purpose I don't understand. Her papers aren't complete enough for that. Then again, I don't know what she can do. She's hidden it from me.

I tilt my head up as raised male voices echo against the pale stones of the pyramid. A glance at Nick shows he's listening just as intently as me. Kai and Ryul's voices are close to us, probably only the next room over.

"You can't just show up here and expect me to give you

free rein on my people! That's not how it works!" Kai's voice rings through my body.

"I already told you; I'm not expecting something for nothing. Can't you see the girl for what she is? A peace offering! A gift! You know that her mother is Minna, she can be useful to you!" King Ryul shouts back.

I shrink against the back of my seat. I may be many things, but useful is not high on my list of chosen adjectives. Nick casts me a sympathetic glance.

"So, you're going to take Minna and leave me with her untrained daughter?"

"I want nothing to do with Minna. She's a traitor to me and my people. The only thing I'm here for is the personal belonging she stole from me!" King Ryul states, calming back down.

The clack of footsteps tells me they're coming closer, even if their voices didn't give their proximity away. Nick sinks back in his seat and looks at me with wide blue eyes.

"So, let's talk about something, huh? What've you been up to? How was Ramsey's house? That place always kind of feels like a museum to me," Nick says, breathless from pushing out so many words so fast.

"I... I," I stutter, my mind not keeping up with Nick's quick plan. "It's actually pretty nice. It's quiet being away from all the commotion of Ret. I had a good time."

I'm blanking on the whole experience, which is not good for pretending we weren't just listening in on their argument. But our time is up, as the men cruise around the corner and into our living space.

"Avi," King Ryul says with a stern glance at me, his already thin lips impossibly thinner. "You're going to go with Kai now."

"I'm sorry, what?" I ask, voice sterner than I mean it to be.

King Ryul grips me by the arm, my flesh turning white

under his hand. "You *will* shut your mouth and you *will* work him or so help me I will rip your arm from its socket right now!"

I can see Nick stand up behind the King, but I don't hesitate to nod my head and accept his terms. He releases my arm and I gasp as blood begins to flow into it again.

"I'm not sure that was entirely necessary," Kai tells King Ryul with a frown, but doesn't press it when he shrugs in response.

"Come girl," Kai says, a hand extended toward me.

I stand on shaky feet and follow him from the room, Nick giving the King a death glare. King Ryul doesn't pay him any mind though, walking out in the opposite direction from where Kai drags me.

Chapter Eighteen

My mouth stays tightly pinched as we sprint through the open rooms of the pyramid palace. Kai doesn't comment on my silence and doesn't say anything to break it either. His broad shoulders knock against the side of my head as we move, but even that isn't enough to get me to speak. King Ryul's threat hangs heavy on my shoulders.

I trip over my feet as Kai leads me up a wide flight of stone stairs. The wide-open spaces of the first floor have been replaced on the second floor by thick walls, torches lit every few feet the only light. He shoulders me into a room to the right, closing the heavy door behind him. I almost laugh at what awaits me in the room, another office. Another desk, another set of chairs. All these people are the same. The only thing that changes in my life is who's sitting behind the desk.

Kai moves sideways past me, settling into the chair behind the desk and motioning for me to take the one in front of it.

"So Ryul thinks you'll be an asset for me. Thinks that you're enough of a benefit to trade whatever Minna has for you. What do you think?" his voice is deep, question serious as he stares across the stone desk at me.

When I hesitate, he folds his arms across his chest. "I'm not sure what good I could do you, sir. I'm just looking for my mom."

"I wasn't aware a nixie could have a child, were you?" He leans towards me.

"I never thought my mother was anything other than what she pretended to be."

He sighs, running a hand through hair so dark it looks like ribbons of sapphire run through it. "Despite what Ryul wants you to be, despite what you are, you're still just a child."

I want to argue with him, insist on my grownup-ness, but he's right. No matter how prepared I may feel for regular life, what I've been exposed to in the last month goes above and beyond anything I ever thought I'd have to deal with. In his eyes, I really am a child. How could I think of myself as anything else as I continually fight to find my mother?

"So what do I do with you now?" he mumbles to himself, dark eyes still boring into mine. "You sure you don't have any of Minna's particular... strengths?"

"Positive."

Ignoring the pain of my heart falling in that statement, I meet his eyes with a relaxed breath. The only thing I've been able to learn so far is how to keep calm. It doesn't matter how I feel about any of this. I must keep myself together.

"Well then, there's not much we can do." He stands, grabbing me by the arm and maneuvering me back out the door and down the stairs.

Picking up the pace until we're almost running, I try to keep up with him. My sneakers smacking against the floor, the sound like a storm in this quiet palace. Kai halts and I'm almost flung onto the floor with the abrupt stop. Picking myself back up after the stumble, I finally investigate the room we've landed in. The colors and style are exactly the same as everywhere else in the pyramid, but there's one thing this room has that the other's haven't.

"Avi?" My mother's voice is soft and disbelieving from where she sits on a flat bench under a glassless window.

For a second, I can't feel my feet. My breath stops coming to my lungs. And then everything floods back and I'm forcing myself not to cry.

"Mom!" I throw myself against her legs, needing to physically feel her myself.

She's warm and firm against my face, and so comfortingly real that tears begin to well in my eyes. Her arms wrap around me, but her face is still directed at Kai.

"What's she doing here? You said she'd be safe!" she accuses him while running a hand through my hair.

"When I told you that I had no idea you were going to bring something with you that would stir everyone up. Do you have any idea what you've done?" Kai asks her, brows creased. "Surely whatever you did before you left you did knowing it was going to cause a mess that your daughter would have to clean up."

Mom's hand stills on my head, her body growing hard under me. "What are you implying?"

"Minna, I'm only saying that perhaps you may have brought this upon yourself." Kai's tone is unapologetic, and my mother pushes me away from her feet to stand and face him.

"You," she says with a pointed finger. "Have no right to talk to me about the consequences of actions. I wouldn't even be here if not for you!"

Kai braces his large hands against his tanned, narrow hips. "You had to make the choice to come here. No one forced you."

Mom laughs. "Yeah, no one forced me. You mean you didn't pressure me for years and years and draw me out multiple times until I felt like the safest option for my daughter was for me to come here after all?"

"I'm not doing this with you right now." Kai waves away her complaint. "Enjoy your reunion."

His flat sandals slap against the ground as he leaves us, my mother standing with shoulders tensed. I stay frozen to my place on the ground, not sure what I should do as I look up at her.

Time has always stood still for my mom. Her long blonde locks are as pale and golden as ever, her waist slender and fragile. Even with our hair color matching, we don't look alike, something that always bothered me before but doesn't now that I understand her unique origins. I can hardly hold her species against her.

She rolls her shoulders back and turns around to face me, finally remembering I'm there. "I never thought I'd see you here, Avi."

"I never thought I'd be here." I try not to bristle at her clipped tone.

"Don't look at me like that," she says; my brows bunched despite my best efforts to appear relaxed.

She hunches down next to where I'm sitting on the floor, her ocean blue eyes slanted with concern. "I really never meant to leave you."

"Or steal my memories?" I snap.

Mom flinches back, pulling her outstretched hand back with her. "How did you find out about that?"

She doesn't even try to defend herself.

"A lot has happened since you left," I tell her, crossing my arms as I become more and more defensive even as I try to remember that this is not the way I wanted our first conversation to go. "I've been passed around a lot. You tend to find out all the family secrets that way."

Her eyes narrow almost imperceptibly, but I've known her

too long for even that small change to go unnoticed. "What do you mean?"

"I'm pretty sure I'm the one that should be asking the questions now. You gave up that right when you left me with some stranger!" My voice squeaks as it reaches such a high decibel.

"Nina isn't a stranger!" Mom yells back, mouth screwed tight. "She's your sister," she finishes quietly.

"My sister? But how is that possible? They told me I was the only one like me, that a nixie had never been known to give birth..." my voice trails off as I keep thinking it over.

Mom grips her hands in mine, the palms smoothing my ragged nerves. "She's been a secret, just like you. I never intended for anyone to know about you two. You were my special secrets, something for only me to know about. That's why I took you to Maine. It was safer for us there. Your sister was grown though, she was having her own adventures."

"Why didn't you tell me about her? Didn't I have a right to know about my own family?" My mind swirls with all the new information and I don't know where to focus first. "Especially if you're going to just dump me with her. I mean you called her my aunt. Don't you think that's a little damaging?"

"I'd love to talk more about this, I really would," she adds seeing my look of disbelief. "But we've got to get going right now."

She stands up and grabs my hand, wrenching me up with her. Her legs are wrapped in the white pleats of her eerily Egyptian getup, matching Kai and the whole aesthetic of the place perfectly as she pulls me through the open window.

* * *

We sprint across the perfect grass towards the front gate, her breath even and smooth next to my haggard hacking. I thought I was in pretty good shape, but the last few weeks have reminded me that there's always room for improvement. That or my Mom is just incredible, which I wouldn't put past her either.

We reach the white pebbles of the walkway, but she doesn't slow down. Rocks fly under our feet as she urges me toward the gates. The guard waiting there braces himself, a trident held across his chest as he watches us approach.

"Let us through," Mom calls out with a voice of authority.

He blinks slowly but pushes the gates open in jerky movements. We fly by him, and I only have a moment to take in his startled gaze before we're out of sight.

"Where are we going?" I gasp as she pulls me down a zigzagging side street, blonde hair flying behind her.

"It's not safe for us in the palace if King Ryul is here," she says, not slowing in her progress.

I jerk her arm for her to slow down. "What are you talking about? Just give him the Trident and then we'll be safe."

At the mention of the Trident, she stops, and I run into her back. Her footing is solid enough that I barely budge her.

She turns to face me, green eyes wide under golden brows. "You have no idea what you're talking about."

Grabbing my hand, she leads us through a narrow alleyway, the bones in my hand protesting her rough treatment. She raps on one of the doors, waits a second and then lets herself in, my limp form trailing behind her.

"Minna?" the person on the other side asks softly as she closes the door behind us.

"Sorry to barge in on you like this," Mom says, pushing me through the room and onto a sinking couch. "But it's time. He knows."

I hear a match strike, and suddenly the face of our host is illuminated. A woman looking very much like my mother lights the lamp on the table in the middle of the room, sweeping blonde hair aside as she does. This quick movement reveals deep gouges running down her cheeks, the flesh there the dull pink of a scar.

I barely remember to close my mouth before she turns to look at me, waving a short knife in my general direction. "What's she doing here then?"

My hand is still firmly grasped in hers, fingers starting to lose feeling at the tips. "She's my daughter."

"Your-your daughter?" the woman gasps, the knife almost falling out of her hand before she gets herself together. "How is that possible?"

Mom just shrugs her slim dancer's shoulders. "I couldn't explain it to you even if I knew."

I glance up at Mom in surprise. I guess I just always assumed that she knew what had happened, how she'd been able to have me, and Nina I guess, even though her kind don't reproduce. It occurs to me in that moment that there could be more of us. How many more siblings could I possibly have out there that she hasn't told me about because she hasn't been caught in her deception yet?

"Well, that *is* something then," the woman says, sinking into the chair opposite us.

This room has none of the glamor of the palace, none of the clean-lined simplicity of the rest of the city. In fact, the furniture we're sitting on looks much more like pieces I would find in the dump than I would in any of the rest of the themed city. I mean faded maroon paisley doesn't exactly go with the rest of the beachy feel.

"So, you said he knows then?" the woman asks my mother, completely dismissing me now that she knows who I am. "He knows the Trident is here?"

Mom nods vigorously, loosening her hair from where she's stashed it behind her ears. "He arrived just this morning and brought her with him. It's a lucky thing I was already in the palace, or I don't know what they would have done with her to draw me out."

Yeah, lucky, I want to scoff. I'm sure it wasn't a coincidence. King Ryul had very clearly studied all the clues my mother had left to her whereabouts, I'm sure he knew she was staying in the palace.

"What are you going to do?"

"I've got to take it away from here. I can't risk Ret getting it," my Mom says, releasing my hand to wring her own.

"Or Amaro," I pipe in helpfully.

Mom glances down at me sharply. "Amaro? What would you know about Amaro?"

I open my mouth to respond, all the different ways I could hurt her with the knowledge of my kidnapping swirling together, when I'm cut off by someone else's interjection.

"Amaro has been interested in you, too," Donovan's voice says, stepping out of the darkness of the corner of the room. He steps forward so the light can reflect off his dark eyes. "Did you think they'd leave her alone when you left?"

Mom's mouth hangs open, but she doesn't try to correct him.

"Ret was right there for her the second you left. Amaro was only behind because you hadn't told me you were leaving," he says, brows pulled down over his eyes. "You can only imagine how happy they were with me about that one."

"How did you get here?" she asks, our host brandishing her knife once more.

Donovan laughs. "The same way everyone else did, by sub."

"Did you know he was here?" Mom asks, turning her accusatory eye on me.

"He made me aware of his presence on the ship. I didn't realize he'd followed me here though."

Donovan steps closer to us. "Just keep her out of this. You

left her so unaware of everything and I've been doing my best to protect her from the mess you left behind. I don't know what you thought you were doing when you wiped her mind. Did you really think that would keep Ret and Amaro from coming after her?"

Mom's jaw screws tight during Donovan's onslaught.

"She was never safe without you. If it wasn't for me, she'd probably be dead by now."

This last jab has my mom leaping off the couch. "What do you know about any of this? You're just a boy."

"A boy that knows where his priorities lie," Donovan says, crossing his arms over his chest.

Mom walks up to him and slaps him across the face, his head jerking to the side from the force of her blow. "Don't talk to me like you understand any of this. Everything I've done, I've done for her. Maybe someday you'll understand that."

She sits back down beside me, but I don't let her get as close as she was before. Donovan glares at her, Mom's handprint outlined in red on his cheek.

"Will everyone just try to calm down?" Our host puts her knife back in the loop of her pants. "I think we're all after the same goal, so just try keep that in mind and *calm down*."

Mom clamps her jaw, the muscles down her throat clenched tight. She doesn't want to play nice, and she doesn't care who knows it.

"She's right," Donovan concedes, sitting on the dusty floor and staring up at my mother in what I'm assuming he thinks is a demure way. "We should be trying to work together, not fighting each other. I'd hate to see the Trident in Ret's hands."

"I'm sure you would," Mom mutters under her breath and I have to work hard to fight the urge to elbow her in the side.

"You're thinking it's time to leave Neopolis?" our host asks Mom, making my heart sink. I've only just gotten here, I'm not ready to go back to the constant back and forth and confusion that happens when I'm on land. "Are you sure that's wise?"

"Yeah, leaving might just make Ret more suspicious. I'm sure they're already watching the docks," Donovan points out, leaving Mom a tangled mass of tension.

She opens her mouth to shut him down, but I place a hand on her arm. "Don't say no to it just because he suggested it. I don't think he's out to get us."

"As your friend has so forcefully pointed out, I can't trust what you think because you have no basis for your opinion," Mom says with a forced smile at Donovan which comes out looking more like a sneer.

Donovan crosses his arms. "You don't have to belittle her."

Mom hisses at him, revealing pointed teeth. Her eyes are more slanted too, the pupils elongated. She's transforming before my eyes, her fingers becoming webbed as she loses control of her anger.

Her friend notices and grabs her arms, kneeling between her legs. "Calm down Minna. You both want the same thing. Just breathe."

Releasing Mom's arms, her friend grabs both sides of her face, forcing her to look into her eyes instead of at Donovan. Mom's shoulders go slack, her breathing loose as she relaxes, and the burgeoning nixie changes slinks back into my mother's skin. I scooch farther away from her on the couch, pulse racing.

Mom pulls herself away from the other woman, eyes wide as she sees the distance between us.

"Avi," she calls to me, arms outstretched. But my body is firmly planted where it is and I'm not sure I'm ready to be any closer to her.

Her hand collapses into her lap and her body seems to fold into itself. "I'm sorry Avi."

"I know." My voice is sad and small. This is all too new to

me. I don't know how to act around my mother like this, but at the very least I do know that she isn't trying to hurt me. No matter what she's done in the past, she didn't do it to purposefully hurt me.

"If you don't think they should leave, what do you suggest?" our host asks, functioning as a much-needed mediator.

Donovan shrugs. "I'm not really sure. I'd say we should just lie low and wait for them to leave, but Neopolis isn't very big. It wouldn't take them long to comb over the city and find us."

"Exactly why I said we should go," Mom says, crossing her hands over her narrow chest. "Staying here is too dangerous when Ryul can just flush us out of wherever we're hiding."

"Surely there's somewhere secure here we could hide. Every city has its hidey-holes, Neopolis can't be that different," I point out, leaning forward over my knees.

Mom just laughs. "You'd think that because you know nothing of the history of Neopolis—"

"Wonder who's fault that is," Donovan interrupts. I wave a hand to shut him up so she'll continue.

"Neopolis was made by our people for our people. We saw no need to create places to hide because Neopolis itself should be enough. Consequently, what you see is what you get here. There is no lower level, no seedy underbelly, just a beautiful city thriving under the sea," she says, ignoring Donovan completely.

"I'm sure that's how it started, but that's how most places start. No one builds their home with the idea that they'll need to hide from it later, but that's usually what happens. I'm sure Neopolis has a place where people who don't fit in can hide," I press.

"If you don't fit in, then you're asked to leave," our host says, voice sad as pale hair covers her face.

Donovan sits up. "All the more reason for Avi to be right. If you're afraid you'll be kicked out of the only home you've ever known just for being different, wouldn't you find somewhere to hide instead?"

A light gleams in Mom's eye. "You might be right."

"I've heard rumors of a spot by the docks, but I'm not sure it's used for what you're wanting it for," her friend tries to argue, but Mom isn't listening to her anymore.

"Where should we start looking first?" she asks Donovan, their mutual dislike for Ret finally bringing them together as the gears in her head turn.

"I'd start by one of the larger docks," Donovan tells her, a finger rubbing through the stubble on his chin. "People like that will want to make sure they have a second option, an easy out if things don't pan out the way they're hoping."

"Let's go then," Mom says, slapping her leg and standing. "We'll have to move quickly."

Chapter Nineteen

Mom leads the way out the door, the artificial sunlight blinding me temporarily. Donovan grabs my hand to guide me out, closing the door behind us. Mom sets a grueling pace, even Donovan breathing heavy as he tries to keep up with her.

The back streets she leads us down wind around haphazardly, feeling more like an old city back home than one more recently built. Even the alleyways are too small for a new city, the buildings leaning over us to the point where I can barely see the ocean sky anymore. I mean to ask Mom when Neopolis was built but am distracted by the dock coming into my eye line.

It rises out of the ground, a huge arch made of brilliantly colored corals haloing a swirling mass of water that hangs in place for no visible reason.

My mouth drops and I have no intention of trying to pull it closed. Everywhere I look there's something new. Stalls are set up along the side of the road selling exotic wares, the people shouting in languages I've never heard of before. The brightly colored flags flutter in the breeze coming from the sea 'hole' and the heavy smells of cooking meats fill the dockside.

Tunnel vision takes over as I don't know what to do or where to look first.

Donovan keeps a tight grip on me, not letting me wander away from his watchful eye. I'm grateful for his attention because Mom hasn't stopped to look back at me once. I try not to let her disregard hurt me, but the sting spreads across my heart all the same.

"Keep close to me," Donovan whispers in my ear, sending shivers down my spine in my already overly sensitized state. He returns the pressure as my hand squeezes his, making me grin even wider.

We press through the crowd of people, my eyes widening at all the people we pass. There are people like my mother and her friend, tall, thin, blond, and beautiful. Then there are others whose dripping and sodden appearance leave me wondering if they truly left the sea behind when they entered Neopolis' dock.

"Try not to stare," Donovan admonishes in my ear when I can't drag my eyes away from a man that has what looks like a large octopus growing out of his head, the tendrils hanging down his face like hair.

"Have you been here before?" I ask him, breathless with the excitement of this place.

He gives me a sidelong glance. "Of course not. Only water folk are welcome here. Why do you think King Ryul's presence was taken so poorly?"

"There were some threats exchanged, and he hinted at a history between them that sounded pretty violent, but honestly I assumed it was just because he's Ryul," I say with a laugh which Donovan is good enough to return. My chest is lighter here in the revelry of market day.

I want to ask him more, but suddenly he's jerking me along, my mother's back lost in the swarming crowd of people. Sweat beads the skin between our hands and I can't tell if it's

Donovan's or mine. I try to peer through the press of creatures, but I still can't catch a glimpse of Mom.

"She wouldn't leave us behind, would she?" I shout to Donovan to be heard over the hawkers selling some form of pink sea-dollar next to us.

He shakes his head, biting his lip. "I'd like to think she wouldn't, but nixies aren't exactly known for being nurturing."

Hardly their fault if they can't have children. I mean really, Donovan thinking she wouldn't come back for me just because they don't have a history of being loving mothers because they *can't* actually be mothers is absurd.

"There she is," he breathes after a long pause, pulling me diagonally through the crowd that moves like a tide around us.

I'm stretched to the point where I wonder if my arm will come off altogether when we finally pop free next to the outer wall of a market building. Mom leans casually against the wall with a wild smile spreading across her face.

"What took you so long?" Her blue eyes glitter as she looks for all the world like a little girl leading a game of hide and go seek.

"I was worried you'd left without us," Donovan says, brows drawn in admonishment.

"You maybe, but Avi never," Mom says without even a hint that she could feel bad for her comment.

Donovan just brushes her off, this isn't new then, the good-natured animosity between them. I wonder if this is what they used to be like before Mom left us and wiped my memories. Breathing deep a few times, I try to clear my mind before those thoughts can poison it again.

"So here we are," Mom says to Donovan. "Where's the seedy underbelly of Neopolis?"

She throws her arms wide, and he frowns. This isn't going to be as easy as I thought it would.

"Can't we just ask someone?" I ask, flushing when they look at me like I'm crazy.

"Sounds like a great way to get some negative attention. I don't think King Ryul would notice us at all then, would he?" Donovan asks sarcastically, making me blush even more.

"It was just an idea," I mutter, but he isn't listening to me.

Something in the alley next to us has grabbed his attention, and Mom presses flat against the wall as she tries to hear what he's picking up.

"I think we might be in luck after all," Donovan says to me with a sly smile.

I'm safely cocooned between the two of them for a moment, their heads almost a foot taller than mine to give the real illusion of protection. I sigh in contentment before it's all over and Donovan drags me around the corner while Mom follows.

"Something going on over here?" Donovan asks the two dripping men huddled in the back of the dead-end alley next to us.

They look up at him with disgust and I notice with shock that one of the men has a large muscle growing out of his cheek. "What do you want land man? You're not even supposed to be allowed down here."

"I just heard you whispering and thought you might be able to help out my friend," he nods to me, but their eyes stray to Mom and stay there, so typical.

"We might be able to help you, for something in return of course," the muscled one's friend says, spittle drooling out the side of his mouth as his eyes stay glued on Mom.

"Of course, of course. I wouldn't try to swindle you guys, we're friends, right?" Donovan tells them with an easy smile. He's really in his element now. "I heard you have somewhere to hide out. Well, these ladies and I are looking for somewhere to hide. Just for a few days, mind you."

"I think we could work that out for the right payment," muscle face says to Donovan while leering at my mother.

Donovan pushes his shoulders back, looking more like the man I first ran into in Nina's apartment than ever before. "What were you thinking?"

The man next to muscle face laughs, receiving an elbow in the gut from his friend. "I think you have a good idea of what we're looking for."

"Then you should know that we're not interested," Mom snaps from behind him, her forehead creased in a frown.

"I wouldn't be so quick to turn us down. You don't know when another opportunity like this could turn up," muscle face says with an ugly smile, cracked teeth jutting out behind his lips.

Donovan flicks something off his jacket. "I wouldn't be so quick to ask for that from this one. You realize she's a nixie, right?"

"Never been with a nixie before," muscle face's friend comments, drool dripping down his chin.

"There's a reason for that," his friend says with a groan. "Fine. What do you have to offer then?"

I'm pulling a blank at this point, terror creeping up to fill the space. We don't have anything. Even my backpack was left behind in the pyramid when Mom dragged me away. I have nothing valuable here, not that I've ever had much regardless.

"How about this?" Donovan pulls a large silver ring from his finger. I've never noticed it before, but it looks heavy as he holds it in his palm. "Should be good for something right?"

"We could melt that down into something useful I betcha," muscle face's friend says, Donovan's eyes narrowing slightly at his belonging being destroyed.

"We'll take it," muscle face says, grabbing it out of Donovan's palm with a grubby little hand. "Follow me."

He walks farther into the back of the alley, and I'm

confused. There's nowhere for us to go back here. His coat makes a wet slap against the side of a rusty trashcan sitting against the side of the wall as he leans over and without warning, disappears.

I start as his friend gives us one more wet smile before following him, leaving behind only the lingering smell of rotten fish.

"Well," Mom says. "Here we go!"

She leaps around Donovan and into the space where the other man disappeared. I follow her, coming around just enough to see the crack in the foundation of the building where my companions have gone. Donovan brings up the rear as I crawl through the jagged hole after my mom.

* * *

The tunnel is dark and damp. I try not to think about the muck my hands sink into as I follow the shuffling sounds into complete darkness. Donovan grabs my ankle as he follows, reassuring me that he hasn't just left us behind.

We crawl along for ten minutes before arriving at our hidden destination. A slow light blooms over us before we're thrust out of the tunnel into a large space the size of a stadium. I stagger back as the salt and fish smell of our new friends increases and the light blinds me. When I can finally see again, we're surrounded by people. The cavern is huge, loud, and completely overwhelming as a continuation of the market from the dock continues around us in a confined space.

I back into Donovan who's also trying to get his bearing. "Some sort of spell I'd guess," he mutters to himself.

That would explain the lack of sound in the tunnel. I never would've assumed this is what would be waiting for us after the dank, dark, silence of the trip here.

Mom finishes taking in her bearings and thanks the men who brought us here, their backs disappearing into the crowd.

"So," she says. "What now?"

"I guess we just wait it out." Donovan keeps his attention focused on watching over the press of people around us.

It's like I'm in a smellier, darker version of the street we just left, and I realize Donovan was right. There *is* a seedy underbelly here of people trying not to be sent back into the real world.

Staring out over the commotion, the place is filled with creatures, very few of them looking completely human like us. The more I see, the more concerned I grow that our humanoid appearance will give us up and have them kicking us out before King Ryul can even begin to search for us.

"Let's hunker down here," Donovan says like he's reading my mind, his eyes also following the people in the market.

The area next to the tunnel is filled with a stack of crates, and it's partially behind these that Donovan decides to make our home. We're still part of the crowd but covered just enough to give us the semblance of privacy and safety.

"It's going to be a long few days," Mom mutters petulantly, her bottom lip poking out like a child. "Maybe I'll just explore a little bit."

I look up at her wide eyed, but Donovan just waves her away, Mom's long blue skirts swishing through the crowd before he can even put his hand back in his lap.

"Are you wanting to explore too?" His voice is slow, and his eyes are tired.

I shake my head. "I'll just wait here with you."

"That's my baby," he says with a small smile, leaning his head against the moist brick of the wall behind us.

"What *is* this place?" I'm still stunned that such a large hiding place could exist under Kai's nose.

He closes his eyes. "Probably just someone trying to

expand on the city. Although they're not doing a very good job."

The back of his head is completely soaked from its contact with the wall. The ocean must still be trying to get in. I think about the dock with the water 'hole' in it and shake my head. It's just copycat work here.

"Are we really just going to hang out here for days?" I wonder how boring it will get sitting here.... just waiting.

He leans further against the wall, his whole back making contact. "I think it's probably the best idea for us right now. I can't see us getting into much trouble if we just stay here."

As if his words directly tempted fate, the other side of the room erupts in enormous applause. My eyes strain as I push them to their limit to see exactly what's going on. Donovan has already leapt from his position on the wall and grabbed me by the wrist, ready to drag me off into who knows where. He stills after a moment, his face peering towards the commotion, and I glance up at him to figure out what's changed in the last two seconds.

"Good grief," he says under his breath. "There goes that plan."

I wrench my gaze to the front of the cavern and make out what's caused his distress. Some sort of wooden stage is set up back there, and my mother has climbed up and is currently performing something. She might be singing, but I can't hear anything from here, I can only see her hips gyrating and her smooth belly twisting in a very distracting dance which has very understandably garnered a lot of attention from the men down here. Just thinking about the two guys who brought us here watching her has me pushing through the crowd before Donovan can stop me.

He doesn't loosen his hold on my wrist, so whether he likes it or not, he's dragged after me through the throng of moist and half wild looking water creatures.

It takes several minutes for me to make my way to the stage. Donovan shouts something to me from behind, but I don't focus on him long enough to make out what he's saying. Honestly, I'm just glad he hasn't let go and left me to tackle this problem on my own. He totally could've if he wanted. Then again after everything we've been through, that doesn't seem to be his way.

I'm so intent on pushing my way through that I don't notice I've made it until I'm thrust upon the rotting wood, palms sinking into the spongy material. Guess I won't have to worry about getting splinters.

"Mom!" I shout, but she doesn't acknowledge me. "Mom! What are you doing?!"

She looks down with slanted eyes and gives me a side smile but doesn't stop her dancing.

"Girl!" the man next to me yells. "If you're going to be here, you'd better join her." With a massive heave of his thick arms, I'm lifted onto the stage, leaving Donovan behind on the ground.

"Mom, what are you doing up here?" I stumble to my feet and reach out to her just a foot away. "I thought you were just going to explore."

"I've got something for her to explore," the man on the floor says to the buddy next to him, his hands vanishing to grab something that I try not to notice.

"Knock it off," Donovan tells him with a shove.

The nasty man takes it as an invitation to punch him in the face, fist landing squarely in the middle of Donovan's nose. They struggle together briefly before other men around them join in, blood spatters flying through the air as my mouth fills with the taste of copper.

"Mom." I come up in front of her, grasping her face between my hands. "We need to get out of here. It isn't safe anymore."

I can't help but be annoyed as I realize how true this statement is. We've been here barely twenty minutes and now we'll have to find somewhere else to hide. She's acting like a child.

Her movements still. "Why do we have to leave?"

"You've caused a scene." I wave my arms to highlight the fighting going on behind me. "It won't take Ryul long to find us if anyone here talks to someone in the main city."

She pouts, her bottom lip sticking out at least an inch from her face. I don't know how she does it, but she still manages to look good through everything.

"Come on." I grab her arm and lead her off the stage, effectively taking the decision from her.

The only memories I have of my mom are from a little girl's perspective. So it's hard to admit just how disappointed I am in her from this point of view. I really thought she would take care of me, that all I had to do was find her and then everything would be fine. That it'd be like when we were home, but now we're together and it's the other way around. I can't even imagine how she managed on her own for so long without someone to protect her from herself. How useful can she really be to Kai like this?

I cut that thought off before it can really grow. I don't want to think about what made Kai feel the need to drag her down here.

Reaching the bottom of the rotted steps, I keep my hand wrapped firmly around her arm as I move us closer to the wall and out of the main melee of fighters. I don't know where Donovan is, and I'm not interested in getting involved in that mess to find him. Instead, I keep us as close to the wall as I can and start working our way back to the tunnel we first came in through. We only have to dodge a few errant blows before we're out of the thick of it.

I'm just getting to our pallet stack temporary home when Donovan meets up with us. He looks pretty bad, the bottom half of his face stained red from the blood pouring out of what is undoubtedly a broken nose.

"I would've thought you were a better fighter than that." My voice is filled with honest surprise. I wouldn't have thought the fight would work out in his favor after the tough guy front I've had to deal with.

He shrugs, face split in a wide grin that reveals pink teeth and I shudder. "You can't really judge me from a fight like that. I barely knew who I was fighting after the first few punches."

I give him a shove in the arm and he just laughs. Mom watches us with narrowed eyes. Her lips purse and I know she wants to say something but instead she turns away. Glancing back at Donovan, I find him watching me, gaze serious under furrowed brows.

"I guess we should go," he finally says, bowing us through the dripping tunnel.

Mom gives him a stern look before crawling through with me right on her heels. Immediately we're ensconced in darkness, the only sound coming from the water dripping around us. I hear Donovan enter the tunnel behind me, one hand giving me a comforting caress against my ankle that lingers just a little too long for politeness.

My mind drifts as we crawl through the tunnel and I wonder what will happen between Donovan and me. There's a connection there. I felt it that day we drove down the coast. Do I care though? He just further represents all the confusing conflicts in my life that I'd rather just forget.

I'm so lost in these thoughts that I don't notice my mother being yanked out of the mouth of the tunnel until I'm being lifted out myself. Hauled to my feet, I stand with Mom, surrounded by guards from Kai's palace, their bare chests gleaming as they block our progress. I stumble towards the tunnel, my back hitting the guard who's moved to block my exit.

"I thought you weren't going to interfere with my work here," King Ryul's voice cuts through the wall of muscle. One of the men moves aside for him to come through, his normally attractive face screwed up. "And look what I have here."

My arms twist behind my back, as one of the meat-headed guards cuffs my wrists together.

"What're you doing?" My back is contorted from the mistreatment.

"Making sure we don't run into any more problems with you," King Ryul says, dismissing me before he turns to Mom. "But what do we do with you, Minna?"

She doesn't even look at him, her body still turned towards me. "Don't listen to them," she tells me with a voice full of venom.

"Don't listen to them?" King Ryul repeats, tone mocking as he stares at my mother with a wry smile. "What do you think I'll say that she shouldn't listen to? Maybe that you were going to start working with me? Maybe that my people helped to put the potion together that stripped your only daughter of her memories? How about the fact that we got her set up in New York for you after you promised to work for us and bring the Trident with you.

"Imagine my surprise when Avi shows up as planned but with no Minna and no Trident. We observed the girl for a few months, making sure she had a friend from us she could confide in, but still no Trident. In fact, Nick tells us she doesn't know anything, not even what you are, which was not our agreement when we discussed developing the potion."

He pauses here and the silence stretches out tensely between us. I wish I could say this was surprising, but, thanks to Ramsey this one at least, hasn't blindsided me. Someday Mom and I will have time to work everything out.

Looking over, I try to catch her eye, but her head is low, gaze glued to the slick cobblestones under her feet. After everything I've been through, I still would've liked for her to try and protect me. Maybe she's hoping I'm still 'not listening.'

"So, now that we have that out of the way, get her out of here." King Ryul gestures to the guards and they haul me off my feet, pulling at the skin on my arms as I struggle to get out of their grip, and they strong-arm me out of the alley.

I'm able to twist my body around just enough to see Mom one more time before the alley leaves my view. One glance is all it takes to see King Ryul slap her across the face, head wrenching to the side.

I start screaming without knowing what I'm hoping it will accomplish. One long ghoulish howl pours out of me until one of the men carrying me uses a hand to slap me across the mouth, the coppery taste of blood spreading where my teeth cut my lip.

"Shut up," he says, voice pitched low in the diminished crowd of the market. "Kai and King Ryul are working together. No one's going to do anything to help you."

The shock from the slap is still working its way through me, but it's done its intended job. My scream is abruptly shut off, my body slumping over in their grip. It's only when the pyramid comes back into view that I realize with a start that they never got Donovan. He must have been more with it than I was and stayed back in the tunnel.

My mouth tightens into a firm line as I try to work out how his freedom could work in my favor, but I can't think of anything. I have no way to get in touch with him, no way to tell him how to find me, and no way to find out what's going on.

The guards march me around the side of the palace, not going up the grand front steps King Ryul brought us through earlier. The back of the palace has a door set into one of the pillars, and it's through this door that the men drag me. They march me down a cramped spiral staircase, necessity making the guards put me down as their shoulders scrape against the rough stones.

It's dark in here, only a few torches set into the pale stone walls, and I'm left feeling colder than I probably should. Logically, I know the temperature can't be that different, but despite that, my skin breaks out in a string of goosebumps.

Quiet in here after the crowds of the marketplace, only my scuffling steps break the silence. The guards say nothing to me or to each other, they know where we're going and that must be good enough for them.

When we reach the bottom of the staircase it's almost pitch black. I can't even see my feet when I look down anymore. Undeterred my muscled escorts keep right on moving until one of them lights a candle, illuminating the small dark room we've entered.

A metal chair sits in the middle of the room, and it's here they deposit me, wrapping my wrists in chains connected to the chair itself. The cold metal burns into my skin and I strain against my restraints to keep the links off my body. Even in the little light, I can see the red marks spreading across my wrists where the chains have touched me. A shocked sob spreads up my throat, but I keep it tamped down.

Standing opposite me, arms folded, the guards don't even bother trying to make eye contact with me. Instead, their bodies stand at attention while their eyes sink into relaxed faces. The clang of a door swinging open against the cool stones has them straightening up a little more, and I hear my mom's voice as she's carried down the stairs.

"You can't do this! I'm a citizen here! You can't just haul me off like I have no rights!"

One guard smiles at the other and I slump against the chains. Somehow, I still believed my mom would take care of everything.

Mom at least had the luxury of having someone carrying a

torch as they descended, the light flaring into view as they come around the last twist and enter our little dungeon.

"Avi?" she cries, collapsing in the arms of the guard carrying her when she sees me. "What's she doing here?"

No one answers her. Not surprising since I haven't heard one of them say a single word the entire day I've been here. She's held up, arms suspended behind her as the remaining guards file in.

"Avi baby, it's going to be alright. Just let me handle every-thing," she says, eyes pleading with me.

I shrug, not saying anything else. My mind whirls. What could we be waiting for and how long will we have to wait? What is there even for her to handle right now? Selfishly, I'm just glad I got a chair, and I don't have to stand like she does.

The soft pad of feet against the tile would've been easily missed were it not for the oppressive silence filling the room. So it's no surprise when King Ryul comes around the corner, his face far more relaxed since our last encounter in the alley. In fact, I might even dare to say he's wearing a slight smile when he looks down on us over his thin nose.

"So good of you to join me," he says, and now I know he's smiling. His face cracks with it, his teeth shining too whitely in the light of the torches. "Now, let's get started."

He turns to Mom. "Where's the Trident?"

In the most unladylike thing, I've ever seen Mom do, which is actually saying a lot despite our nearly hippie lifestyle, she hacks a wad of spit into his face. I sit shocked as I gaze at the green slimy wad as it trails down between his eyes along the bridge of his nose.

"It's going to be like that is it?" His voice is deathly quiet as he pulls out a handkerchief and wipes the offending material off his face. He meets the eye of one of my guards, waving his hand at him.

I'm so busy watching King Ryul that I miss it when the

guard steps closer to me and delivers a well-aimed punch at my cheekbone. Knocked back, I'm breathless as dark spots flitter across my vision. My mouth gapes like a fish while Mom screams.

"Don't you touch her! She has nothing to do with this! Hit me!"

King Ryul just smiles, his lips thin as they stretch over his teeth. "Where is the Trident?"

Mom doesn't say anything, panicked eyes going from him to me and back again. Mumbling under her breath, I watch as King Ryul loses his patience and waves to my guard again. My hands pull against their chains as he rears up to punches me again. My body braces for the impact this time as my heart beats raggedly. I take a deep breath and the air moves in the room like the wind off the sea. I close my eyes, letting the salt wash over my skin. The punch lands, but I don't feel it.

As the numbness subsides, I'm hit with the burning pain from the double impact, my chest moving in shallow breaths as I try to clear my vision. Already, I know that if I touch the spot still tingling on my face, I'll feel swelling. The skin under my eye begins to well up enough that I can see it without having to look down. Tears run down my face as the guard turns toward me again.

I want to look at my mom. I want someone to comfort me and make it okay. But there's no comfort here, no hope. Mom only makes things worse. I'm alone here. It's only me and the promise of more pain.

"Where is the Trident, Minna?" King Ryul asks again. "Let's move on to somewhere else," he says to the guard when she doesn't respond.

The guard lifts one of my fingers away from where I've clamped it against the arm of the chair. Groans whisper past my clenched teeth as he continues to bend the finger back toward my wrist. I make eye contact with Mom, triggering her breaking point.

"Stop! I'll tell you!" she says, legs completely giving out as she hangs suspended by the guard's white-knuckle grip on her armpits. "Just leave her alone."

The guard releases my finger and I clench it into a tight fist of protection. Breathing quick and heart pounding, I try not to think about how close I came to breaking my first bone today. Silent tears begin to stream down my face against my will, but the adrenaline fleeing my system has taken over.

"Just let her go first," Mom pleads with King Ryul, but he shakes his head. She's in no position to negotiate. He knows he has her in a tight spot, and there's nothing I can do to change it.

"Where is the Trident?" he asks her once again.

"Just let her go, let her go," Mom pleads one more time, the tears in her eyes matching my own.

"You know I can't do that. Tell me where the Trident is and then I'll let her go," he says, crossing his arms over his chest.

Panicked, Mom's eyes flicker over to me and linger just a second too long, and King Ryul turns to look at me as well. Chained and sullen, I meet his gaze, but his eyes light up the longer he stares at me.

"So that's how you did it," he says, soft and whispering to himself. "That's how you kept it a secret for so long. That's how none of my spies were able to find it no matter how hard or how long they searched."

"No!" she shouts, straining in the arms of her guard, her body tense as she pulls and pulls, trying to get free. "Leave her alone!"

He walks in slow measured steps towards me, his feet making no sound against the tiled floor. One long manicured hand reaches out for me, his eyes lit from a fire within making his grin menacing in the flickering torchlight.

Gripping my chin in his cool fingers, he wrenches my face up to meet his. I turn my eyes away, doing what little is in my power to take his away.

"Look at me." His voice is soft as it brushes against my cheek.

"Don't do it!" Mom yells again, face red from the strain of pulling against her captor.

His fingers dig into my face as he wrenches me toward him again. "Look at me!"

The pressure within me mounts as he pulls on my head until finally, I look into his icy blue eyes. They narrow in concentration as he stares at me, my own eyes as wide as they can be despite the swelling as fear overwhelms me and his fingers dig into my already bruised skin. I struggle to pull my head out of his grip but strapped to this chair I have nowhere to go.

With a small gasp, he pulls harder on my chin, eyes widening in surprise. "How is this possible?" he says to Minna, voice loud in my face.

I can't see Mom anymore, I can only hear her sobs, her words incoherent. Fear creeps up my throat and I manage a strangled plea to my mother. "What's he talking about?"

"I can see it," King Ryul whispers. "It's right there. How did she do that? How do I get it out?"

"What are you talking about? Someone answer me!" I beg, fresh tears forming new tracks down my face.

He's so intent on peering into my eyes, that he misses the slight shuffle in the hallway behind him. Mom quiets down, hearing it too. I do a mental count of the men in here, five guards, the two with me, the one with Mother, the two for King Ryul, and King Ryul. I'm hoping beyond hope it's Donovan waiting in the hallway for me, but I don't know what good that will do me. There's too many of them for one man to take.

"Tell me Minna, tell me how you did it," King Ryul says to my mom, eyes locked so tightly on mine that he misses as someone else enters the room.

"Ryul," Kai's voice breaks across his back. "What are you doing down here with my men and my employee?"

My heart sinks with the confirmation that it isn't Donovan, even as I realize how much better off I am to have Kai here. He holds some power, unlike Donovan who'd be kicked back out into the ocean if Kai found out he'd been hiding here.

Staring past Kai, I wish I were surprised to find he hasn't come alone. A couple guard's stand behind him, but only one of them catches my eye. The one staring with grey eyes.

"Kai," King Ryul squeaks, spinning around on one heel to block me from Kai's view. "Sorry for the inconvenience, I just knew I had to act quickly to get the information I needed. You can take her back with you if you want, and I won't need your men any longer."

Kai lowers one black eyebrow over his kohl-lined eyes. "You didn't answer my question. What are you doing down here?"

King Ryul makes some half-hearted excuse, and I watch sweat darken the material of his shirt through his shoulder blades.

Then a pair of cool hands runs down my arms and over the chains holding me in place.

"Don't move," Donovan says in my ear, his breath sending tingles down my spine.

I stay still, keeping my gaze on my father as he gives me a slight nod. A heated argument grows between King Ryul and Kai. I hold my breath to make myself as nondescript as possible. The last thing I need is to become a distraction.

Mom stands in the arms of her guard, quick eyes watching Donovan's deft movements. She hasn't noticed Bracken in the room yet.

Donovan catches the chains as they're loosened, making sure they don't clank on their way to the floor. Then he moves over to the right side, making quick work of those as well. Kai's just starting to leave with his guards and my mother in tow when Bracken makes his move.

With a quick shove, Donovan pushes me into the safety of the guards, my father taking a swing at King Ryul. All sense of decorum lost now; King Ryul swings back. Bracken places a well-aimed kick at his temple, and he thumps against the ground, all without noticing my growing absence behind him.

Although it's only taken seconds, my heart's beating a mile a minute when Bracken joins Donovan and I and we start climbing up the staircase.

"Thank you." I breathe, trying to watch my feet on twisting staircase.

Donovan shrugs. "I'm just sorry we didn't get to you sooner."

We get to the top of the stairs, and he grabs my face with his gentle hands, tipping my head up to the light while he stares into my eyes, Bracken watching over my shoulder. Their sharp intake echoes King Ryul's only minutes before.

"What is it?" I ask, assuming his eyes are lingering on the puffy bruises that are only growing.

Bracken's mouth gapes open and closed a few times before he answers. "It's your eyes. I can see the Trident in them."

"What?!" I step back from him, pulling my face out of his reach while I try to process what he's said.

Donovan doesn't try to come after me, instead he leaves his hands open at his side. "It was you. It's been you all along. Avi, you're the Trident."

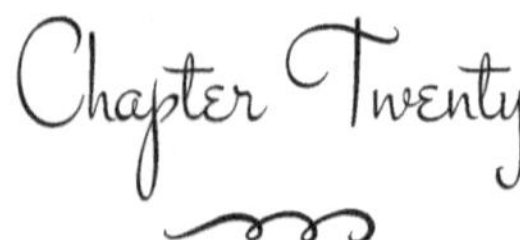

Chapter Twenty

"You're the Trident," Donovan repeats, running a hand through his hair as he steps back with wide eyes. "All this time, everyone was looking for this giant metal trident, when we should have been looking for the girl with the trident in her eyes."

"My eyes?"

He nods, grabbing my hand and leading me farther out of the shadow of the pyramid. I stumble across the white pebble path as the sky around us grows dark. My face throbs, and the finger the guard thought about breaking pulses in Donovan's grip.

I have no idea what he's talking about. *I'm the Trident?* I've looked at my face a million times and never seen a trident there. He has to be wrong. But then...

That feeling I had when we got to Neopolis... maybe that had nothing to do with the city's magic. Maybe that was all the Trident. Coming here must have awoken something in it.

"Stop, just stop a second," I gasp, pulling my hand free once we're outside the palace gates.

"Are you okay?" Bracken asks, as Donovan runs his hands

through the air by my face in a phantom touch. "He really got you good."

"No kidding." I push past Donovan's shoulder and farther down the street, setting the pace much slower this time.

Donovan catches up with me easily and leads me back down toward the dock. We haven't talked about it, but I know we can't stay here anymore.

"We need to get out of here. It wasn't safe before, and it's certainly not safe now, not with King Ryul on our trail," Bracken says, glancing at me as he speaks to Donovan.

"I've got a boat ready to go. I knew we needed a backup plan," Donovan says to him. "We couldn't rely on Minna."

Bracken's face darkens, his jaw tensing. He grabs me by the shoulder. "I didn't get to be there for you before, but I'm here now."

I give him a sloppy smile, the swelling in my face making sure it's lopsided. "I believe you."

"Should we try to go back for her?" Donovan asks, referring to my mother.

Shaking my head, I realize what I should have known all along. "She can't help us now."

The men nod and push us farther into the city, lifting me by the underarm when I slow down.

Donovan links his arm through mine as we get deeper into the city, buildings looming over us once more, blocking out the faint lights of deep-water fish moving across the dome of Neopolis.

Sighing, I lean into his shoulder. Against the odds, we've made it through together and I know he's the one person I can count on to never let me down. Every time I've turned around and needed help, Donovan's been there. Not Nick, not Ramsey, not even my mother.

But Donovan came back, and so did my father.

"Let me show you something," Donovan whispers into

my hair as he turns toward me. "You need to see what I just saw."

He leads me down a side street, Bracken keeping watch on the main road as our footsteps echo off the cobblestones. "It's just over here."

Glancing back at me with a smile, Donovan loosens his grip, his eyes lingering over my bruises. I spare a thought for my mom as we pass a small doorway so reminiscent of the one she took me to earlier. I hope she'll be okay, but I really can't worry about her right now. She's a grown woman and she left me with enough problems and questions of my own to deal with.

Donovan stops when we reach a small square, where one of the fountains I heard earlier sits in the middle, a few street-lights illuminating the dolphin frozen in the middle of breaching the water. The fountain isn't running and the square is deserted, leaving us ensconced in silence.

"Look at yourself in the water," he says, voice soft as we lean over the fountain.

I brace my hands against the cool stone that is a constant theme of this place. Looking down into the still water, at first all I can see are the spreading raspberry bruises and the swelling around one of my eyes.

"Very funny, Donovan," I say with a fake laugh, brushing the limp strands of hair back from my face.

Donovan's figure materializes in the water next to mine as he places a hand on the small of my back. "Look closer."

I lean forward further, staring at myself with narrowed brows. Honestly, I'm disappointed that all that's reflected back at me is a scared little girl. I would've though that after everything I've been through there would have been more growth physically reflected on me.

"Closer," he whispers again.

I'm so close to the water that my nose is practically

touching it, the teal tile of the fountain inches away through the clear water. With an exasperated sigh, I try to see myself again.

My eyes are the only thing I can make out at this distance, but it's all I needed to see. My stormy grey eyes stare back at me through the water, looking as normal as ever, but there in the darkness of my pupils is a small light I've never seen before. Leaning forward further, I finally see what King Ryul saw.

Outlined by a pale line of fire is the image of a trident reflected at me. Gasping, I try to get a better look. My hair spills forward into the fountain, ruining the reflection I've been staring at.

"Did you - did you see that?!" I breathe, looking back at Donovan while my hair leaves wet streaks against my shirt.

"Yeah." He sits next to me. "That's what I was saying. You're the Trident."

The blood cools in my veins. "I'm the Trident."

Donovan's eyes narrow as he glances around the empty courtyard. "We need to go."

"Can't we- can't we just sit for a second, I need to process this," I ask, staring at nothing as the implications of what's been done to me roll over my mind like an earthquake.

Hearing Donovan say that I'm the Trident, hearing myself say it, changes something within me. The pain is still there, but now I feel a power building. There's a charge in me.

"I wish we could, but we have a boat to catch, and it's too dangerous for you here." Donovan takes my uninjured hand, eyes soft as he looks at our joined fingers. "We'll figure this out, together."

As crazy as it sounds, I believe him.

* * *

Heavy footsteps beat down the road behind us as we make our way to the dock. Donovan glances back, the muscles in his jaw tightening.

"Here comes trouble," he mutters to himself, watching Bracken as he slips free a knife from his pants pocket.

Pushing me towards the side of the road, Donovan keeps his gaze in front of us. Shadows grow as the road twists, loud voices echoing off the stone houses ahead of us. With a muttered curse, Donovan ducks through a door left cracked open. Bracken follows behind us, pulling the door closed as the groups before and behind us meet in the straight section of street.

We huddle against the door, muffled light coming through a gauzy curtain covered window. Shelves sit half full of plastic-wrapped wares, the cash register abandoned despite the early hour.

Shouting filters in through the cracks in the door, Bracken flinching as we hear King Ryul's voice.

"Patrice," he calls. "Never thought I'd see you down here with the fish."

"You didn't give me much choice," she huffs. "Where's the Trident?"

I flinch, Donovan's arm wraps around my waist, pulling me closer to him. Bracken holds the knife at the ready despite the relative safety of the closed door.

"You know it was never yours, Patrice, the Trident is the instrument of kings."

"If it were up to you, it would be the instrument of repression," she retorts.

"We have to get out of here," Donovan whispers to Bracken, his breath warm against my skin.

Bracken nods, peeling away from the door as he takes in the rest of the room. We trail behind him, grateful to have someone trained in this to help us out.

He approaches the dark back of the shop, where the light can't travel. "There's got to be a back door. We find it, we get to the dock. You don't look back." He gives me a pointed look that I ignore.

I can feel the power in me now. I can't deny that the Trident is within me, no matter how much I wanted to. The salt-coated breeze from the dock winds through my hair, begging me to use it.

"Avi, we need to go." Donovan grabs my arm, pulling me toward where Bracken is moving.

I shake my head. "I'm not leaving Patrice and Ryul to follow us."

Now that I know what's in me, I will never go back to being their pawn. Not even for my mom. The Trident is alive in me and I'm going to use it.

They still haven't spotted us, and I'm not going to give them the chance.

I exhale a long slow breath and I can feel the power flow through me to the ocean beyond the dock. Blue light flickers along my arms, drifting through the air towards the ocean gate. A crack echoes through the building and there's silence for a moment as everyone waits, listening.

With a roar, the ocean hits the weak wood of the building. It shudders, splintering under the weight of the water. There's a high-pitched screen that I can only assume is Patrice and then Donovan grabs me, forcing me to run. I can feel his racing pulse where my arm is around his neck. He's afraid.

It's funny, I would have been afraid of the water too, but now there's nothing but peace. The water runs around us, protecting me. I control it. There's nothing to be afraid of now.

I wriggle until Donovan puts me down. We keep pace with Bracken as we run from the mess I created. I run a hand along the uneven wall, unable to make out much in front of me. Bracken curses in the darkness and then a bright crack of light washes over his tight face.

The boys were right, a back door was sitting behind tall shelves of unorganized inventory. Bracken's dark hair catches the light as he peers around the edge of the door. Releasing a breath, he waves us forward, Donovan using his body to block for me just in case.

This back alley lies abandoned, a few papers floating in the influx of the ocean. Gunfire comes from the road we left. The wave I brought must not have taken care of everyone. I don't know if King Ryul or Patrice survived, but in the fight for the Trident, every man is equal.

The area around the dock is empty, water swirling knee height around Bracken's legs. A large silver boat shaped like a bullet sits next to a wooden dock that extends into the swirling ocean hole.

"Oh good, we're not too late," Donovan says under his breath as he ushers us along the dock.

He presses a hand on the side of the boat and a panel flips up, revealing a small cabin within.

"You set this up?" I ask, not quite believe that we're really getting out of here.

He shrugs. "I knew we needed a backup plan to get out of here. I wasn't going to leave you with all the crazies down here. Too much time under the sea has left these people with fish brains. When I found out your father was with us, it wasn't hard to rope him into my plans and get this boat ready for us."

Donovan grins and I laugh as he helps me into the boat, my father is tense as he climbs in behind us. There's a small aisle of airplane seats inside, and I climb into one and buckle myself in as Bracken closes the door behind us.

Donovan leans over me for a second, hand hovering by my face like he wants to touch me.

"Thanks," I tell him, staring up into his brown eyes. "For everything."

"Of course. Don't you know? I would do anything for you," he says, wrapping a hand around the back of my neck and pressing me to his lips. Our breathes mingle, and the tight pain in my face is nothing as I pull myself closer to him.

Bracken coughs, and with a strangled sigh Donovan releases me. "All right, let's get out of here."

My lips tingle as I watch him climb into the front seat and press a few buttons.

"Good riddance," I sigh as we shoot into the water and leave the city and Amaro far behind.

The ship shifts around us, and through the window at the front of the boat I can see the pull of the water through the swirling hole penetrating the Neopolis bubble.

I'll be back, I realize as I watch the city disappear into the darkness of the deep ocean. I feel it as surely as I feel the new power coursing through my veins.

I'll be back, not as a captive. Not as a prisoner.

But as the Trident.

<h1 style="text-align:center">From the Publisher</h1>

Thank you so much for reading Seeking Neopolis, Book One in The Trident's Reckoning Duology!

We hope you enjoyed the journey and characters as much as we loved bringing them to you. We'd love for you to leave a review on Amazon and Goodreads while the story is fresh in your mind. Reviews are writing fuel for authors and help their books get into the hands of other hungry readers. If you're a big fan of speculative young adult and middle grade fiction, we invite you to join our street team. Get copies of our books in advance, early access to covers, and other freebies!

Stag Beetle Books
www.stagbeetlebooks.com

Acknowledgments

This book has been so many years in the making and has been through so many eager hands to get to this point. I've been so grateful for all of you who have stuck with me from the beginning. Can you even believe this book finally made it? I'm sure you're not even surprised. You always believed in me.

Danny, thank you for the years of support and for having to listen to me complain about characters who wouldn't behave. I know you don't understand it, but you support me anyway and I couldn't do it without you.

My parents, I'm sure you never expected that promise you made to a thirteen-year-old fan fiction writer to turn out like this, but I hope I've made you proud.

Kristina, Megan, and Jake, thank you for always being there for me. From brainstorms to first drafts to writing events that take all day, I have never once had to question if you were going to be there, and that has made all the difference in my ability to believe in myself.

Alan and Steve (and the rest of the fellowship gang), you guys have pushed my writing into credibility. I can't thank you enough for knowing my weaknesses and being the gentle support that enabled me to take them on and fix more than a few plot problems over the years. Every writer should have people like you in their life, and I'm beyond grateful that you're in mine.

Laura, this has been an incredible journey together and I'm so thrilled that we've been able to accomplish this together. Thank you for believing in my books and for the many edits and hours spent looking over book covers. My books get to see the light of day because of you! There's not enough thanks in the world I could give you for something like that.

To my many readers, you're amazing and more than I could have asked for. Thank you for your sweet reviews and for loving my characters as much as I do. I can't wait to see more of you in the coming year. You guys are what it's all about.

Most importantly, to my Heavenly Father. Thank you for this talent and for placing people in my life at the right time, and for never letting me give up. All my blessings I owe to you.